Praise for Adi Alsaid

Never Always Sometimes

"There is a kernel of truth in every cliché, and Alsaid cracks the teen-lit trope of friends becoming lovers wide open, exposing a beautiful truth inside."

—*Kirkus Reviews* (starred review)

"An utterly charming and thoughtful meditation on love, friendship and all the territories in between."

—Nicola Yoon, #1 *New York Times* bestselling author of *Everything, Everything*

"With all the fun of a classic teen movie, this one should fly off the shelves."

—*Booklist*

"A refreshing novel about friendship and romance that defies cliché, *Never Always Sometimes* will win readers over with its hilarious musings and universal truths."

—Adam Silvera, *New York Times* bestselling author of *More Happy Than Not*

"Exploring universal feelings of friendship and love, Alsaid offers a colorful depiction of two teens discovering what they have in common with others. Their escapades and realizations will evoke laughter and empathy."

—*Publishers Weekly*

"This fun romp will appeal to students looking to push beyond the edges of their own comfort zones."

—*School Library Journal*

Let's Get Lost

"Reminiscent of John Green's *Paper Towns*, Alsaid's debut is a gem among contemporary YA novels.... An achingly beautiful story."

—*School Library Journal*

"This will likely be a popular summer hit, especially for older teens about to embark on their own journeys of self-discovery."

—*Booklist*

"With equal parts heartache and hope, this debut is a fresh interpretation of the premise that 'home is who you're with.'"

—*Horn Book*

"*Let's Get Lost* is a touching debut novel and worthy of addition to young adult collections."

—*VOYA*

Also by Adi Alsaid

Let's Get Lost

NEVER ALWAYS SOMETIMES

ADI ALSAID

HARLEQUIN® TEEN

Recycling programs for this product may not exist in your area.

ISBN-13: 978-0-373-21210-1

Never Always Sometimes

This edition published by arrangement with Harlequin Books S.A.

For questions and comments about the quality of this book, please contact us at CustomerService@Harlequin.com.

Printed in U.S.A.

For Sylas and Lucy.

PROLOGUE: THE LIST

DAVE DROPPED HIS backpack by his feet and slid onto the bench that overlooked the harbor at Morro Bay. He loved the view here: the ocean sprawling out like the future itself, interrupted only by the white tips of docked sailboats and the rusted railing people held on to watch the sunset. He loved how far away it felt from San Luis Obispo, even though it was only fifteen minutes away. Most of all, he loved when Julia would appear in his periphery mock-frowning, how she would keep her eyes on him, trying not to smile as she walked up, then she would slide in right next to him like there was nowhere else she belonged.

"Hey, you goof. Sorry I'm late."

Dave looked up just as Julia was sitting down. She was wearing her usual: shorts, a plaid blue shirt over a tank top, the pair of flip-flops she loved so much that they were now made up of more duct tape than the original rubbery material. Her light brown hair was in a loose ponytail, two perfect strands looped around her ears. If the lights ever went out in her presence, Dave was pretty sure the brightness of her eyes would be more useful than a flashlight.

"S'okay. How was hanging out with your mom this weekend?"

"Greatest thing ever. Don't get me wrong, the dads are awesome. But my mom is the coolest person alive."

"Hyperbole foul," Dave said.

Julia crossed her legs at the ankles and looked around the harbor. "Did I miss anything interesting?"

"There was a couple breaking up by the ice cream shop. I couldn't hear what they were saying, but the girl was such a sad crier. I wanted to go give her a hug, but that might have been a little weird."

Julia gave him a smile and stole a sip from the bubble tea he'd been holding.

"Tell me more about your mom. What makes her so cool?"

"Everything," Julia said. "She lives the kind of life that I didn't even understand was an option. She once biked from Canada to Chile. On a bicycle. For, like, months. Other adults work from nine to five and then go home to watch TV. She bikes a whole continent."

"Huh," Dave said, impressed. "That is pretty cool. How come she's never come by before?"

"She's too busy being awesome," Julia said. She glanced around for a little while, swirling the drink in her hand. Dave followed her gaze to a little boy riding his tricycle down the harbor, his parents walking calmly behind, beaming with pride. "So. High school tomorrow. Big day."

"Yup," Dave said with a shrug, reaching for his tea back.

He imagined what other kids might be doing in anticipation of starting high school. Picking out outfits, getting haircuts, quarreling with parents and siblings, texting each other messages that made more use of emoticons than proper punctuation.

"Any thoughts? Concerns? Schemes?"

"Oh, you know. Nothing specific to high school. Take over the world."

She scrunched her mouth to one side of her face, then looked straight at him, which always made Dave feel like he was either lucky or about to turn into a puddle. A lucky puddle, that's what he'd felt like ever since he'd met Julia. "We're still gonna be us?"

"What do you mean?"

"I mean...we're kind of different from most people, right? We don't do what everyone else does. We're more likely to bike a continent than watch TV all afternoon."

"I guess so."

Julia drank from his bubble tea, aiming the fat straw at the dark spots of tapioca that settled on the bottom of the cup. When she'd sucked up a few and chewed on them thoughtfully, she looked down at the ground. "As long as we don't get turned into something that looks more like high school, more like everybody else and less like us, I'll be okay."

She glanced at him, then looked across the harbor at the bay, where the water was starting to take on the color of the sun.

"So I'm not allowed to become the high school quarterback that dates the cheerleading captain?"

"I'm going to throw up this bubble tea right in your face."

He bumped her lightly with his shoulder, thrilled as always at the weight of her next to him, the warmth of her skin beneath the plaid shirt. "I don't think you have anything to worry about. You couldn't be a cliché if you tried."

Julia smiled at that, tucking a strand of hair back behind her ear. She grabbed the bottom of the bench with her hands and leaned forward a little, stretching, and the brown tress slipped back in front of her face. She kicked at the backpack by his feet. "You have any paper in there? I have an idea."

The Nevers

or

Dave and Julia's Guide to an Original High School Experience

1. Never be recognized by your lunch spot. Keep moving.

2. Never run for prom king/queen, student body president, or any other position that would have its own page in the yearbook.

3. Never attend a party at the Kapoor brothers' house. (Or any party where the invite is just the word "BEER.")

4. Definitely never host a "BEER" party while parent(s) is/are out of town.

5. Never dye your hair a color found in a rainbow.

6. Never streak, skinny dip, or do anything else that could result in a viral nude pic.

7. Never hook up with a teacher. (Substitute teachers are acceptable.)

8. Never pine silently after someone for the entirety of high school.

9. Never go on an epic "life-changing" road trip.

10. Never date your best friend.

PART 1
DAVE

ALMOST FOUR YEARS LATER

THE KIDS WALKING past Dave seemed to be in some other universe. They moved too quickly, they were too animated, they talked too loudly. They held on to their backpacks too tightly, checked themselves in tiny mirrors hanging on the inside of their lockers too often, acted as if everything mattered too much. Dave knew the truth: Nothing mattered. Nothing but the fact that when school was out for the day, he and Julia were going to spend the afternoon at Morro Bay.

No one had told him that March of senior year would feel like it was made of Jell-O. After he'd received his acceptance letter from UCLA, high school had morphed into something he could basically see through. When, two days later, Julia received her congratulations from UCSB, only an hour up the coastline, the whole world took on brighter notes, like the simple primary colors of Jell-O flavors. They giggled constantly.

Julia's head appeared by his side, leaning against the locker next to his. It was strange how he could see her every day and still be surprised by how it felt to have her near. She knocked her head against the locker softly and combed her hair behind her ear. "It's like time has ceased to advance. I swear I've been in Marroney's class for a decade. I can't believe it's only lunch."

"There is nothing in here I care about," Dave announced into his locker. He reached into a crumpled heap of papers on top of a history textbook he hadn't pulled out in weeks and grabbed a single, ripped page. "Apparently, I got a *C* on an art assignment last year." He showed the drawing to Julia: a single palm tree growing out of a tiny half moon of an island in the middle of a turquoise ocean.

"Don't show UCLA that. They'll pull your scholarship."

Dave crumpled the paper into a ball and tossed it at a nearby garbage can. It careened off the edge and rolled back to his feet. He picked it up and shoved it back into the locker. "Any notable Marroney moments today?"

"I can't even remember," Julia said, moving aside to make room for Dave's locker neighbor. "The whole day has barely registered." She put her head on Dave's shoulder and let out a sigh. "I think he ate a piece of chalk."

It was pleasant torture, how casually she could touch him. Dave kept exploring the wasteland of his locker, tossing out a moldy, half-eaten bagel, occasionally unfolding a sheet of paper with mild curiosity, trying not to move too much so that Julia wouldn't either. He made a pile of papers to throw out and a much smaller one of things to keep. So far, the small pile contained two in-class notes from Julia and a short story he'd read in AP English.

"Still on for the harbor today?"

"It's the only thing that's kept me sane," Julia said, pulling away. "Come on, why are we still here? I'm starving. Marroney didn't offer me any of his chalk."

"I do not care about any of this," Dave repeated. Liberated by the absence of her touch, he walked over to the trash can and dragged it toward his locker, then proceeded to shovel in the entirety of the contents except for the books. A

USB memory stick was wrapped inside a candy wrapper, covered in chocolate, and he tossed that, too. A few sheets remained tucked into the corners, some ripped pieces stuck under the heavy history textbook.

But something caught his eye. One paper folded so neatly that for a second he thought it may have been a note he'd saved from his mom. She'd died when he was nine, and though he'd learned to live with that, he still treated the things she left behind like relics. But when he unfolded the sheet and realized what he was holding, a smile spread his lips. Dave's eyes went down the list to number eight: *Never pine silently after someone for the entirety of high school.*

He looked at Julia, recalling the day they'd made the list, suddenly flushed with warmth at the thought that nothing had come between them in four years. She was holding on to her backpack's straps, starting to get impatient. Everything about Julia was beautiful to him, but it was the side of her face that he loved the most. The slope of her neck, the slight jut of her chin, how the blue in her eyes popped. Her ears, which were the cutest ears on the planet, or maybe the only cute ones ever crafted.

"David Nathaniel O'Flannery, why are we still here?"

"How have we been best friends for this long and you still don't know my full name?"

"I know most of your initials. Can we go, please?"

"Look at what I just found."

"Is it Marroney's mole from sophomore year?"

"Our Nevers list."

Julia turned around to face him. A couple of football players passed between them talking about a party happening on Friday. She was quiet, studying Dave with a raised eyebrow.

"You wouldn't lie to me, would you, O'Flannery? I could never forgive you."

"Gutierrez. My last name is Gutierrez."

"Don't change the subject. Did you really find it?" She motioned for him to hand the paper over, which he did, making sure their fingers would brush. The linoleum hallways were starting to empty out, people were settling into their lunch spots. "I was actually thinking about this the other day. I even wrote my mom about it," Julia said, reading over the list. A smile shaped her lips, which were on the thin side, though Dave couldn't imagine wishing for them to be any different. "We did a pretty good job of sticking to this."

"Except for that time you hooked up with Marroney," Dave said, moving to her side and reading the list with her.

"I wish. He's such a dreamboat."

Dave closed his locker and they peered into classrooms they passed by, watching the teachers settle into their lunchtime rituals, doing some grading as they picked at meals packed into Tupperware. Dave and Julia wordlessly stopped in front of Mr. Marroney's room and watched him try to balance a pencil on the end of a yardstick.

"This is your one regret from high school?"

"There's a playful charm to him," Julia said, in full volume, though the door was open. "I'm surprised you don't see it."

They stared on for a while, then made their way out toward the cafeteria. The line was at its peak, snaking all the way around the tables and reaching almost to the door. The tables inside the cafeteria and out on the blacktop had long since been claimed. "Kind of cool that we never did get a permanent lunch spot," Dave said, gesturing with the list in hand. "I hadn't even remembered that it was on the list. Had you?"

"No," Julia said. "The subconscious is weird." She reached

into her bag and grabbed a Granny Smith apple, rubbing it halfheartedly on the hem of her shirt. "How do you feel about the gym today?"

He shrugged and they walked across the blacktop to the basketball gym tucked behind the soccer field. They had a handful of spots they sometimes went to, usually agreeing on a spot wordlessly, both of them headed in the same direction as if pulled by the same invisible string. They entered the old building, which used to smell of mold until a new court had been installed, so now it smelled like mold and new wood. The walls were painted the school colors: maroon and gold. Next to the banners hanging from the ceiling there was a deflated soccer ball pinned to the rafters.

Julia led them up the plastic bleachers. A group of kids was shooting around, and one of them looked at Dave and called out to him. "Hey, man, we need one more! You wanna run?"

"No, thanks," Dave said. "I had a really bad dream about basketball once and I haven't been able to play since."

The kid frowned, then looked over at his friends who shook their heads and laughed. Dave took a seat next to Julia as the kids resumed their shooting. "I think you've used that one before," Julia said, taking a bite out of her apple.

"I'm kind of offended on your behalf that they don't ask you to play."

"They did once."

"Really?" Dave rummaged through his backpack for the Tupperware he'd packed himself in the morning. "Why don't I remember that?"

"I was really good. Dunked on people. Scored more points than I did on the SAT. Every male in the room suppressed the memory immediately to keep their egos from disintegrating."

Dave laughed as he scooped a plastic forkful of chicken and

rice. It was a recipe he vaguely remembered from childhood, one he'd found in his mom's old cookbooks and had taught himself to make. His dad and his older brother, Brett, never said anything about it, but the leftovers never lasted more than two days. "So, you've heard from your mom recently?" Julia had been raised by her adoptive fathers, but her biological mom had always lingered on the fringe, occasionally keeping in touch. Julia idolized her, and Dave, who'd been yearning for his mom for years, could never fault her for it.

"Yeah," Julia said, unable to keep a smile from forming. "She's even been calling. I heard the dads tell her the other day that she's welcome anytime, so there's a chance that a visit is in the works."

Dave reached over and grabbed Julia's head, shaking it from side to side. Long ago, in the awkward years of middle school, that had been established as his one gesture of affection when he didn't know how else to touch her. "Julia! That's great."

"You goof, I'm gonna choke on my apple." She shook him off. "I don't want to get my hopes up."

"*Her* hopes should be up. Her biological daughter is awesome."

"She's lived in eight countries and has worked with famous painters and sculptors. No offense, dear friend, but I think her standards for awesome are a little higher than yours."

Dave took another forkful of rice and chewed it over slowly, watching the basketball players shoot free throws to decide on teams. "I don't care how great of a life she's led, if she doesn't come visit you she's a very poor judge of awesomeness."

He glanced out the corner of his eye at Julia, who set her apple core aside and grabbed a napkin-wrapped sandwich out of her bag. He was waiting to catch that smile of hers, to know he had caused it. Instead, he only saw her eyes flick toward the Nevers list, which was resting folded on his knee. They turned their attention to the pickup game happening on the court, each eating their lunch languidly.

For the last two periods of the day, Dave could feel the seconds ticking by, like bugs crawling on his skin. He reread the Nevers list, smiling to himself at the memory of him and Julia stealing the pen away from each other to write the next item. He gazed out the window at the blue California sky, texted Julia beneath his desk, scowled at the two kids in the back of the room who somehow believed that what they were doing was quiet enough to be called whispering. Next to him, Anika Watson took diligent notes, and he wondered how she was mustering the energy. He wondered how many of the items on the Nevers list she'd done, whether she was going to the Kapoor party that he'd overheard was happening that Friday night. Looking around the room, he imagined a little number popping up above each person's head depicting how many Nevers they'd done.

At the final releasing bell of the day, Dave and Julia met up in the hallway, silently making their way out to the parking lot, where Julia's supposedly white Mazda Miata should have been glimmering in the California sun but was barely reflective thanks to the year-long layer of dust she'd never bothered to clean off.

Before Julia said anything, Dave knew what she'd been thinking about. He knew her well enough to read her silences, and there'd been only one thing on her mind since he'd found the list. He smiled as she spoke. "What if we did the list?"

Dave shrugged and tossed his backpack into her trunk. "Why would we?"

"Because two more months of this will drive me crazy," Julia said. She unzipped her light blue hoodie and threw it into the car on top of his backpack, then stepped out of her sandals and slipped those into the trunk, too. "We've got nothing left to prove to ourselves. High school didn't change us. Maybe it's time to try out what everyone else has been doing. Just for kicks. God knows we could use some entertaining."

It was one of those perfect seventy-five-degree days, more L.A. than San Francisco, though San Luis Obispo was perfectly in between the two cities. A breeze was blowing, and now that Julia was wearing only her tank top it almost tired him how beautiful she was. It'd been a long time of this, keeping his love for her subdued. It'd been a long time of letting her rest her head on his shoulder during their movie nights, of letting her prop her almost-always bare feet on his lap, his hands nonchalantly gripping her ankles. He'd been a cliché all four years of high school, in love with his best friend, pining silently.

He opened the passenger door and looked across the roof of Julia's car, which was more brown than white, covered with raindrop-shaped streaks of dirt, though it hadn't rained in weeks. "I hear there's a party at the Kapoors' on Friday."

Julia beamed a smile at him. "Look at you. In the know."

"I'm an influential man, Ms. Stokes. I'm expected to keep up with current events."

Julia snorted and plopped herself down into the driver's seat. "So, no Friday movie night, then? We're going to a party? With beers in red plastic cups and Top 40 music being blasted and kids our age? People hooking up in upstairs bedrooms and throwing up in the bushes outside and at least one girl running out in tears?"

"Presumably," Dave said. "I've never actually been to a party, so I have no idea if that's what happens."

Julia lowered the top of the car, then pulled out of the

school's parking lot and turned right, headed toward California One and the harbor at Morro Bay.

"So, we're doing this?" Dave asked. "We're gonna join in on what everyone else has been doing?"

"Why not?" Julia said, and Dave couldn't help but smile at the side of her face, the way the sun made her eyes impossibly blue, how he could see her mom on her thoughts. "I'll come over before the party so we can decide what we're going to wear."

"And we can talk about how drunk we're gonna get," Dave added.

"And who we're gonna make out with."

"Yup."

Dave turned to face the road and sank into his seat. He lowered the mirror visor and stuck his arm out the side of the car, feeling the sun on his skin. He kept smiling, too experienced at hiding to let the tiny heartbreak show.

FRIDAY AT THE KAPOORS'

BY FRIDAY, DAVE had mostly forgotten about their plans to attend the party. It was only during homeroom when he asked Julia what movie she wanted to watch that night that she reminded him about their plans to attend the Kapoors' party. A mild dread filled him as he pictured his night full of drunken jackasses and shitty music rather than sharing snacks with Julia in a darkened theater, getting coffee at a diner afterward.

At six, Julia came over to get ready. She was wearing the same clothes she'd worn to school, shorts and a T-shirt with the logo of a bookstore in San Francisco. Her feet were bare, but she was holding a plastic bag through which Dave could see a pair of high heels and a few boxes.

"You're joking with the shoes, right?"

"Hey, if I'm taking part in a cliché, I'm going all the way." She entered the house, moving past him with a light touch to his ribs. "I can't wait for that moment when all the other girls take their high heels off to go barefoot and they finally see what a genius I am for not wearing shoes in the first place."

"I don't think that's a high school thing," Dave said, following her into the kitchen. "I think high heels are more of a grown-up cliché."

Julia plopped the bag down on the counter and scowled at him. "Don't take this away from me, Dave. Tonight the universe vindicates my disdain for footwear." She reached into the bag and took out cupcake mix, some eggs, and a container of rainbow sprinkles.

"What's all this?"

"The dads said it's rude to show up to a party empty-handed," Julia said.

"So we're gonna bake the Kapoors cupcakes?"

"If I'm being honest, I fully expect the two of us to eat most of these. But yes."

Dave picked up the cupcake mix and examined it, uncertain about how the gesture would be received by their classmates, but finally deciding that if he was going to get made fun of for being considerate, as confusing as that would be, it was something he could live with. "If we're going to this party, I guess there may as well be sweets involved."

"Damn right," Julia said, leaning over to preheat the oven.

"You are the only two high school seniors in the world that would be baking on a Friday night." Brett stood at the entrance to the kitchen for a second, shaking his head before going to the fridge and grabbing himself a beer. Dave wasn't a small guy, six feet and an above-average build, but when Brett stood at his full height, Dave couldn't help but feel small. Dave was almost a carbon copy of his dad, but in Brett, their mom's features lived on: the sharp nose and lighter eyes.

"For your information, Judgey McHigh Horse, we're going to a Kapoor party tonight." Julia opened a few cabinets until she found a mixing bowl.

"You two?" He looked at Dave, who could only shrug. "I wish I could see that."

"I'm sure you would take any chance you got to hang out around high school girls again."

"With you over all the time, I don't really have a choice, do I?" Brett took a swig from his beer. He'd just turned twenty-one, which was a huge relief for their dad, who'd been letting Brett drink for a while now. After their mom had died, Brett had helped take care of Dave, and in his dad's eyes, that earned him the right to do anything he wanted. "So what's with the baking?"

"It's rude to show up empty-handed," Dave offered.

Brett laughed.

"Okay, then. Good luck with that." He lingered by the fridge for a few minutes, finishing his beer. "How are there still Kapoor brothers going to that school? I thought the youngest one graduated the same year I did."

"The triplets are juniors," Dave said, pouring sugar and cream into a mixing bowl for the frosting. "And I think there was an oops baby that's in junior high now."

"I heard a rumor that the Kapoor parents only procreate because they're building up an army," Julia said. In the few minutes since they'd started working on the cupcakes, Julia had managed to get herself covered in cupcake mix. It coated her brown hair and the tip of her nose, and there was a smear of batter on her chin. Dave had to resist the urge to take a picture of her or call her adorable. "They've been planning to take over San Luis Obispo for generations."

"I could actually see that," Brett said, tossing his beer into the recycling bin and grabbing another can, letting loose a burp that sounded less like a burp and more like a bass line. "Dad, you want a beer?" he called out into the living room, where their dad was likely watching college basketball. There was a grunt of a response, so Brett grabbed another one and set it on the counter next to him.

"Don't open that," Dave said to Brett. "We need a ride to the party."

Brett popped open the new beer defiantly, sucking up the

foam that hissed out. "You really need to get your license already. You're eighteen."

"This is more of a situation where we intend to, as you and your brainless friends would call it, 'get wasted,' and less of a Dave-not-having-a-license thing," Julia said. "I could have driven if I wanted to."

Brett shook his head. "You two are so codependent."

Dave blushed, but Julia kept on mixing cupcake batter without missing a beat. "It's not codependence, it's attachment," she said.

"Attached at the hip, maybe," Brett said, drinking from his beer. "You should take it easy on the booze; you two probably share a liver. You won't last an hour at that party."

Julia scowled at him, then clapped cupcake mix off her hands in front of his face. "Why the hell not?"

Brett coughed, brushing the white cloud away from his face. "You're too…I don't know. Artsy."

Julia laughed. "I don't paint, write, sculpt, or play any music. I don't think you know what *artsy* means."

"I think he's trying to call you *intelligent*, but in a derogatory way," Dave said.

"I mean that you go to parties ironically, barefoot, and you bring cupcakes." He took another drink, mulling something over in his head. "You're right, *artsy* was the wrong word. I should have said *clueless*. The Kapoor parties are legendary for being wild. I don't think you know what you're getting yourselves into."

"I'm sure the beer-pong tournament will be really intimidating," Julia said, turning back to the cupcake batter. "You know, I had second thoughts of going before you came in. But now I'm sure it'll be a blast. I can't wait until I see that glimmer in someone's eyes when they start thinking high school days are the glory days. Like the look in your eyes, Brett."

Brett looked around the kitchen, giving his derisive laugh that was more like a snort. Dave could tell he was trying to think of a comeback. After a while, Brett scowled, muttered something about cupcakes, and then went into the living room to rejoin their dad. Watching TV was their favorite thing to do. They did so silently, never acknowledging that it drew them together. Sometimes Dave felt like joining them, but it seemed to belong just to the two of them. Dave didn't mind so much; he had his own silent way of feeling close to his dad: They cooked for each other, meals that Dave's mom used to make for all of them.

"You have to teach me how to do that. I never get the last word with him," Dave said, dipping a finger into the frosting to taste it. There was something delightful about watching Julia move about the kitchen recklessly, a trail of batter and eggshells in her wake. The tiled floor was a mess when she was done with it, polka-dotted with vanilla extract. Her fingerprints were all over the black cabinets and on the stove. A pile of dishes sat in the sink, way more of them than she had needed. On his own, Dave was a bit of a neat freak. But when Julia was nearby, messes seemed beautiful, life's untidiness easier to comprehend.

"So this is how tradition falls," he said, taking a seat on one of the stools at the breakfast counter. "With cupcakes and the Kapoor army."

"Better a bang than a whimper," she said, easing onto the stool next to him. She reached over and brushed something off his shoulder, as if he were the one covered in ingredients. "Plus, don't be so dramatic. It doesn't suit you. We'll watch a movie next Friday, when we get bored of this. And them."

Dave nodded, understanding what she was getting at, though maybe not in the exact way she'd meant it. Julia kept mostly to herself at school, and by extension he did, too. He was friendly enough with classmates, though, especially when Julia wasn't around to draw his attention. There were a couple of guys he might even go so far as to call friends, though he never really spoke to them outside of school. Once or twice he'd hung out with them, gone to lunch and then played video games in a curtain-drawn den. There'd been dog hair on every surface, a stale smell of Doritos in the air. Their conversations had bored him, and within an hour or so he'd found himself longing for Julia's company, an urge so sharp it felt like homesickness. He had no trouble being alone. But if he was around anyone, he wanted it to be Julia.

"You're right," Dave said, the worry over the party melting away. "I might even try breaking the promise to never go streaking while we're at it."

"I'll make sure that the picture goes viral and you live the rest of your life in regret and shame."

"You're such a good friend." Dave put a hand on top of her head and shook lightly. "I don't know what I'd do without you."

"Show up to parties empty-handed, for one."

Dave chuckled, dipping another finger into the frosting. "You have to admit it's kind of weird, though. Doing this after avoiding it for so long."

Julia shrugged, using her pinky to steal the frosting from his finger before he could lick it away. "I don't think it'll be that bad. Just see it as a brief social experiment." She hopped off the stool and went to the oven, peering in through the glass to check on the cupcakes. "My mom did this once."

"Went to a Kapoor party?"

She rolled her eyes at him. "No, goof. She came back to the States, got a regular job. This was when I was around nine or so. She worked at a bank, tried to go back to school. She calls it her 'social experiment with the sheep.' Six months later, she'd taken off again, even happier to return to her unordinary life."

Julia leaned back against the counter, crossing her arms in front of her chest, not really meeting Dave's gaze. She knew she was being transparent, but she'd never been good at hiding her feelings when it came to her mom.

"I see what you're doing. You're drawing parallels between us and your mom so I will feel as cool as she is."

Julia smiled and tossed a towel at him. "If it is too lame we'll just leave. We can even have a secret signal."

Dave groaned. "Why a secret signal? We could just turn to each other and say, 'This sucks,' and then leave."

"Will you get into the spirit of this thing, please? Our secret signal will be to start a dance-off."

"You're ridiculous."

"And you love me for it," she said, smirking.

o o o

The Kapoor house was near school, about a fifteen-minute walk away. It was a route they were deeply familiar with, having driven it, walked it, and ridden their bikes down it countless times. But the streets took on a strange feel that Friday night, like walking into your own house and finding the furniture rearranged. The trees looked funny somehow, leafier than usual, or taller, or ominous. Okay, they looked pretty normal, but it felt weird noticing them while on the way to the Kapoor house for a party. Even walking next to Julia joking around felt a little strange in this context.

When they arrived, Dave rang the doorbell, confused by the relative silence coming from inside the house. He'd expected the rhythmic thumping of what passed for pop music. He crinkled the tinfoil covering the tray of cupcakes as they waited for someone to answer. Julia leaned on his shoulder as she stepped into the high heels, the soles of her feet gray from the sidewalks. Once she was in them she grimaced at him. "Why," she said, not a question, he knew, but a complaint.

One of the Kapoor triplets opened the door, the collar of his polo shirt popped up, the sight of which always caused a dull ache somewhere in Dave's chest. Julia let out a short "Ha!" at the sight of the red plastic cup in his hand.

"Beer's in the fridge, the sink, and the bathtub. We've got a game of beer pong going if you guys want next. Shots of tequila start once someone brings tequila." He closed the door behind them and then peeked under the tinfoil of the cupcake tray. "You guys made cupcakes?"

"Um," Dave said, eyeing the closed door with an increasing sense of regret.

"Cool," the Kapoor said, letting the tinfoil drop back down. Then he walked past them through the empty living room and toward the kitchen.

"I think we've made a terrible mistake," Dave whispered.

"Of course we have," Julia said. "That was the point." Then she started making her way across the shag carpet, gingerly stepping ahead as if tiptoeing through poisonous bushes. She held out her arms for balance, and Dave walked by her side so she'd have him to lean against.

"I'll have you know that I'm about to start a dance-off."

"Oh, shush. We've only had one interaction. And he wasn't all that amusing."

Dave stopped walking, nearly causing Julia to tip over. "Julia. A red plastic cup full of beer *and* a popped collar. On a polo shirt. The only thing that would have topped that introduction to the party was if he *WOOH*ed at us."

"Your standards are too low. This might be the only high school party I ever go to. I want to see plenty of it."

"So you can look back fondly at the glory days?"

Julia poked him in the stomach, which he kind of took as the equivalent of when he grabbed her head and shook. "Goof."

They stood there in the empty living room for a second, mostly just smiling at each other. Dave imagined that if anyone walked into the room at that point it might look like they loved each other in the same way.

"Come on," Julia said. "The night is young. We have a lot of people to make fun of."

In the kitchen, the two other Kapoor triplets stood at one end of a plastic lawn table. They were setting up red plastic cups into a triangle on the table, pouring little measures of beer into each one. They, too, wore polo shirts, though each a different color and with the collars blissfully kept down. Three other guys, vaguely recognizable from school, lingered by the table, arguing about who had called "next." A girl was at the speaker system choosing songs. She was wearing sneakers, not high heels, but Dave decided not to point that out.

"Not exactly what I'd imagined," Dave whispered to Julia.

"Pretty underwhelming," Julia agreed.

They waved hello to the six people at the party, and after casually obliterating a couple of cupcakes, they each grabbed a beer and stood near the beer-pong table, listening to the Kapoors trash-talk the two guys who'd won the argument and taken next game. Every now and then Dave would help by picking up the Ping-Pong ball and handing it over, then wiping the dirt-flecked remnants of beer against his jeans.

"What about this did Brett feel we couldn't handle?" Dave asked.

"The excitement, I'm sure." Julia sipped from her beer can and looked around the room, disappointed. Good, Dave thought. Next week they'd be back to their movie night.

It wasn't long before more people started showing up and the Top 40 hits started blasting. The beer-pong players kept getting louder, the trash talk unraveling into something a little more ridiculous but, Dave had to admit, a lot funnier ("My mom could have hit that shot while conceiving me!"). In came Grant Stephens, wearing of all things his letterman jacket. "I didn't even know those existed in real life," Julia said. The rest of the football team showed up, too, some of them hulking inside their striped polo shirts. Juan and Abby, the longtime basketball couple, arrived with their arms around each other. Dave had always thought that they pushed the limits of the school's PDA policies, but in comparison to their performance that evening, they apparently held back quite a bit of affection on a day-to-day basis.

All the recognizable cliques came by, and so did those ungroupable stragglers who were known by their little circles of two or three, friendships that were fairly similar to Dave and Julia's; people they knew the names of but not much more. Every one of them was pulled in the direction of the beer, then they regrouped into their little planets of social comfort, slowly orbiting around the room and briefly interacting with other planets before making it back to the beer and then hurtling away from it again, their voices louder and their arm gestures more erratic with every trip. Here they were, all these people gathering to drink in abundance and in a variety of ways, chugging beers, taking Jell-O shots from tiny cups like the kind they gave you in the nurse's office, writing with Sharpies on Melvin Olnyck's face as soon as he passed out on the couch, Alexandra and Louise from Dave's economics class making out against the wall right by family photos of the innumerable Kapoor children, even though Dave had never guessed that they were friends, much less a couple.

"This is kind of weird, isn't it?"

Julia nodded. "I can't believe this has been happening the whole time we were in high school."

"I was just thinking that," Dave said. He finished off his beer and took a few steps to place it atop one of the many beer can pyramids that had started popping up around the house. "I'm gonna try to find the bathroom. Don't get swallowed up by this madness."

"Wait, Dave, before you go."

"Yeah?"

God, she was beautiful. Her cheeks were slightly flushed from the alcohol and the warmth of so many people inside the house. She stepped out of her high heels, suddenly the height he'd always known her to be. Relief visibly washed over her. She closed her eyes for a second, her toes curling and uncurling against the sticky kitchen floor. "That felt so good I might start wearing high heels just for the pleasure of removing them." She sighed with a smile. "Okay, I just wanted you to witness that. You can go pee now."

He smiled at her, then made his way through the groups of increasingly drunken classmates to find the bathroom.

EMPTY COLORING BOOKS

DAVE FLUSHED AND washed his hands, drying them off on his jeans since the single hand towel was clearly soaked through. He glanced briefly at himself in the mirror, wondering what he would look like in a polo shirt and then shaking off the thought, or more like shuddering it away the way he did with nightmares. This had been an interesting experiment, but now it was time to find Julia and go back to their little world of two.

Except that the party had rearranged itself while Dave was in the bathroom. The number of people in the kitchen had doubled. Beer pong was over and now there was a new game being played, one he'd seen Brett and his friends play, though he'd never really cared enough to try to understand it. Julia wasn't where they'd been standing for most of the night.

He surveyed the room but couldn't spot her, which surprised him. He was so used to looking for her that he felt unreasonably skillful at it, as if no matter how many people were around his eyes would easily land on her. Her presence called out to him like a beacon.

"Dave!" Vince Staffert shouted on his approach, clearly drunk. "Yo!"

"Hey, Vince."

"Come play flip cup with us. We need one more." He put

his arm around Dave's shoulders and started pulling him away from the wall.

"Uh, I don't really know how to play," Dave said, trying to hold his ground.

"Dave, you got into UCLA. I'm sure you can figure out a drinking game."

Caught off guard by Vince knowing that about him, Dave stammered, "I—I shouldn't. Julia and I were just about to go."

Vince sometimes asked Dave for help in math class, and from those few interactions, Dave had always thought of him as a nice guy. He knew there was another side to Vince, football player that he was, but all he'd ever seen was someone big and quiet and not so good at math.

"This house is not that big. She'll find you." Vince pulled him to the kitchen table. Cups were scattered and stacked across the surface, little puddles of beer pooling together. The other team consisted of two guys and two girls, none of whom Dave knew on a first-name basis, though he'd seen them around school.

"Guys, I'm not sure you want me on your team."

"Yeah, I agree," one of the other football players said to Vince.

"AJ, don't be a dick. Here," Vince said, pouring some beer in a cup, which by the looks of it had been used many a time throughout the night. "The game's easy," he declared and explained the rules in a few seconds. "Got it?" Once, Dave and Julia had misread a flyer and, thinking they were about to see an author they loved, had accidentally attended a reading at the library by the West Coast's leading researcher on menopause. So it'd be hard to say that this was the most out of place Dave had ever felt. But it was close enough.

Dave sighed. He and Julia had avoided all of this because

they'd wanted their high school years to be a little more unique than everyone else's. And yeah, they were here to see what they'd successfully avoided, but Dave had meant to just be an observer.

Dave surveyed the room one last time for Julia. The blue of her eyes, those three freckles on her neck. But she was nowhere around, and so he checked his phone. A text from her was waiting on his screen. Went off to explore the craziness on my own. Best story at the end of the night wins. Godspeed.

He smiled at the words, at what a great idea it was. Julia could turn any situation into something inherently more interesting. You're on, he wrote back, already looking forward to reuniting with her, though he had no doubts she would have the better story.

Then he gave Vince a nod and turned his attention to the game.

o o o

Seventeen wins in a row later, Dave could feel the alcohol practically bubbling in his veins. It felt a little like doing a somersault underwater and then coming up really quickly, your head spinning and sending a warm tingle down your spine. Dave, it turned out, was prodigiously good at flip cup. He'd yet to fail at flipping a cup over. Every time it was his turn, he'd swallow the beer down in a second or two, and with one deft move of his hand, the cup would be upside down on the table without so much as a wobble.

Vince was nearly in hysterics, throwing a meaty arm around Dave's neck, high-fiving everyone in the vicinity with his other hand, yelling about them being the world champions until no one else wanted to play them.

He and Vince walked outside without discussion, as if they were magnetically drawn to the fresh air. Dave looked around for Julia, wanting her to be nearby, longing to just exchange stupid jokes back and forth like they'd been doing for so long. He was going to break away and look for her, but then he noticed the briskness of the air and the way everyone seemed to be smiling and he took a seat with Vince on a bench.

"How come we've never hung out before, Dave?"

"I don't know," he answered. He burped, then chuckled at the thought of two dudes drinking beers and burping together. "Probably 'cause of Julia," he added. "I'm usually trying to spend my time with her."

"I've always wondered, are you two dating?"

"Nah. Just friends," Dave said, a line he was used to delivering with as little emotion as possible, as if he were a spy trying not to be discovered.

Vince crushed his beer can in his hand and placed it by his feet. He put his hands on his knees—smaller hands than Dave would have expected from someone Vince's size. "Since the truth serum known as Keystone Light is coursing through my veins, I'm gonna open up a bit here. You ready for it?"

"I'm ready," Dave said, wondering what Julia would make of the conversation.

"You can handle it? Peering deep into my soul?"

"To be honest, right now it kind of feels like I can peer into everyone's soul."

"That sounds pretty scary to me," Vince said with a smile. He ran a hand over his head, which was shaved recently, only the thinnest layer of fuzz starting to show through. "I am so in love," he groaned, putting his elbows on his knees and slouching over. "Two years, man. She's like some sickness I can't get rid of."

"Who?"

"Carly," he said quietly, though no one was paying enough

attention to them to hear. "She's all I think about." Vince looked so sad all of a sudden.

"Does she know?"

"I was always waiting for the right time to tell her, then she met some guy from Pacific Beach. At one of our games, no less. She's been dating him for over a year, and I've barely been able to sleep since. I wake up at four A.M. thinking of things to say to her, and I repeat them to myself until my alarm goes off and it's time to go to school to stop myself from saying it."

Dave made a little hum of agreement in the back of his throat. Inside the house, people were taking pictures of themselves on their phones, making faces, kissing each other on the cheek. Their eyes were glazed over, and everyone seemed to be either shouting across the room or whispering into someone else's ear. He couldn't remember who Carly was. "You could tell her anyway. Just to get it off your chest."

"I don't want it off my chest, though. It keeps me close to her. Plus, she's happy, and it's not my place to disturb that." He sat back against the bench and smiled sadly. "Is that weird?"

"Nah, it's not weird. Actually, Julia and I have this list…" He stopped himself when he couldn't think of how to phrase what he wanted to say without calling Vince a cliché. So many people were quietly in love that he and Julia considered it part of a normal high school experience and had therefore sworn it off. But Dave hadn't really thought about it in those terms in a long time. Pining silently was a cliché, which meant that people were constantly in love with each other without saying a thing about it. How much unrequited, unspoken love filled up the halls every day? How many kids in class felt exactly like Dave did on a day-to-day basis? "You're probably not alone," Dave finally settled for. "I'm sure most of us are thinking about someone else when we're in class."

"Yeah, but that's mostly horniness."

They chuckled, then Dave finished his beer and crumpled it like Vince had. "Do you want to talk more about Carly?"

"Nah," Vince said, standing up. "Just saying it out loud every now and then makes it more bearable. Thanks for listening. Let's go inside and get drunker and talk to other people who are being gently eaten alive by longing."

Dave smiled, and then took the hand Vince was offering to help him off the bench. Dave strolled around the house, reveling in everyone's drunkenness, and how different it was than he'd imagined. It made him think of the title of one of his favorite albums, *You Forgot It in People* by Broken Social Scene, and he was a little embarrassed that he'd assumed all of his classmates were cartoons of teenagers.

When he couldn't spot Julia anywhere, he checked his phone again and saw that the battery had died. There was a flutter of worry when the screen didn't click on, Dave feeling like a shitty friend for being unreachable, for maybe causing her to worry. Then the mood of the party settled back into his bones and he pocketed the phone, sure that Julia was elsewhere in the house, enjoying herself in just the same way he was.

He'd ended up in the den, where he stared at the hundreds of books in the Kapoors' library, turning his head slightly to read the spines.

"I do that, too," a girl's voice said.

He looked up to find Gretchen, a girl from his AP Chemistry class. Her back was to him, but he could recognize her by her hair, which was wavy enough to maybe be considered curly. It was dark blond, lightening up toward the ends, though he didn't know enough about her or her hair to know if the blonder tips were natural or the evidence of a past dye job.

She turned to look at him, big brown eyes and the hint of

a smile. At a glimpse, he could tell that her bottom teeth were slightly crooked. The world was full of details he'd failed to notice before.

"Do what?" he said.

"Check out bookshelves at strangers' houses," she answered, stepping up next to him and looking at the books as if to prove she wasn't lying. "I'm usually a bit awkward in houses that I haven't been to before, so it's a way to not look weird. If I find something I've read before it automatically makes me more comfortable."

He looked over at Gretchen, who fixed her eyes on the books. She was in a simple blue dress and—Dave couldn't help the thought—looked lovely. "Is that what you're doing now?"

She met his eyes for just a moment and turned them away again, trying to hide a grin. "Oh, I don't know how to read."

She was laughing as she said it, showing another glimpse of her crooked lower teeth. They weren't unsightly, just imperfect. Dave liked the look of them, for some reason.

Dave chuckled. "That was one of the worst attempts at a lie I've ever seen."

"Dammit, I know." She blushed a little and rolled her eyes at herself. "I've been trying to get better, but I smile every time. I think I could be one of the greatest pranksters of our generation, but my mouth just doesn't want any part of it. Stupid smile."

"I'm Dave. We have AP—"

"AP Chem, I know. Come on, Dave, I live, like, a block away from you. We were in the same lab group that one time."

"Right. Sorry, I just usually assume people don't know me."

"I know you," she said. A lock of blond hair fell in front of her face and she pulled on it, examining the lighter ends for a few seconds before letting it drop against her dress. "So, have you read any of these?"

"All of them," Dave said. A silent, funny look passed between them, acknowledging the fact that he'd delivered the line with a straight face.

Gretchen reached over and pulled a maroon book out at random. "What's this one about?" She turned the book over and pretended to read the back copy, though there wasn't any. She furrowed her brow and concentrated, but the corners of her mouth twitched anyway, begging to smile.

He took a step closer to her and pulled the book up to read the title, *California Real Estate Law 1987–1992.* At this distance, it was hard not to notice Gretchen in her entirety. He'd always seen her out of the corner of his eyes, blond locks and not much more, talkative, active at school in the way that he and Julia inherently disapproved of. Her legs were tan from soccer practices in the sun, and she wore scuffed beige sneakers that didn't really go with her dress. "This one's an adventure-slash-love story," he said, looking at the faint dimple in her chin.

"Ooh, that's my favorite genre! And here I was judging the book by its cover."

"What was your guess? Judging by the cover."

"Erotica," she said, nodding. "I would have definitely thought hard-core erotica."

He laughed, the image of her reforming itself, starting to fill up with color.

"So tell me about this adventure-slash-love story."

Maybe for the first time, he looked at her and saw more than just her face. The words that he would have used to describe her yesterday—that she was just another popular pretty girl, a soccer player who maybe ran for student council or worked on the yearbook or something like that—suddenly seemed to lack any real description. That was true of many of the people at the party, he realized. It was like he'd been carrying around a coloring book that hadn't yet been drawn in. He and Julia knew the outlines of people, but not much more.

"Well," he said, and he took a seat on the leather couch behind them. Gretchen sat down next to him, the space between them hard to distinguish because of how her dress fell onto his jeans. "It's about this guy named..." He struggled for a name, then grabbed the book from Gretchen's hand and flipped to a random page. "A guy named Californian Tort Law."

"He sounds cute."

"So cute."

"Is there a girl?"

Dave smiled at her, at the way she'd positioned herself to face him, at the way she was smiling back, at all the unexpected turns his night had taken, normal as it may have been to everyone else at the Kapoor house. He wondered only briefly about how Julia's night had gone since they'd split, whether she'd discovered some of the same things he had about their classmates.

"Well, I wouldn't want to give it away. You'll just have to read it yourself."

"No! Don't be like that. I want to hear the whole story tonight."

"I don't think there's much left of tonight," Dave said, looking back toward the living room, which had definitely quieted down. The party was emptying out. Julia must have left to go home by now, and he should probably do the same soon.

"Come on. Tell me about the girl. What was her name?"

"Her name," Dave said, looking down at the open book in his lap, "was Section 16520 of the Family Code."

"Interesting name."

"Swedish," Dave explained.

Gretchen beamed a smile at him and gave him a head nod to continue. With a quick, appreciative thought for the Nevers list he'd found stuck in his locker, Dave continued his story.

° ° °

When Dave walked out of the Kapoor house, it was past three in the morning. Tiredness was starting to dull the edges around the thrill of the night, a faint headache building up as payback for all that beer. He was so ready to go to bed that he almost missed Julia sitting on the curb in front of the house, her head on her knees, arms curled around herself. He leaned over and could hear her softly breathing, asleep.

"Julia," he said, putting an arm on her shoulder. When she stirred, eyes darting, confused, he asked her how long she'd been waiting for him.

"I don't know. An hour, maybe. Where the hell did you run off to?"

"Nowhere. I was in the den downstairs."

"You weren't answering my calls." She put her hands on either side of her and stretched her back out. "What gives?"

"My phone died, sorry."

"Fuck, Dave, you couldn't have come to tell me that?"

"I tried." He stuck his hands in his pockets, not knowing what else to do with them. He hated making her upset. "I couldn't find you anywhere, so I thought you'd left."

"Without you? Please." She yawned. "You know you're an awful human being for letting your phone run out of battery. Come on, David Montgomery Burns, it's the twenty-first century. Stay plugged in. You made your friend worry."

"Why didn't you go home?"

"Again. Without you?" She let out a groan and then reached her hand out. "Help me up, you forsaken supposed friend."

"I'm sorry," Dave said, pulling her up gently. "I feel like shit."

"Good. Wallow in that for a second."

They started walking down the middle of the road, the streetlights casting hazy shadows. Earlier in the night, it had felt so bizarre to be walking toward a party. Now the fog was starting to roll in and the trees looked beautiful. Julia's arms were crossed in front of her chest, her jaw tense. He tried to read her silence, just how angry she was at him. But the booze was interfering, making his mind return to the wonders of street lighting at three A.M. Feeling guilty, Dave cast his eyes down at his shoes.

"Well, don't look so freakin' glum," Julia said, rolling her eyes when he looked up. "Come on, let's go have coffee at the diner."

"Really?"

"Yeah," Julia said. "If you buy me a slice of pie, all is forgiven. We still have to exchange stories from the night."

Dave thought of Gretchen, the strange appeal of those crooked teeth. It felt weird to bring her up, though; he'd never talked to Julia about girls. She'd talked to him about the few guys she'd fleetingly dated, and had on occasion tried to pry out from him some admittance of a crush on anyone. But for obvious reasons he'd always said there was no one he was interested in. Bringing it up now felt somehow wrong. Plus "a girl and I talked for a while" was not much of a story, so the next thing that came to mind was the flip-cup tournament. He chuckled to himself, though a distinct feeling of shame goose-bumped up his arms. "Embarrassing is good, right? We were here to fit in in an almost gross way?"

"Oh God, what'd you do?"

"Let's say I really embraced the spirit of the Kapoor party."

"Eww, Dave, did you buy a polo shirt? I'm going to have to cut you out of my life, aren't I?"

Dave put his hands in his pockets, turning the corner toward the street where the diner stood, lit up against all the darkened storefronts. "I don't think I'm ready for that," Dave said, adding a chuckle.

HOMEROOM & HAPPY HOUR

THERE WAS NO greater proof of an underlying human connection than the universal hatred of Monday mornings. Everyone wore it on their faces: students with hair sticking out in every direction, as if trying to get away. Teachers sat at their desks scowling at their lesson plans. The principal looked as if he was suffering a nervous breakdown. The halls were practically an obstacle course with people lying down with their legs sprawled out, backpacks tossed in front of their lockers as pillows.

Dave had slept in most of the day Saturday and then stayed up on Sunday night supposedly trying to do homework, but really just rebelling against the thought that they were still assigning homework to seniors in March. He'd gotten into college—couldn't they just accept that he'd succeeded at this whole high school thing and leave him alone?

He'd slept less than four hours, and when Ms. Romero took attendance in homeroom, saying "here" physically hurt. Julia arrived a couple of minutes late, her earphones still in, a yellow tardy sheet from the office in hand. She hadn't bothered to change out of her pajama pants, and her hastily combed hair made Dave think of what it would be like to wake up next to her. She gave the tardy slip to Ms. Romero wordlessly and then plopped down next to Dave, pulling one of the earphones out and handing it over, as per tradition.

Julia hated talking in the mornings, and so Dave knew to listen to the music until she was ready. Neko Case crooned beautifully for a while as Ms. Romero struggled to put the morning's announcements up on the projector. This was how to combat the awfulness of Monday mornings. The PA went off, but no one cared to listen. A succession of yawns made its way across the room, knocking a couple of heads down to rest on their desks.

"I'll be right back," Ms. Romero said, at which point the silence in the room started coming apart. Bouts of isolated whispering grew into all-out conversations that filled the room.

Neko Case's voice stopped abruptly, and Dave heard Julia's sandals fall to the floor. He kept the muted earphone in, always happy to be tied together to her.

"How was Carmel?" Dave asked. She'd left early Saturday morning with her dads to go visit her grandparents, returning on Sunday when Dave was knee-deep in unjust homework assignments.

"Pretty. It's always pretty." She put her arms on her desk and lowered her head down, looking up at Dave with tired eyes. "I was thinking more about the party."

Dave raised an eyebrow at her. At the diner after the party, Julia had told him about her misadventures while they were split: a couple of guys' awful attempts to make out with her, their worse attempts at interesting conversation. She'd ended up playing video games in the basement with a group of juniors—stoner clichés that she hadn't expected to run into at the party, but clichés nonetheless. They'd joked about Dave's embarrassing flip-cup skills. Throughout the weekend, Dave's thoughts had returned to Gretchen, how he'd kind of fallen in love with the mood of the party. He'd assumed Julia had talked it all out of her system, though.

"Really? What were you thinking? How much fun you had?"

He smirked, but Julia surprised him by answering, "God, yes. It was so awful, I couldn't help but enjoy myself."

She pulled out her earphone and then plucked Dave's out, wrapping the cord around her phone. "There were so many clichés, I don't think we even touched on all of them at the diner. Did you see the girl puking in the bushes? I thought it was you for a second and I was really proud of you, but then I realized that she was five feet tall and had red curly hair and way bigger boobs than you do."

"You mean April Holmes? She was in a miniskirt."

"You could have been in a miniskirt. I think you have the legs for it." She sat up and put her phone away in her bag, which was this hand-stitched, colorful knapsack thing that her mom had sent her as a gift from Ecuador. "Anyway! I think we should do more." She'd talked herself fully awake now. In the background, Ms. Romero had finally succeeded in getting the projector to work and was asking if anyone had any questions about the bulletin. She said it in a way that made it sound like she had no interest in answering any of those questions.

"More parties?"

"No. Well, yes. But I was thinking of more Nevers. Do you have the list?"

Dave rummaged through his backpack until he found the folded sheet of paper, a little bent at the corners from whatever it is that happens inside backpacks that ensures all papers get ruined. He pulled out a chocolate muffin as well and peeled off the Saran Wrap while Julia looked at the Nevers.

His mom had loved those chocolate muffins, and now his dad kept them stocked in the house, making trips to Costco specifically to get them. Dave made eye contact with Nicky Marquez across the room, whom he had talked to at some point at the party. He hadn't known a thing about Nicky before, but now he knew that his parents were migrant workers, and that he hadn't learned English until he was nine.

Julia drew a red line across Never number three. "We can have so much fun with these." She brought the paper closer to Dave, so he could read with her. It always drove him crazy how easily she minimized the distance between them, as if it didn't mean anything. And then, almost out of nowhere, he thought about sitting next to Gretchen, how he was looking forward to seeing her in chemistry third period.

"We're definitely dying our hair crazy colors."

"We are?"

"This week," she said, folding both hands on the desk and resting her chin on top of them, continuing to read the list, the matter not up for discussion. "Actually, we're doing all of them." She sat back up quickly, smiling. "It's the perfect way to end the year," she said. "It's been so boring; this'll be the perfect end-of-high-school celebration. Embrace the clichés so tightly they'll suffocate. I think my mom would approve."

Dave eyed the clock. Homeroom was almost over. His tired brain tried to process doing all the Nevers, and the first thing he could think of was the chance at running into Gretchen more often. He grabbed a chunk of his muffin and chewed on it.

Julia was eyeing the list, chewing on her lip. He did one of those mouth-shrug-raised-eyebrow things that meant, "Sure, why not?" Which he immediately regretted when Julia spoke again.

"Mom'll probably want to be here to see her daughter go to the prom with the prom king. Side note: You're definitely running for prom king."

Muffin crumbs fell out of his mouth. "Is that so?"

"Yeah. That hasn't happened yet, right?" She tapped the girl next to her on the arm. "When do we vote for prom king stuff?"

Margot—petite, nerdy, shy—had never looked so confused in her life. "Uhh, prom, I think?"

Julia turned back to Dave. "We'll have to research with Brett. I'm already seeing big things for your campaign. Fundraising galas." Her leg started racing up and down under the table. She was radiant when she got excited about something. Her mouth scrunched over to one side of her face but somehow remained a smile. It was indescribably cute.

He watched her eyes go wide, a smile that was about ninety-five percent mischief spreading her thin lips. "Marroney. Number seven." Her finger pointed at the line. *Never hook up with a teacher.*

"You can't be serious."

"Why wouldn't I be?"

"Julia, the man collects food in his mustache. He wears pocket protectors, which I'm pretty certain have been out of production since the eighties, right around the time his kind-of-sometimes mullet-hairdo thing went out of style. He makes jokes about irrational numbers. He's a total cliché of a math teacher. I'm almost certain that he's not a real person; he's Frankenstein's monster but made up of math-teacher clichés. I heard a rumor that he's got all the known numbers of pi tattooed on his ass."

"That's a stupid rumor. And I can't wait until I undress him and dispel it once and for all."

Dave was mostly sure the comment was a joke, but he still felt a pang of jealousy. The bell rang, and everyone gathered their belongings, rushing toward the door as if already free for the day. Jenny Owens said, "Shit," and tried to scribble in a few last-second answers.

Julia stood up, folding the Nevers list neatly and grabbing her belongings. She stepped into her sandals and gave Ms. Romero a little wave as they walked out into the hallway. Dave followed behind, still trying to figure out if Julia was joking.

o o o

"I've never been a stalker before," Dave said. They waited for the Chili's hostess to find them a table near where Marroney and a handful of other teachers had gathered to enjoy a Friday afternoon happy hour.

"This isn't stalking. This is organizing a coincidental run-in."

"That's a stalkerish way to put it."

After obsessing for the rest of the week over how to best seduce Marroney (Dave shuddered every time she said it), Julia declared Friday to be a Never day. After school, they'd go to Julia's house and dye their hair in a bright display of their individuality—individuality purchased from a box at the CVS. But before they could do that, Julia and Marroney had to have their meet-cute. "Prepare for a lot of flirtatious giggling and some charming repartee," Julia had said when they were outside the school, waiting for Marroney to leave so they could follow him. "And that'll just be coming from him."

Now Dave watched Marroney struggle to find the straw in his margarita, his tongue flicking out blindly. He wondered if Julia would call her own bluff anytime soon. Marroney was wearing a mustard-colored short-sleeved button-up shirt with a coffee stain on his collar. His tie had little calculators on it.

Five other teachers were at the table, including Ms. Romero and Dave's AP Chem teacher, Mr. Kahn. Each of them had a giant fluorescent-colored frozen margarita in front of them.

Dave and Julia sat in a booth perpendicular to the teachers so they could both see as the teachers delved into a bottomless basket of chips and salsa. On his first attempt, a fat blob of red salsa fell from Marroney's chips and landed squarely on his tie.

"You know, I didn't get it at first," Dave said, turning to look at Julia, who was smiling in Marroney's direction, "but you're right. This has the makings of a great seduction."

"Your tone says you're trying to be sarcastic, but I'm failing to understand the joke."

"Julia, he's hideous."

"That's an ugly thing to say." Julia picked up her menu and propped it up so she could stare without being caught. "Okay, so here's the plan." She leaned across the table conspiratorially, refusing to speak until Dave leaned down, too. It was their classic pose for plotting mischief; they'd done it when figuring out which movie to go to, or when planning the surprise party for Julia's dads. They'd huddled together like this when they wrote the Nevers on their bench in Morro Bay. Dave loved seeing the details on her fingers when she put them flat on the table in front of her, the way her orangey smell seemed stronger in just those instances. They always adopted a tone more serious than was called for, whispering to each other, craning their necks around, pretending to study the room skittishly, as if someone was after them. The rest of the world felt exterior to them, like their friendship was some idyllic cove only they had access to.

"We wait until he gets up to use the bathroom."

"You are getting creepier by the minute," Dave whispered.

"Listen," she hissed. "When the romantic interest has been isolated—"

"You mean the victim."

"David Gostkowski, you interrupt me again and I'll dye your hair bright green."

"Isn't that happening anyway?"

"We wait until he gets up to use the bathroom," Julia said, her eyes getting big, warning Dave to keep quiet. "At which point, we follow." She stole a glance over the menu to look in Marroney's direction again. He was halfway done with his margarita, sprinkles of salt on his mustache catching the light and shimmering. The table was already getting louder, breaking up into a couple of conversations. It was curious to see them behave so much like students in a classroom. "Your job," Julia continued, "will be to go into the men's room and make sure no one else is there. When you've cleared it, you give me the signal by starting a dance-off, and I go in."

"What happens once you corner him in the bathroom?"

"Flirtation," Julia said, drawing the word out long under her breath. It was easy to forget what she was talking about. No one could make him laugh like she could, even if it was hidden away like this, the laughter quiet but understood between them. How had he not learned to be happy with just this? How had he not managed to stifle the desire for more?

"This is by far one of your best plans."

"I appreciate that," she said, ignoring his sarcasm. "But you're clearly forgetting the snow fort I designed freshman year."

"We live in California, Jules."

"Just because it never snowed doesn't mean it wasn't a fantastic fort. The planning itself was pitch-perfect; it was the execution that, at no fault of mine, fell short." She smacked her palms down on the table and looked over at the teachers. "We're getting away from the point. I need to do what many a teenage girl has done before and seduce the sexy older man."

Dave stole a glance at the side of her face and then joined in spying on them. They'd decimated the chips and were raising their hands, looking around for their waitress to ask for refills. Mr. Kahn was polishing off his first margarita and grimacing from a brain freeze. "Shocking that none of them have had to use the bathroom yet," Dave said.

"I know, right? Those are some sizeable drinks. Maybe Marroney is much younger than he appears. God, he must be so virile."

"I'm going to puke all over you. Good luck with the seduction covered in my puke."

"The stench of another man on me will only make him jealous."

For the next twenty minutes, after they'd placed an order with their waitress, they watched the teachers. At first they attempted to be inconspicuous, but the teachers seemed to be in their own little world, and once their drinks were refilled, they didn't care much for anything on the outside. Julia refined her strategy, and despite the dull ache in his chest at the thought of her seducing anyone at all, Dave helped. By the time Marroney stood up, Julia's plan had been tweaked to perfection. Or at least that's what she said when she stood up and pulled Dave by the arm, motioning for him to follow.

As per their revised plan, Dave sped up past Marroney and cut him off before he got to the bathroom. No one else was in there. He checked the two stalls for feet, just in case. Then he went to the faucets and pretended to wash his hands as Marroney came in. Dave tried to hide his face so that Marroney wouldn't recognize him, then said, "Urinals aren't working. Gotta use a stall."

"Thank you," Marroney said. He entered the first stall without so much as a glance at the functioning urinals. As soon as he shut the door, Dave walked out of the bathroom, where Julia was waiting. She was so excited, shifting her weight from one foot to the other, her hands balled up into little fists.

"Okay, phase one complete," he said. He put his hand on the back of his neck, a nervous habit. "You realize this is insane, right?"

"You're mispronouncing 'genius.'"

She took a breath, like someone about to attempt swimming the length of a pool underwater. And with that she walked into the men's bathroom.

Dave anxiously watched the door close behind her, casting a glance to make sure no one had noticed. The hostess was on her phone; a waitress was waiting at the window for a dish; the manager stood by the bar, looking at something on a clipboard. Chili's was probably the best place for covert operations; no one cared enough to look around.

It was only about thirty seconds later that she came back out, a huge, goofy grin on her face, color in her cheeks. She put her hands on Dave and urged him back to the booth. "Retreat! Retreat!"

"What happened?"

"Dammit, man, fall back!" Julia cried, laughter on the edge of her voice. When they slipped back into the booth, back in their conspiratorial hunch, she erupted into cackles while Dave could only sit there and watch.

"I take it the meet-cute didn't go as planned."

"We should get the bill before the cops arrive."

"Julia, what the hell happened in there?"

"I may have tickled him," she said, still red and laughing, looking over her shoulder toward the bathroom. "Accidentally."

Dave stopped looking for the waitress to signal for the check. He slouched closer to Julia. "How do you accidentally tickle someone?"

"I froze up, okay. He walked out of the stall and I was standing there trying to figure out how to break the ice. We stared at each other and then I just kind of…tickled him." She reached for her glass of water and took a long swallow. "Which, by the way, was an awful plan. Cornering him in the bathroom and expecting flirtation to just happen naturally? That's sloppy planning. I expect more from you."

"It was your plan!"

"Don't split hairs now; it's too late to apologize. Just do better next time." She looked over her shoulder again and gave a little gasp when she saw Marroney coming out of the bathroom. "I may have yelled something inappropriate, too."

Dave held his breath as Marroney walked past the table, his eyes fixed on Julia's. "I told him I wanted to lick his face," Julia whispered quickly, right before Marroney's mustard shirt passed by their lowered heads.

MAKING A MESS

WHEN THEY LEFT CHILI'S, Dave felt wonderful. Things had gone wrong, but in the exact way they should have. Now he had the evening with Julia to look forward to. He sincerely doubted bright green hair would look good on him, but he had succumbed to Julia's rationale about the Nevers making the end of the year more interesting. So what if it was some insane attempt to prove herself original, probably in an attempt to win her mom's approval; the Nevers brought out a joy in Julia that he loved being a part of. As long as nothing between them changed, he didn't have much to complain about.

"Why'd we add this to the list anyway?" Dave asked after they'd left the CVS and were parking at Julia's house. He was holding the boxes of green and pink dye in a plastic bag in his lap.

"My mom," Julia said. "She's always told me that changing looks has nothing to do with leading a unique life. It's usually the sign of a pretty ordinary inner self."

They walked up the driveway to Julia's house, a modest two-story with the garage open, her dad's workstation glistening with tools. The lawn was lush, almost overgrown. A porch swing hung slightly off-balance and in need of a paint job. Julia pushed open the door, placing her bag on the little entry table, which held a basket for keys and loose change and which was often piled up with unopened mail. A pleasant smell wafted toward them from the kitchen.

"Hey, homies," Julia said when she entered the kitchen. Tom and Ethan were sitting at the kitchen island hunched over a couple of notebooks. Someone Dave didn't know was standing by the stove, tending to about a million different things: a wok, two saucepans, a cutting board stockpiled with vegetables. He turned over his shoulder to glance at Dave and Julia, then wiped the sweat off his forehead with a dish towel before returning to cooking.

"Hello, hello," Tom said, moving to kiss Julia on the cheek and hug Dave. "How was your day?"

"Impossible to summarize in small talk," Julia said, walking over to Ethan, who was frowning at his notebook and tapping his pen against the counter of the kitchen island. Julia gave his back a hug. "You look stressed, Dad."

"Restaurant stuff." He sighed and tossed the pen down, sitting up and rubbing a hand through his graying hair. He almost always wore checkered shirts with the top button undone. He kept a cigarette tucked into his ear, though Dave had never seen him smoke. He'd started an Internet company before they'd adopted Julia, then sold it to start a string of businesses in the last two decades, none of them quite as successful as the first one. The latest venture was a restaurant. "Say hi to Chef Mike. We're doing menu testing."

"Hi, Chef Mike!" Julia and Dave said at the same time.

Julia walked over to Chef Mike to see him work while deflecting her dads' questions about her day, probably since the only mentionable thing about it was tickling a possibly middle-aged (it was hard to tell exactly how old Marroney was) teacher. Meanwhile, Dave sorted their mail into little piles on the counter: bills, junk, personal/miscellaneous. Dave never got any regular mail himself, save for last year's college recruiting packets. Aside from that, he was convinced that ninety percent of the mail in the world was credit-card offers. He came across a postcard mailed from Mexico, the handwriting familiar and addressed to Julia.

"Postcard for you," Dave said, holding it out to her. Her bare feet pitter-pattered against the kitchen tiles and she snatched it from his hand.

Julia read quickly, almost breathing the words out loud. Then she laughed and said, "She sends her love," to Tom and Ethan. The postcards didn't come often, so when they did, Dave knew, Julia read them over and over again, as if they were poetry. Then she'd put them up in her room connected by strings to pushpins on a map indicating where they'd been sent from. Ecuador, China, Australia, Belgium, Chile, Mexico. Julia traced her mom's journeys around the world and used the few details she knew to imagine the days when she would be able to travel as well. Without question, the best night in Dave's life was the night he and Julia sat staring at the map, splitting a bottle of wine stolen from the garage and planning travels the two of them would go on together.

"Is she still in Mexico City?" Tom asked, dipping a spoon into one of the sauces simmering on the stove to take a taste. "More ginger?" he said to Chef Mike, who shook his head.

"Yup," Julia said. "Working at an art gallery and part-time at a bar-slash-restaurant-slash-art-house movie theater."

"That sounds about right," Tom said with a smile. "That's gotta be the longest she's spent in one place since you were born."

"She says it might be her favorite place she's lived in. Although I'm sure she says that about everywhere she's been, because she only picks amazing places." She slipped the postcard into her shirt pocket. "We're gonna go upstairs to dye our hair. Call us when some of this amazing-smelling food is ready."

"That's funny, I thought I heard you say you were dyeing your hair," Ethan said, looking up from his notebook. Julia nodded with a smirk and Ethan looked over at Dave.

"I'm going with green," Dave said with a nod.

"Don't you have to ask permission from us to do something like this?" Tom said.

"I'm a college acceptee," Julia said. "That pretty much grants me freedom to do whatever I want, except for felonies."

"How'd you get talked into this?" Tom asked Dave.

"Your daughter has a talent for corrupting the youth."

"Don't I know it," Tom said. He crossed his muscular arms in front of his chest and appraised the two of them. "I don't think I'm ready to let go of my iron fist of authority in this household."

"Don't worry," Julia said, grabbing the CVS bag with the hair dye off the counter and kissing him on the cheek. "You can still tell Dad what to do all the time."

"Hey," Ethan called halfheartedly, his attention slipping back into his work, "I resemble that remark."

"Resemble? What, are you having a stroke, old man? Don't you mean resent?"

"It's a *Three Stooges* reference," Dave explained.

"There is hope yet," Ethan said, giving Dave a smile as Julia dragged him out of the kitchen by the arm. "Don't make a mess," he called out after them.

"We are definitely making a mess," Julia whispered to Dave as they went up the stairs toward her room.

"Which of us is going first?" Dave said, reading the tiny print on the side of the box.

"Let's do yours first. Your hair's darker, so we should probably let the bleach sink in longer for you."

They grabbed some old towels from the linen closet and spread them around the bathroom in Julia's room. Julia snapped on the gloves that came in the box, and Dave sat on a stool in front of the sink, watching Julia go over the instructions again. She had the most hilariously exaggerated reactions to every step of the process, and Dave sat back and watched, relishing each expression. Just as she was about to dab a bit of the dye on Dave's arm to test for skin allergies, Debbie the cat jumped onto Dave's lap, getting a green streak down her back.

"Oops. Dad's not going to be a fan of that."

As the bleach began to do its thing, whatever it was bleach actually *did* to lighten hair, they swapped spots. Dave draped a towel over Julia's shoulders and she undid her ponytail, her hair a light brown cascade that brushed against his fingers. "Have we sufficiently researched this process?"

"Depends on what you mean by 'sufficiently.'"

"Um."

"It might not look like a professional dye job but I won't get us killed."

"I guess that's reassuring?" Dave said, making sure the question mark was understood. After the bleach had magically transformed them into blondes—Julia pulling off the look much better than Dave ever could, though he admitted he was biased—Dave took a seat in the chair and watched a slightly different version of his best friend pour out the dye into a little container provided in the kit.

"This stuff smells great," Dave said.

"Don't you dare get high off the fumes. Sit still," she said, straightening his head and focusing on the dye job.

It didn't take her long to finish, since Dave didn't have all that much hair. The instructions said to let it sit for at least twenty-five minutes, though the Internet suggested much longer, so while they waited for his hair to really grab hold of the green, they changed spots again. He tested the dye against her arm, then mixed the two liquids together as she had. He shook the bottle, careful not to spill. When he took his finger off the top, though, a single pink drop that clung to his gloved hand dripped off and landed right in the middle of Debbie's forehead.

"That's what she gets for being so in love with you," Julia said, looking down at her cat rubbing her side against Dave's leg, unaware of the splotchy dye job she was receiving.

Dave squeezed out the dye onto his fingers, and for the next twenty minutes he became lost in the task. He worked slowly, not because he wanted to stretch out the time, but because it was Julia's hair, and everything to do with Julia he did with care. When he was done, he decided to wait with Julia, so that they would rinse the dye off at the same time. They tried to wipe Debbie clean, but she kept moving around and the drops of pink and green she'd absorbed spread across her fur.

"She looks like a tie-dyed shirt gone wrong," Julia said.

"That doesn't bode well for our hair."

Julia sat on the counter and looked at herself in the mirror, leaning in to examine the pink stains by her hairline. "The genius in this is that if it turns out shitty it's even more of a cliché."

"That'll be a comfort when everyone's laughing at us."

"Look at you worrying about what others think. Way to get into the spirit." She smiled, then gave him a friendly tap with her foot. "I think that's long enough. Time for the big reveal." She hopped off the counter and turned on her shower, grabbing the removable head and waiting for the water to warm up a bit.

They helped each other rinse the excess dye from their hair, which resulted in more dye getting all over the bathroom. "It looks like a couple of cartoon animals were blown up in here," Dave said.

They turned to face each other, and when Julia asked how her hair had turned out he had to swallow down the word *sexy*. "It looks pretty good," he said. "How's mine?"

She cast her eyes up at his hairline and bit her bottom lip. "I couldn't have hoped for better," she said, then laughed. "Maybe you should just look for yourself." She moved aside to let him step in front of the mirror.

"My God."

"I think the lighting in here is bad," Julia said, suppressing another laugh.

"Julia, it looks like someone vomited on my head."

Dave looked at her in the mirror, petrified. She brought her hands up to her mouth, her perfectly pink hair framing that lovely face of hers as the laughter tore through her.

"This is seriously the worst shade of green I've ever seen." Dave turned on the faucet and ran water through his hair, and the pretty shade of green water that poured into the sink only made the joke crueler. "There's no way I'm walking around with this on my head."

"Oh, come on. You really pull it off." Julia was doubled over in laughter, trying to catch her breath.

"I'm shaving it off."

"No, don't! The Nevers!" She dropped to the floor, not taking her eyes off of him, her hand clutching at her stomach. "Oww, Dave, the laughter hurts."

"The Nevers just said dye your hair. They didn't say anything about keeping vomit on my head for the rest of the school year. I'm gonna go to the mall to get this cut. Right now."

"If I keep looking at it, I might pee myself." She laughed again, either pretending to wipe a tear from her eye or actually doing it, Dave couldn't tell at this point. "Wait until the morning. Maybe it'll look better in daylight."

Dave grimaced but stayed put. "Only because I'm such a good friend and you're clearly enjoying this." He lingered by the mirror for a second, looking down at Julia, who was trying to fight off another giggling fit. It was hard *not* to want this to go on, whatever his hair looked like, hard not to chase after the idea of the Nevers, too, when the result was a whole day spent with Julia laughing at his side, her cheeks as pink as her hair, her eyes suffused with joy. "It's going to be a strange end of the year, isn't it?"

○ ○ ○

The next morning Dave's hair not only looked like puke, but like puke that had been allowed to sit out overnight.

Julia practically woke up laughing, and she refused to let Dave go until her dads saw his hair. They made their way downstairs, where Tom, Ethan, and Chef Mike seemed to have never left the spots they'd been at the day before.

"Good timing, we're just about to test the Sunday brunch menu," Ethan said when he heard them entering the kitchen. He was typing on his computer while Tom peeked over Chef Mike's shoulder, watching him crack an egg into a steaming pot of water. Julia held her laughter, waiting for them to look up. She took a seat at one of the stools positioned by the kitchen island, and finally Ethan looked away from his screen and gasped.

The other two men turned to look at Dave. Tom immediately broke out in laughter. Chef Mike just said, "Yikes," before returning to poaching eggs.

"Yup, going to the mall right now," Dave said.

"You probably should, I might lose my appetite otherwise."

"Ouch," Dave said, though he took a seat next to Julia and Ethan.

Ethan pulled his glasses off and reached over to touch Julia's hair. "This actually suits you."

Dave loved sitting in the kitchen with Julia and her dads, loved the ease with which they talked and laughed with each other. He wished him and Brett and their dad had it, too. Dave had always wondered how Tom and Ethan handled Julia's infatuation with her mom, whether they were ever hurt by it. But when he sat with them in their kitchen, it became clear that there was plenty of love to go around. No matter how much she longed for her mom, Julia never neglected her dads.

"How does your bathroom look?" Tom said, pouring a mug of coffee and offering it to Dave.

Julia quickly cupped her hand over Dave's mouth. "Spotless."

"You're grounded," Tom said, shaking his head.

"We had this discussion yesterday. Your reign of terror over me is done. Let it go." Julia pulled her hand back and reached for Dave's mug, blowing slightly at the surface. There was a hint of a chemical smell around the two of them from the hair dye, and Dave was thankful for the aromatic tendrils of steam rising from the coffee. He rose from his chair and went to the fridge to grab the milk, adding just a splash, the way Julia liked it. "So how's the restaurant going? When do I get to see the dream come true?"

"More like a nightmare," Ethan muttered. He put his glasses back on, then looked over at Julia. "Just kidding. Don't panic."

"Julia panics?" Dave asked, sitting back down.

Julia gave Ethan a light smack on the arm. "I have a rep to live up to; don't tell people stuff like that."

"Is there really anything this kid doesn't know about you?"

"Not the point." Julia drank from her mug, then slid it across the marble top to Dave.

They spent the morning in the comforts of the kitchen and the joys of the banter that Julia had learned from her dads. She filled them in vaguely on the Nevers, stating that she and Dave were conducting important sociological research into the world of the modern teenager. It sometimes felt like Dave belonged in that kitchen, though he knew he was just using Tom and Ethan's warmth as a reason to think he and Julia were meant for more than friendship. When the afternoon started looming, Dave forced himself to leave the house, to cut his hair and maybe see his own family for a bit.

The mall was a slight detour on the way home, and throughout the walk he wished he were the kind of guy who wore hats. There weren't a lot of people around, but it was still embarrassing to be out in public. He imagined even the squirrels, usually nonchalant about human hairstyles, staring down at him from the trees and making disgusted faces.

When he walked through the glass doors of the mall, he knew right away he was going to run into someone he knew, someone from school, someone who would be witness to the atrocity he and Julia had committed on his head. The mall was swarming with families, couples in their twenties, packs of middle school girls sharing cups of lemonade. Huge banners hung from the rafters announcing a special weekend-only sale.

He sighed and kept his eyes cast down on the floor, trying to maneuver his way around the crowd without running into too many people. Before he knew it, he was at the Supercuts, and the hipster girl with the red hair and the half sleeve of tattoos had written his name down on her clipboard and told him to take a seat in the waiting area.

Just as he was sighing in relief, he saw that the only chair available was right next to Gretchen. She was reading, but almost as soon as his eyes landed on her, she looked up at him. She smiled at him—all lips, though, no imperfect lower teeth—and raised her hand in a wave.

He raised his hand up and mouthed *hello*, hoping she'd somehow missed his hair. Which, of course, she hadn't.

"Wow. What happened there?"

His stomach clenched as he took a seat next to her. "I know, I know."

"That couldn't have been by choice."

"I wouldn't have done it if I'd known it would end up looking like…" He motioned with his hands, pointing at the hair and trying to find a word that accurately described the fiasco sitting on his head.

"Like a wound festering in the eighteenth century before antibiotics were discovered?"

"That's very specific. But yes."

Gretchen smiled wide. She was in a simple white T-shirt and jeans, the beige sneakers that, he'd noticed lately, she wore most days. Dave felt his face flush and hoped she'd get called up to get her haircut soon, so she wouldn't have time to memorize what he looked like. He didn't know what to say, but was saved from a comment by a blow-dryer that went off nearby. Dave tried to seem casual as he looked around the Supercuts—two other guys waiting for their turn were on their phones, a woman sat with tinfoil in her hair reading a magazine, an old lady had one of those silver dome things over her head—but his eyes kept flicking back toward Gretchen. She kept her book on her lap, picked at a split end, smiled at him whenever their eyes would meet, looked away as shyly as he did.

"Sorry I haven't talked to you in class this week," Dave said once the hair dryer stopped. "I kept wanting to. But the more I thought about it, the more the other night at the Kapoors' felt like a dream and I wasn't really sure it happened. It did happen, right?"

Gretchen brought her book up to her face like she was smelling it, but Dave had the notion that she was just trying to hide a smile. He could see it in her eyes. "It happened," she said.

"Okay." Dave watched as a woman came in with her baby stroller and argued about the wait for an appointment. "I'm gonna talk to you in class, is what I'm trying to say," Dave said, feeling strange that he had the urge to tell her such a thing. "If you're okay with that."

"Good. You can help me improve my prank skills."

"You really feel strongly about keeping a straight face, huh?"

Gretchen shrugged and crossed her feet at her ankles. "I've got two older brothers. I was the butt of too many jokes when I was younger, and now I'm basically bitter at life and seeking revenge."

"You sound really bitter."

"Good, that's the whole shtick I'm going for." She motioned the length of her body, as if she was clearly exuding bitterness, as if she was dripping with anything other than sweetness.

Whoa. Where did that thought come from?

"It's working," Dave said, and the two of them smiled at each other for a second until Gretchen was called up by one of the stylists. He watched her lean her head back into the shampooing faucet and close her eyes as the water washed over her blond locks. She played with the book in her hands, flipping the cover over. Her nails were flecked with baby-blue polish.

Dave waited for his turn, trying not to get caught looking in Gretchen's direction as she got a trim. The two guys waiting next to him were still on their phones, occasionally glancing up at his hair. Dave was pretty sure one of them took a photo while pretending to search for a signal. But the embarrassment he'd felt only a few moments ago had faded some.

When it was his turn, the only open spot was once again right next to Gretchen. She was reading and this time she didn't notice him right away. The hair stylist—tall, black, wearing a tight shirt that showed off his sleek muscles—draped one of those protective sheets over Dave and then Velcroed it at the back. "What are we doing with this?" he asked, bravely running a hand through Dave's hair.

"For the love of God, take it all off."

"Wise choice," the stylist said. He grabbed an electric razor from his tools on the counter. "You kids never learn to let a professional do it."

Gretchen stopped reading and smiled at Dave through the mirror. Dave had never understood why people associated cheekbones with beauty, but now that he noticed Gretchen's, he got it. "You should save all of the hair in a bag," Gretchen said. "I don't know exactly what you'd do with it, but there's a prank in there somewhere."

"I don't think I'm ready to be the guy that collects hair in a bag."

Gretchen laughed in a way he hadn't seen before, this goofy laugh that showed off her front teeth and sounded like it came from a cartoon character.

"When I hit rock bottom, that's when I start collecting hair."

"What do you think people who collect hair do with it?"

"I don't know if those people actually exist. I think that's just something TV shows and movies made up for the creepiness factor and to get some laughs."

"Oh, they exist. I'm sure of it."

"You think?" Dave said. Just then, the redheaded hipster girl who'd been cutting Gretchen's hair brushed off the clippings from Gretchen's shoulder and said they were all done. Dave found himself thinking, *Don't go.*

Then his stylist turned on the razor and kept his head still, and Gretchen disappeared from Dave's sight. It was an abrupt and disappointing good-bye. Still, it was a little thrilling having a good conversation with someone who wasn't Julia. It was a little liberating, truth be told, to think of someone else for a while. When Dave stood up to pay, now sporting a completely shaved head, he saw that it hadn't been a good-bye at all; Gretchen was waiting for him at the front.

"I don't know if you drove here," Gretchen said, "but I can give you a ride home, if you want. Since we live so close." Without waiting for an answer, she reached up and ran a hand over his shaved head. "This feels nice."

"Thanks," he said, wondering if she could spot the goose bumps she'd given him. "I'd love a ride."

"Good." She smiled, then motioned with her head. "It's this way."

PARTICULAR SHADES

ANOTHER PERFECT CALIFORNIA DAY. There were plenty of them throughout the year, so many that they were nearly indistinguishable, a string of blessings that were mostly taken for granted, except for when there were three or four chilly days in a row and everyone suddenly longed for perfection again. So when Mr. Patch, Dave and Julia's AP English teacher, decided to have class outside, it was less an impulse to take advantage of the weather and more of an excuse to allow everyone to waste an hour.

They were supposed to be working on practice essays, but even Mr. Patch was lying against the tree where most of the seniors gathered for lunch, pretending to keep an eye on things. Some people from class were sitting at the picnic tables near the cafeteria, their notebooks (paper or computer) nowhere to be seen. A handful of people had put in their earphones as soon as they'd stepped outside. Julia and Dave separated themselves from the class immediately, and they lay out at the edge of the soccer field, where a little hill faced out at the blacktop and the rest of the school. Julia was resting her head on Dave's stomach, her pink hair just as bright as when they dyed it. The weight of her against him was like warmth added to the day. It quieted everything, as if the touch of her head on his stomach was a mute button, and all that existed was the two of them.

In the days since the hair coloring and the shenanigans with

Marroney in the Chili's bathroom, Julia had been in a fantastic mood. All she wanted to do was plan out the rest of the Nevers, starting with Dave's prom king campaign. It was hard not to get caught up in the excitement. Yes, he'd sat next to Gretchen during their last two classes together, and walked with her to her next class, even though his was on the other side of school and he'd arrived late. She was fun to talk to, and the more he found out about her, the more colorful she seemed. But this was Julia, and a maybe-crush could not compare.

Another class joined the unofficial festivities. An art class, judging from the large sketch pads the students carried with them. The teacher was reading a paperback as she walked, smug in her knowledge that if anyone could get away with having their class outside it was the art teacher. Dave spotted Gretchen among the art students, a dark green sketchbook with a pencil in the spiral binding tucked under her arm. She was talking to Joey Planko, a junior soccer player who, from what Dave had heard at the Kapoor party, was already getting scholarship offers. Frankly, he looked like he could receive scholarship offers solely for having muscles. He looked like the human version of a sports car.

Dave watched them walk across the blacktop, passing in front of where he and Julia were lying. He kept preparing his arm to wave at Gretchen when she noticed him, but her eyes were turned in Joey's direction. The two of them and a couple of other people made their way across the lush soccer field to the far goal, none of them casting so much as a glance in Dave and Julia's direction, and Dave was somewhat thankful to not have to explain to Julia his newfound friendship with Gretchen, or whatever it was.

"Debbie's been trying to kill the pink spots on her tail. Sometimes I catch her looking at my hair and I can just tell her brain is whirring, making the connection. She's going to come after me soon."

Dave looked down at Julia, whose eyes were still closed. "You're a goof."

"You can't use 'goof.' I use 'goof' about you." She raised her head a bit and adjusted her ponytail, then laid back against his sore ab muscles. "I bet that when we travel the world and we're hanging out with other travelers at hostels and stuff like my mom does, we're gonna fight each other for whose turn it is to tell people about the Nevers. 'You told it last time!' 'No, you did! Let me tell it.'"

"I don't think you've ever been as excited about anything as you are about this."

"Don't be hyperbolic. Remember that time when I asked for just one donut hole and they not only refused to charge me, but gave me three of them?"

"Yeah." Dave smiled at the memory. "You couldn't stop giggling for the whole car ride." He picked out a blade of grass that had gotten stuck in her hair. A shriek broke out across the soccer field, and when Dave looked in the direction it had come from, he saw Joey bear-hugging Gretchen, lifting her feet off the ground. She was laughing, allowing herself to be wrapped up.

"Kind of like the time that author you like responded to your e-mail."

"I was not giggling," Dave said. "My voice just cracked while laughing."

"I've never seen you happier," Julia said, poking his side, making him squirm.

All of a sudden it felt silly that he'd even thought he might be developing a crush on Gretchen. A few good conversations and noticing that she was prettier than he'd realized did not amount to anything. Okay, so she was friendlier than he'd given her credit for. But Dave was an outsider. Without Julia, he'd probably be a loner, and Gretchen was not one for loners. Her ex-boyfriend, the one who had graduated last year, he vaguely remembered, was very much a Joey Planko type. Athletic and popular and not even a dick about it. Dave couldn't recall the guy's name, but now flashes of the two of them last year came back to him. The guy had tattoos and could go from clean shaven to hipster beard within a week. Dave could grow exactly three hairs above his lip on each side.

The principal, Dr. Hill, walked out onto the blacktop and everyone held their breath, hoping that their temporary idyll wasn't quite over yet. But Dr. Hill squinted against the sun, lingered for a second at the entrance to the building, then took a seat at a picnic table and smiled his approval. Dave pulled his phone out of his pocket and played one of his favorite songs, Beck and Daniel Johnston singing "True Love Will Find You in the End." It felt a little cheesy and cliché, and therefore perfect, especially since the meaning would be lost on Julia. *Never pine silently*, the Nevers said. This felt like speaking up.

As the beautiful harmonica hook rang out, Dave put his hand on Julia's forehead, right above her temple. "My mom used to do this to me to get me to fall asleep," he said, starting to run his fingers gently in a circle.

Julia sighed. "I can see why. That feels nice."

She seemed to sink deeper into his stomach. Beck's honey-coated voice sang into the perfect California air, Dave mouthing the words. "You'll find out just who was your friend."

Dave glanced back at Gretchen and her circle of friends one last time before closing his eyes and putting her out of his mind.

○ ○ ○

When school let out that day, there was a palpable sense of happiness in the air. Dave knew that there were still interminably boring days to come. But for now they were forgotten.

Dave met Julia by her locker, though she didn't bother replacing any of the books in her bag. They ambled to Julia's Mazda, for once in no rush to leave. "That was actually nice. This even feels like a nostalgic walk down the halls," Dave said. He pretended to choke up. "I'm gonna miss it so much!"

"Maybe that nap in the sun fried my brain, but I can see myself looking back fondly on some parts of high school."

"You mean homecoming football games?"

"And the Kapoor parties." She reached out her hand and brushed her fingertips against the lockers they passed by. "I mean things like that resolution we wrote for Model UN last year where we blamed Disney for all the world's ills, or having class outside. That group video project for French where I convinced everyone that we should do an infomercial for tampons. I've been noticing lately that I laugh a whole lot more in class than I ever realized. I kept track today. Guess how many times someone laughed in class?"

They turned a corner and pushed open the doors that led to the parking lot. A few stringy clouds had shown up, the kind that really took hold of color during sunsets and lit up the sky in a way the sun just simply couldn't on its own. "I don't know. Six."

"Twelve on average per period."

"Twelve?"

"Twelve!" Julia said, slipping out of her moccasins as soon as they were off school grounds. "I know school in general can kind of suck, and a lot of people here haven't had an original thought their entire lives, but this place isn't always awful."

"Speaking of awful," Dave said, pointing out Marroney walking to his car, this time not feeling a pang of jealousy at all, but an appreciation for Julia, for how long she'd been in his life, for everything she brought into it. "Seduction, part deux?"

"His shirt is the exact same color your hair was."

"I'm kind of surprised he isn't constantly being seduced by someone."

"David Ruth Gonzalez, I detect a hint of sarcasm in your voice, and I'm telling you I won't have you insulting the love of my life."

"He's not the love of your life yet."

He grabbed her car keys from her hand. "I'll make us a playlist to listen to as we drive around, enjoying the beautiful day and talking about our strategy for my prom king campaign and how to get your mom to come down and see it all happen. But first, you're going to go over there and awkwardly court your math teacher. Try not to tickle him this time."

"I don't know what you mean by 'awkward.'" She removed her hair tie and slipped it on her wrist, then mockingly whipped her hair around. "Careful, it's about to get sexy in this vicinity."

"Eww."

"Sticks and stones, Gonzalez. Sticks and stones."

"It's Gutierrez. Go take your awkward womanly charms to that strange little man over there before he gets away and I puke all over the place."

Julia beamed a big smile at him, the kind of smile that had been making his day for years. There was love in the way she looked at him. Maybe not the particular shade of love that would suit him best, but he'd be a fool not to take as much of it as he could get.

He leaned back against Julia's Mazda and watched her sneak across the parking lot toward Marroney, crouching behind cars and rolling clumsily over their hoods in action hero/ninja fashion. A preppy kid yelled at her to get off his car, alerting Marroney to Julia's approach. He sped up, jiggling his keys when he got to his car door like the victim in a horror movie, escaping right before Julia could get her hands on him.

VIRAL

"IN ALL THE years you've known me, have I ever even hinted at the possibility that I could perform a double backflip off the roof and land safely on my feet?"

"There've been some hints."

"No, Julia."

"Well, I don't hear you coming up with any ideas, baldy. All we have right now is 'Hi, I'm Dave Gutierrez,' which isn't even your real name. If we don't add some excitement, this promotional video is only going to promote how uninteresting you are."

"That hurt," Dave said, plopping down on his bed. "Why don't we just make some really badass posters?"

"You know I didn't mean it like that. And there's no such thing as badass posters. A poster's not gonna win you the crown. The people want sexy viral videos, and sexy viral videos we will give them."

Dave picked up a little stuffed soccer ball that he'd had since he was little and had never thrown away because his mom had gotten it for him. He tossed it up a few times, trying to get it to graze the ceiling. "Why don't we switch? You run for prom queen and I'll try to seduce a teacher."

"You're not stealing Marroney away from me." Julia took a seat at Dave's desk and searched the Internet for some more prom king campaign videos. "So far, the basic trend I'm seeing here is a halfhearted attempt at being funny and low production value. Pop culture references, pop music, friends that are really bad actors. The occasional 'cool' teacher cameo and school inside jokes." She spun around to face Dave and propped her feet up on the corner of his bed, placing his computer on her lap. Her soles were permanently gray and callused and Dave loved the sight of them, even if they were, objectively speaking, gross. "Some of these are seriously awful. If ours is this bad I don't care how many people vote for you, we're committing seppuku at graduation."

"That might be an overreaction." He sat up, his back against the headboard, rolling the soccer ball back and forth on the bed until a bad spin caused it to fall to the ground. "I hate to admit it, but we might need Brett's help."

"Now you're talking. To think like them we have to associate with their kind."

"Your word choice has been concerning lately. You sound vaguely fascist." Julia stared him down and Dave sighed. "Throw me my phone, I'll see if I can bribe Brett with pizza to get him to help us out."

Julia reached for his phone on his desk and tossed it at him, then turned her attention back to prom campaign videos. He wasn't quite used to the pink hair yet, but her face was still as beautiful as it always had been. Sometimes, Dave wondered if maybe he saw more beauty in it than others did, if it was love alone that attracted him to her. Why other guys weren't constantly chasing after her was impossible to understand, though it wasn't something he questioned either. Sure, she'd seen a couple of guys over the last few years. But she did not receive the kind of attention he thought she deserved.

"How many times do you think I can use 'bro' in one text without him thinking I'm making fun of him?"

"Two, tops." She brought her index finger to her mouth and absentmindedly chewed on her nail. "Actually, he might get offended if you don't 'bro' him a few times."

"'Hey, bro. Julia and I are doing this prom king stuff and need your help, bro….' Ugh, I already want to punch myself in the face."

He deleted the message, checked his e-mail and social media, then opened up the text function again and retyped the message as it was. "Wouldn't it be interesting if every text message you received told you how many times it'd been edited before being sent?"

Julia shivered. "Don't talk about that stuff. It makes me get existential."

"How do text messages make you feel existential?"

"I start thinking about exactly that: how people can edit a thought before sending it out to the world. They can make themselves seem more well-spoken than they are, or funnier, smarter. I start thinking that no one in the world is who they say they are, then my mind goes to how I also edit myself, not just online but in real life, except for those rare instances like right now where I'm ranting—even though that's a lie because I've had this train of thought before and damned if I didn't tweak it in my head a few times to make it sound better—and then my mind starts racing so furiously I can't control my thoughts, and I start thinking about robots and wondering if I'm even a real person. Then I have to watch cartoons to shut my brain off."

Dave blinked at Julia. "Sometimes I forget how truly insane you are."

"That's what I'm saying! Sometimes I wonder why I'm so popular at school." Julia clicked a few times on the computer.

"There are far too many prom king campaign videos that involve white kids rapping."

"White kids are allowed to rap."

"Not like this," Julia said.

"Speaking of popularity, have you noticed people being more talkative with you in class since the Kapoor party? It's like we accidentally initiated ourselves into a higher level of acceptance just by showing up there."

Julia glanced up at him over the top of the computer. "Maybe with you, flip-cup champion. People still avoid me like a slightly more contemporary version of the plague."

"You sure you aren't insulting people somehow? Giving off a closed-off vibe by, I don't know, puking on them or something?"

"Puking on people is not an insult."

Dave stood from the bed to go retrieve the stuffed soccer ball. While he was up the doorbell rang, not that pleasant one-two chime that other houses had but a horrifying singsong melody that stretched out far too long. Dave ran out his bedroom door before whoever was there had a chance to ring again. He jostled down the stairs, steadying himself with the handrail in case his socks and the hardwood floors decided to conspire against him.

When he reached the door he took a second to catch his breath, chastising himself for being out of breath from going *down* the stairs. Why wasn't exercising on the Nevers list? He swung open the door, expecting Brett to have forgotten his keys.

"Hi," Gretchen said. She was in her soccer uniform, a grass stain on her knee. Her face was flushed. "Your house was on the way," she said, looking down the street from the direction she came. The wind whipped her hair in front of her face. "I thought after we ran into each other at the mall you might try to do more than just say hi at school. I thought you might..." She looked down at her soccer cleats and shifted the weight of her backpack, which was black with a white scuff mark across the bottom and a red button pinned on the right shoulder strap. "Anyway, since you live so close, I figured I'd come by and tell you that I want us to talk more." She looked back up but only met Dave's eyes for a second before glancing away. A smile tugged at the corners of her mouth, like it had when she had tried making a joke at the Kapoor party. "You're easy to talk to. And you're nice. And you make me laugh a lot." A strand of hair had blown across her face and into her mouth, and she laughed and pulled it back behind her ear. "You seem great, Dave. And I thought that maybe you might be thinking the same about me, but..."

A car rolled past the street behind Gretchen, blasting Mexican ranchera music. Dave realized he'd been smiling for a while, and he felt himself blush just at the realization. His T-shirt was dotted with yellow stains from the Thai food he and Julia had had for lunch. It was only yesterday that he'd given up on the prospect of anything but friendliness with Gretchen, and now he felt a giddiness rising so quickly it was useless to deny that it was there. Dave leaned against the open door. "I'm glad you came. I've been trying to figure out what to do with a bag full of human hair. Any ideas?"

Gretchen smiled, her big brown eyes lighting up. Her smile made him feel like she'd just handed him a tray of freshly baked chocolate-chip cookies.

"Dave, I have an idea!" Julia called out from inside the house. He turned around to see her coming down the stairs, his laptop in her hands. "We might have to hire hundreds of people to help make it happen, but with Brett's help we—"

She stopped on the stairs when she noticed Gretchen at the door. "Oh. Hi."

"Hi, Julia," Gretchen said, offering a shy wave. She looked back at Dave. "Think about what I said. I'll see you later?"

"Yeah." Dave nodded. Gretchen gave him one last smile and then turned away, taking the steps at the front of his house with a little hop. Dave closed the door and turned to face Julia, his heart pounding. For some reason he felt like he'd been caught at something. At mingling with the clichés, at hiding a crush.

"Getting in with the popular kids," she said, raising an eyebrow. "Savvy political move."

"Thanks," Dave said, stuck by the door, waiting for his heart to quiet down. His hands were shaking.

Julia lingered at the stairs, and Dave wondered if she could tell that political savvy was the furthest thing from his mind. Then she came down and joined him by the front door, showing him the computer screen. "Check this out. We can hire an explosives expert for only three hundred dollars an hour, plus supplies. That's cheaper than a lawyer or a therapist! A bake sale for charity isn't on the Nevers, but maybe we can whip up some cupcakes with the PTA and raise money for some dynamite."

The rest of the evening, Julia rattled on about how blowing stuff up was the sure way to win the public's heart. She found epic music for the video's soundtrack, looked up junk cars on eBay, searched Google Maps for nearby fields where they could blow up a car without anyone getting hurt. She even started writing a script for the video, chock-full of references to movies released in the last five years. She took over his phone and started texting Brett about what he would need to see get blown up in exchange for his vote for prom king. She was funny, and charming, and energetic, and yet all Dave could think about was Gretchen.

SOLVE FOR X

DAVE, JULIA, AND Brett were at one of the tables outside Fratelli's, the tangy smell of pepperoni thick in the air. Brett and Julia were discussing the viral video, but Dave was lost in his thoughts.

Ever since he reached the right age for it, basically since he met Julia, he'd considered himself a romantic, an advocate of love, of people getting tangled up in each other. He liked hearing about people hooking up because it was just more evidence of human chemistry, that sparks occurred and brought two people together, if only for a moment. But because he'd only ever loved Julia, and only ever in that particular way that he loved her, he'd never experienced getting tangled up firsthand.

He'd kissed exactly one girl in his life: his cousin's friend sophomore year when he'd gone to Fresno for a family reunion. That kiss had happened only because the girl was deceptively quick and, despite her awkwardness, had aimed really well when she'd nosedived at Dave's lips. It'd been a strange first kiss for someone who'd romanticized them for so long, and Dave had fled as soon as he could. Since then there'd only been the constant longing for Julia. He'd never pursued anyone else because there wasn't anyone who could ever pull his interest away from her. In the process, he'd missed out on a lot of normal high school experiences, clichés that even Julia hadn't avoided: crushes; first kisses; the slow, stumbling, eager approach to sex, with various successes or failures. He'd reserved all of it for Julia, never admitting to himself that it might not come. Rather, never admitting to himself that it wouldn't, that Julia loved him in a completely different, yet faultless, way. That she loved him, she always had, just in a way that shouldn't be interfered with.

Maybe, finally, it was time to pursue. He pulled his phone out and went to his contact list. At the Kapoor party, Gretchen had grabbed his phone and entered her name as *Section 16520 of the Family Code.* He clicked on her name and went to the message screen. Nothing had been said yet between them, and it was a little intimidating to know where to start. Just hi? Ask her out? A knock-knock joke? He held his thumbs over the keyboard, waiting for something to sound right in his head. Then he realized he'd been ignoring Brett and Julia for a long time and resolved to text Gretchen later that night.

"Look, I'm all for blowing shit up," Brett was saying, sprinkling, as usual, way too much Parmesan cheese on another slice of pepperoni-and-mushroom pizza, "and to be honest I didn't think an artsy girl like you would have such a badass idea. But the prom committee would probably disqualify you for it."

"There's a prom committee? People care that much?"

"Says the girl who's buying me pizza in order to get her friend voted onto the ballot."

"Oh, I'm sorry, did I offend the Man Formerly Known as Prom King by implying that prom is not important enough to necessitate a committee? And I can repeat all of that in monosyllables, if you like."

"Don't use a five-dollar when a fifty-cent word will do. Your boy Mark Twain said that." Brett was only a couple of years older than Dave, and though he sometimes acted like he was still twelve, he looked much more grown-up, his features aged by all the time he spent in the sun during his construction jobs, by losing his mom at eleven and having to look after his little brother.

"Shit, that was actually a good one." Julia tossed her napkin at Brett.

"What ballot?" Dave asked.

"Welcome to the conversation," Julia said, breaking off a piece of crust and dipping it in her side order of marinara sauce. "The campaign isn't actually for prom king; it's just to get voted onto the ballot. That vote is in April. Then people vote for prom king from the four or five people on the ballot at the prom."

"If you wanted Dave to be prom king, you should have tried talking to other people for the last four years. People vote their friends onto the ballot, so the people with the most friends get on. Dave has one friend."

"But she's such a great friend!" Julia cried out.

"Hey, I have more than one friend."

"Like who?" they both said at the same time.

"Jinx!" Julia cried out.

"No one plays jinx anymore," Brett scoffed.

Julia stuck her tongue at him. "You owe me a bibliography citing your sources. People definitely still play jinx. Oh, and by the way, no one 'plays' jinx. They adhere to the unmalleable rules of jinx, much like they do gravity."

Brett rolled his eyes, though a smile remained. Sometimes, he and Julia joked around as easily as she and Dave did, though mostly they were the butt of each other's jokes. "The point is, if you guys really want this to happen—and I'm still having trouble understanding why you're all of a sudden interested in prom—you have to either make a ton of friends, or do something memorable that'll have people thinking about Dave when it's time to vote."

"How are explosives not memorable?"

"Forget the explosives! It sounds awesome but it won't work. A viral video could do the trick, provided it actually goes viral."

"How do we get the video to go viral?" Dave asked.

"If I knew that I wouldn't be here eating pizza with you. I'd be busy cashing in on Internet fame and all the groupies that come with it."

"Gross," Dave and Julia said at the same time, sharing a look at the second jinx of the conversation.

"There's no formula you can follow. If it's funny it'll help, but that doesn't guarantee anything. Some videos go viral, some don't." He took a bite of pizza, the excess Parmesan raining down onto his plate and sticking to his chin. The table next to them, a family of four, stood up to go, leaving their trash behind.

Dave watched them walk away and, like they often did, he and Julia got up to clean their mess. "Bunch of savages," Julia muttered to herself when they rejoined Brett at the table.

"You guys are so weird."

"Why? Because we clean up after savages that can't do it on their own?"

"No," Brett said, wiping his face with a napkin. "Because you did it at the exact same time, without saying anything to each other. It's like you're twins who can communicate telepathically." He chuckled and then threw the napkin down on his empty plate, pushing it away from him. "Why are you guys doing this anyway? It doesn't seem like you."

"You'd never understand," Dave said, giving Julia a look.

"Never," Julia repeated, almost in a whisper.

"Never," Dave said, even quieter. They kept going back and forth until they broke out laughing.

Brett stared blankly at them. "So weird. But seriously, why the sudden interest?" He looked at Julia. "Are you finally admitting that all you've ever wanted is to go to prom with the prom king?"

"That comment was so gross that I'm taking away all the credit I gave you for your Mark Twain zinger."

"I don't hear a denial."

"Brett, you're shaming the family name. Please stop," Dave said.

In the back of his mind, Dave was thinking about prom, the long understanding that he and Julia would go together. It was silly to think about how Gretchen would affect all of that, ridiculous to already be thinking that far ahead. But there it was anyway, the thought taking root. A picture flashed in Dave's mind, quick and without warning, of Gretchen with her hands around his neck, pulling him close.

"Shit, we're late!" Julia said, rising suddenly from the table.

"Late for what?" Dave asked.

"It's a surprise." She collected the trash on the table and tossed it in the nearby trash can. "But we have to get going now or we're not gonna make it in time."

"You guys need a ride?" Brett asked.

"No, thanks. It's at the Broken Bean. We'll walk."

"All right. Thanks for the pizza. Good luck making all your secret fantasies come true," he said to Julia. He unlocked the doors to his pickup truck but instead of getting in he lingered, as if waiting for Julia's retort.

o o o

Dave knew it was going to be an interesting night as soon as he saw the sign in front of the Broken Bean that announced it was slam-poetry night. But he didn't quite understand how interesting it would be until they took a seat just as Marroney made his way to the stage.

"My God."

"I know," Julia said. "I'm already getting chills. Prepare to swoon."

"You're not gonna give up on this are you?"

"True love persists, my friend," Julia said, starting to whisper, since Marroney was adjusting the microphone. He was wearing a maroon button-up shirt that had full sleeves, for once, and though his jeans appeared to have zippers all over them, he was also wearing a fedora that actually looked good on him, even with his mullet poking out the back. He ran a thumb and forefinger in opposite directions across his mustache, smoothing out the hairs or simply preparing for his performance. Then he pulled out a little red notebook from his back pocket and cleared his throat in that resounding way that only the middle-aged can. A shriek of feedback rang out through the coffee shop.

Then he closed his eyes and the coffee shop quieted down with anticipation.

"Everything about me was shaped by the boy who died." He paused for effect, letting the silence thicken the room. "No, no, don't be sad, this was a long time ago and all the tears that were meant for him have already been cried. I was little, too, a tiny blob of a human being, not yet formed, life's pounding fists had yet to tell me who I was going to be. I've seen parents, grandparents, uncles, and aunts die, but it was the first funeral I attended that taught me to love life."

Marroney had the confident, assertive cadence of slam poetry down perfectly, which was bizarre to see from a guy who looked like Marroney. He was more animated than Dave had ever seen him, although Dave had never had him as a teacher, and it made him wonder if that's what he was like in class. At one point the crowd let loose a round of applause, whistles, and *Ohh!*s that Dave knew happened only when the poet had said a really good line. Julia was smiling wildly, whooping along with the crowd.

Marroney snapped his fingers and the room quieted back down. "This is going to sound like a cliché, but what's that matter when it's true." He snapped again. "It takes less than a second for the sound of the friction between my fingers to reach your ears." Another snap. "That's the line between life and death, and you can't see it but you sure as hell can hear it." Another snap. "Listen." Snap. "To." Snap. "Every." Snap. "Second."

When Marroney left the stage to the sound of applause, the emcee, a fat guy in a bowling shirt and a rainbow-colored tie, read out the scores from the judges. Then he announced that they were going to take a short break and the last round of poets would have their turn. "First up after the break is Julia," he said, reading from a clipboard. "So, Julia, get ready to slam."

Dave turned to Julia. "You're not."

"Oh, I am."

"You're going to embarrass yourself, aren't you?"

"Not at all. But if Marroney doesn't fall in love with me tonight, I might need to hire some outside help, because I don't know what else to do." Julia pulled out a folded piece of paper from her pocket. Before she unfolded it, it looked a lot like the Nevers list had, her loopy handwriting showing through on the back of the page.

Dave caught a glimpse of the title. "He's going to file a restraining order."

"That or a marriage certificate," Julia said, grinning. "After his performance, I really wouldn't mind."

"I don't know if it was *that* good."

"Dave, it was so good, you're probably pregnant right now, just from the sexiness of the words."

When Julia took the stage, with her bare feet and pink hair, she looked like someone who belonged at a slam-poetry reading. She was wearing a high-waisted skirt and a soft cotton gray T-shirt with the words PURA VIDA printed across the front. Dave glanced over to see Marroney's reaction, but he didn't have a good angle.

"Hi," Julia said, making her voice a little lower and throatier, affecting a shy look in her eye that Dave knew perfectly well was meant to be seductive. "This one's called *Solve for* X, *or Why Mathematicians Must be Good at Sex*."

A few chuckles spread across the room, but Julia didn't drop the act. She lowered her head, hanging on to the mic stand like a rock star, her pink hair hanging in front of her face like a curtain waiting to be pulled up. Someone shifted out of his line of sight, and Dave turned to see Marroney put a hand to his forehead to hide his face.

"There's something about the slope of his"—Julia paused with a smile—"cosine that drives me to irrational equations. There's something about how he can recite pi to forty digits that makes my…heart swell exponentially. If *X* is the point where two lines meet, let my tangent and his intersect and repeat." Someone in the crowd let out a whoop. Dave sipped from his coffee, unable to hide his smile. "I plotted him on my graph, and he touches *all* my quadrants."

A few more shouts let out, and one of the judges was nodding. Julia pulled the microphone from its stand and started speaking louder, not even giving the audience time to react before moving on to the next line.

"We'll never be apart but he still calls me his *x*-axis because I'm *always* horizontal. When he's near, I'm not multiplying or subtracting or dividing, I'm just picturing us with no added variables. I must be his prime number because there's only room for him inside my equation."

The crowd was starting to buzz. Even the soft clink of dishes being put in the kitchen had quieted down. Just a week or so ago, Dave would probably have felt humiliated that Julia could muster up a whole poem full of math sex puns aimed at Marroney when she had never felt as much as a pulse in his direction. But tonight, with Gretchen taking up his thoughts, Dave felt only pride at Julia's cleverness. There was a certain letting go within him, like something inside his chest was literally relaxing its grip. It was time to appreciate everything about Julia without fretting about what she couldn't provide.

Apparently, Marroney didn't feel the same way. As Julia continued her performance, Marroney leaned over to whisper something to the redheaded woman sitting next to him, then grabbed his blazer off the back of his chair and squeezed past the people in his row, his cheeks a bright shade of red.

"And if—" She stopped as soon as she saw him leaving the coffee shop, and immediately her shtick fell away. She dropped the microphone to her side and bit her bottom lip. "Dammit," she said. Then she shrugged and tucked the microphone back into its stand.

As she hopped off the stage, the crowd, confused at the abrupt ending, broke out into scattered applause. "Get that look off your face, David O'Neal Macbeth. He'll be mine in the end."

"You know what, Julia, I don't doubt it. He'd be a fool not to take the opportunity."

Julia laughed, then grabbed her Ecuadorean bag from the back of the chair she'd been sitting in. "When you say it like that, it actually sounds gross." Julia slung her bag over her shoulder. "I know it's a weeknight but you wanna have a sleepover? Feeling pretty good right now."

"Always."

"Actually gonna Skype with my mom, too. You can say hi."

"Wow, moving up to Skype dates, huh?"

Julia couldn't contain her smile. Dave understood more than anything Julia's affection for her mom, though as long as he'd known her that affection had been tinged with disappointment, with longing. He could see the way it colored everything she did. The Nevers list had been written with her in mind, he knew, and it was now being acted out for her. Like a girl at the edge of the pool, refusing to dive in until Mommy looked, Julia wanted her mom's attention. He would never say anything like that out loud. But it made him protective of Julia, of the next disappointment her mom would inevitably deliver. While Dave had nuggets of bittersweet memories of his own mom to return to and occasionally talk about with his dad—the day they'd all gone to the harbor, rented a boat on a whim, the fine white mist of the ocean rising up the sides of the boat—Julia had nothing of her mother to hold close. There was no past life that included her; there was only the longing for her. It was the only thing she'd ever had.

Later that night, Julia set up her computer on the kitchen island, chatting excitedly with her mom. Her mom had the same radiant blue eyes as Julia, and her hair was mostly auburn, with the odd gray hair shimmering in the light of her Mexico City living room. She wore a silver ring in her nose, and every now and then a guy would cross the room behind her, though she didn't acknowledge his presence. Dave stood by the fridge, rummaging through mounds of Tupperware, opening each one, taking a taste, then leaving a Post-it for Tom and Ethan with his thoughts.

"What's with the hair, Jules?"

"You like it?" Julia said, tugging a tress down in front of her face. "I did it ironically. We did Dave's hair, too, but it turned out not so well." She went on to explain the Nevers, all they'd done for it and all that was still to do. Dave listened, wincing at the naked longing in Julia's voice, hoping that Julia's mom wouldn't disapprove, because he didn't want Julia to lose interest. For whatever reason, without the Nevers Dave pictured things with Gretchen fizzling out, a return to normalcy that no longer included anyone outside him and Julia.

"Where are those fathers of yours? I wanna say hi," Julia's mother cut in, without any comment on the Nevers. Dave watched Julia try to hide the disappointment that, for him, was so clear to see. "I miss their faces. Plus, I have a little proposition for them."

"They're out. They've been stressed 'cause of restaurant stuff, so they went out to watch a movie and have ice cream. What's the proposition? I'm pretty much the head of the household anyway."

Julia's mom's laugh was throaty; it sounded like a few decades' worth of cigarette smoke. "Very well, then, head of the household. I'm thinking about coming to visit."

"Fuckin' do it!" Julia said, her mood bouncing back immediately. Her legs started jittering, as if she were trying to keep the excitement offscreen.

"Nothing's for sure yet. But I miss the Bay Area and there are some events on the West Coast this summer that I want to go to. I figured that, if it was okay with your dads, I'd come hang out for a week or so. Near the end of the school year."

"Ooh! Are you going to be my prom date?"

"Easy tiger." Julia's mom laughed again. "I was thinking sometime around graduation. I have no interest in going to the event itself, because commencement speeches are the worst thing in the world. But maybe the after-party. Do your dads let you party?"

"I let myself party."

"How Beastie Boys of you. Good. E-mail me about dates and stuff so I don't forget, and I'll keep in touch. Again, no promises. But I do wanna see you. I gotta run, kiddo."

"Okay," Julia said. "Talk to you later."

"Bye. Oh, and, Jules? That Nevers list? Awesome idea. Keep doing that. No point in living a life less ordinary if you don't know what the other side looks like." With a flair for the dramatic, Julia's mom cut the call off. Julia shut her computer calmly, beaming.

She was so excited they'd stayed up talking until two in the morning, even though they had school the next day. The kind of conversation that quickly deteriorated into laughter, conversation that wasn't really about anything other than the desire to not fall asleep. Finally, during a lull in laughter, Dave had looked up and seen Julia asleep peacefully.

He was sprawled out on the floor between Julia's bed and her window, barely covering himself up in the ratty sleeping bag that he always used on their sleepovers. He was giving himself goose bumps thinking about Gretchen, looking at her name on his phone. Behind him, Julia was curled up near the edge of the bed, her face tucked beneath the covers, one bare knee poking out from the sheets. She was a sound sleeper, breathing so imperceptibly that after all these years Dave still sometimes sat up, checking to make sure she was okay.

Debbie was curled up at Dave's feet, and a sliver of the moon was visible through a crack in the blinds. There was a stale smell to the sleeping bag, a smell that had always been comforting because there was only one place he ever smelled it. He used to fall asleep in this spot on the floor fantasizing chastely that Julia would simply climb off the bed and lie next to him, their noses and foreheads touching, hands clasped together.

Now, free of those daydreams, Dave looked at his phone. The message history between Dave and Gretchen was still completely blank, but he finally knew what he wanted to say.

Hi, Gretchen. It's Dave. I think you're great, too.

TREE HOUSE

THE IDEA TO do another Never came to Dave one morning at the same moment as he took his first bite of sugary breakfast cereal. He hadn't outgrown kids' cereals, or the simple pleasure of playing the games on the back of the box. It reminded him of his mom, truth be told, the way she'd let him pick out which cereal he wanted when they'd go grocery shopping together, the way she'd scowl as he slurped the leftover milk and its swirls of artificial coloring. Some days were like that still, everything a reminder. That no one ever brought her up in his house didn't mean she was absent. It was actually in the silences that he remembered her most often, and today his dad hadn't spoken a word, just poured himself a bowl of the same cereal.

Dave skipped the bus that morning and decided to walk to school, and to do it slowly. It was a cool morning, and Dave had not brought a sweater with him. But the cold felt good against his skin, maybe because he felt liberated. Liberated to enjoy his best friend's company, to enjoy the rest of the school year without having to always fret about what to do with that love that had been festering for so long. Gretchen had texted him back the next morning, and they'd been talking ever since.

Before the Nevers, summer had felt like a far-off place, surrounded by swamps of boredom that he'd have to lug his way through. But now it felt more like a pleasant hike, with plenty of pretty views and maybe some hot springs along the way. Okay, it was a little early in the morning for similes, but Dave was now looking forward to the last couple months of high school. The Nevers would be fun to complete, especially if he didn't have to worry about how things went with Julia. Who knew how things would play out with Gretchen, but there were possibilities there, more than he'd ever really had. In the fall he'd be at UCLA and Julia would be nearby in Santa Barbara and maybe by then his life would be entirely different. He'd be dating Gretchen, or would have at least experienced love firsthand. Or maybe nothing would happen with Gretchen and his life would be exactly the same, just unburdened by unrequited love. Maybe that was enough.

He arrived to homeroom almost at the same time as Julia, right before the bell went off. He accepted one of her earphones as they took a seat together and waited for her to be awake enough for conversation. When she paused the music, he told her about the idea he'd had to break the first Never on the list: *Never be recognized by your lunch spot.*

○ ○ ○

They met Sunday night at school, Brett driving his pickup truck straight onto the blacktop where Julia was already waiting, early for once. In the darkening light of the evening, Dave could barely see her silhouette leaning against the tree that they'd be, according to Brett, "pimping out." Brett had brought work gloves and goggles for everyone, along with all the supplies: planks of wood, and two-by-fours, and even a generator with some work lights. He claimed to have borrowed it all with permission, which Dave found highly unlikely, although he couldn't help but feel flattered by his brother's efforts. Brett had even drawn up some plans after talking with Dave and Julia on Friday about how they envisioned the project. Before they started work, Brett pulled out his camera and started recording.

"Why are you filming this?"

"Because," Brett said, "*this* is how you get voted onto the prom king ballot." He got some shots of the tree where the seniors gathered for lunch, which, over the weekend, would become the tree house known as Dave and Julia's lunch spot. He zoomed in on the plans he had drawn out, then set up a tripod on the hill by the soccer field for a time-lapse video.

"You're being strangely helpful," Julia said, putting on her gloves and eyeing Brett. "I didn't know you could be…"

"A nice person?" Brett said. "I'm a little hurt by that."

"I wasn't trying to insinuate anything, I was actually struggling for a way to complete the thought. But, yeah, 'nice person' works. I thought you were just going to be critical of the plan. Like with the explosions."

"Truth be told, I've been waiting for years for you guys to come out of your shells. I wanted to be around to watch it happen."

"Shells? What shells? I'm not shy."

"It has nothing to do with shyness. The little tortoise shell the two of you live in without letting the rest of the world in," Brett said, turning on the generator, the whirring cutting off Julia's chance to retort. She looked over at Dave, who could only shrug. There was probably some truth in what he'd said.

At first it didn't seem like they were accomplishing much. Dave and Julia stacked piles of wood around the tree. Brett would hand Dave a few pencil-marked boards and tell him where to hammer in nails, which Dave would do it slowly, careful not to miss the neat little *X*s. Music playing from Brett's truck filled the night, though it was often drowned out by sawing, drilling, and Julia making fun of Brett's taste in music.

Then, all of a sudden, there were stairs leading up the tree to where the first of the branches spread out to cast a shade that the seniors claimed as their own. The skeleton of a tree house had appeared almost as if through magic. It was nothing that Dave would dare to get into yet, but if he squinted at it he could see it coming to life, like a connect-the-dots drawing that was still a missing a few lines.

With each plank that was hammered into place, each branch sawed out of the way, a palpable sense of accomplishment built in the air, or maybe that was just happening in Dave's head. Every now and then Julia's arm would brush against his, bare despite the chilly night—they'd all started sweating early, and long sleeves were quickly rolled up, sweaters discarded into a small pile in the bed of the pickup truck, which early in the night held tons of supplies and now was mostly bare. It would be a lie to say he felt nothing at the touch of her skin—skin doesn't forget so quickly—nor would it be honest to say it didn't make him happy—hearts are even worse at learning new habits—but it didn't feel momentous anymore. In fact, the shiver down his spine rather quickly led to thoughts of Gretchen, and it was with her face in mind that he put together the tree house.

When the sun started to bruise the sky with its approach, the three of them put their tools down and looked at the tree. Dave was sweating, and he could hear Julia and Brett breathing heavily beside him. While Brett made a run to a nearby deli for a huge thermos of coffee and a box of bagels, Julia and Dave added the finishing touches: applying a coat of varnish on the outside, sanding away the rough edges on the counter that faced out at the entire school, arranging an armory of pillows purchased at a Goodwill store and sprayed with disinfectant before being spread around the tree house floor. Everything was now ready for seniors in their last two languid months of school before freedom.

They broke it in together, spilling grains of sugar and drops of creamy coffee over their work and talking giddily, despite the accumulated exhaustion. Dave and Julia were an hour or so away from having to sit through class, but there was a sense that they'd done something lasting and meaningful.

"Hold this pen with me," Julia said, pulling out the Nevers list from her back pocket.

"Have you seriously been carrying that with you every day?"

"Shut up and hold this pen," she said. He wrapped his fingers around the pen and then Julia's hand covered his own. She moved the pen across the page. "There. We have a lunch spot now."

Brett swallowed down a bite of bagel. "Shit, I wish I would have gotten that on tape. That would have been perfect." He wiped some cream cheese from the corner of his mouth and went to get the camera. "Say it again."

Julia laughed and shook her head, folding the list away as if it were a treasure map. "Too late, man. It's done."

Brett folded up his camera, then turned on his stool to admire the work. "Not too shabby."

They joined him, identical threefold smiles on their faces. "Thanks for doing this, Brett. This was really cool of you."

Brett nodded, took a sip from his coffee. After a moment or two, he stood up, folding his gloves into his back pocket. "It was fun hanging out with you guys," he said, and he extended his hand for Dave to shake, which he did. It struck him that Brett might have been one more person he'd mistakenly assumed he knew all about. He wondered how much he missed their mom, whether he, too, wished his dad were better at bringing her up. "Thanks," he said, the word suddenly inadequate for what he was feeling.

Brett nodded, then offered his hand to Julia, who looked at it and chuckled. "A handshake? Please." She put her coffee down on the counter and rose to give Brett a hug. "I underestimated how cool you are."

"I think I did, too," Brett said, pulling away from the hug somewhat awkwardly.

"But I still don't think you know what 'artsy' means."

"Fine. I'll call you a pyromaniac from now on." He smiled, then disappeared down the staircase.

A few minutes after Brett's pickup had pulled away from the blacktop, the first of the teachers started showing up, their classroom windows sliding open, their silhouetted heads looking down at their desks, most of them not even looking outside. "How many more Nevers to go?" Dave asked.

"I'm not counting Marroney or prom king yet, so three down, seven to go."

Dave drank from his coffee, thought about the last Never. At the start of it all, he probably wouldn't have said anything. But now that he was liberated from certain things, his curiosity got the best of him. "What about the last one? We're not going to date each other, are we?"

Julia smirked, looping a strand of hair behind her ear. "I'd actually thought about that already." She spun around on the stool she'd taken, one of the dozen that lined the edge of the tree house. The sun was getting ready to peek out from behind the hills, though the morning fog would probably make for an unimpressive sunrise. "We were always gonna go to prom together, right? We can just call that a date. Our one and only date."

"Okay," Dave said simply, finding a sort of comfort in the words being spoken out loud.

○ ○ ○

By lunchtime, Brett had sent the video through his system of friends, many of them still closely linked to current SLO High students. Everyone knew who was responsible for the tree house that had sprung up magically over the weekend, and when Dave walked into the courtyard, the assembled seniors broke into applause. Julia had gone to nap in the library, but she insisted that Dave continue his ploy to get in with the popular crowd for the sake of his campaign. He might have shied away from going alone if he hadn't seen Gretchen climb the stairs he'd helped build.

"Dave!" Vince Staffert called to him from the corner of the tree house. "I saved a spot for you, man." He stood and waved him over, a bag of chips in his hand. The tree house was packed, people on every stool and sprawled out on the floor, making use of the pillows. Underclassmen gazed up with wonder, peering like tourists drawn in by a crowd, wondering what they were missing out on.

As it turned out, Gretchen and Vince were friends, and when Dave took the seat that Vince had reserved for him, Gretchen was only two stools away. Vince and a few others kept talking about what a cool thing Dave and Julia had done, but Dave could barely focus on what they were saying. He and Gretchen kept exchanging looks so obviously that it was a shock no one called them out on it.

He chatted amicably with everyone around, even laughed a little with Vince, who was all the time proving himself to be nicer than Dave had ever given him credit for. That other clichéd football-player side of him that Dave assumed existed never made an appearance. But at one point he decided there was only one person he really wanted to talk to, and when the girl sitting next to Gretchen stood up, he immediately moved over.

"How was your weekend?"

"Not quite as constructive as yours," Gretchen said, plopping a piece of papaya into her mouth with a smile.

"I see what you did there."

"I've been thinking of it for, like, six whole minutes."

Dave laughed, leaning into her shoulder with a nudge. "Come on, how was your weekend?"

Gretchen chewed thoughtfully for a while. "Not too shabby. I think some weekends feel wasted if you don't have a ton of fun, and some feel wasted if you don't have a ton of sleep, and I did a solid amount of both."

"What did you do for fun?"

"I slept," Gretchen said, picking out another piece of fruit from her Tupperware.

"You are on a roll today."

"I think you bring it out of me," Gretchen said with a shrug, pushing the Tupperware in his direction to offer him a piece. He reached his fingers in for a piece of pineapple, feeling a little cheesy in longing for their hands to brush against each other.

When the bell rang and lunch was over, Dave and Gretchen separated themselves from the group. It happened almost magnetically, the two of them drifting off from the rest, keeping pace only with each other.

"So," Gretchen said, hoisting a binder to her chest the way nerdy kids in movies did, "you built a tree house."

"I had some help." Dave shrugged.

"Still, pretty cool. Was it your idea?"

"Inspired by a desire for us to have our own lunch spot," he said, aware that he'd purposely avoided saying Julia's name but not sure why. "But yes, my idea."

"I wonder what your grandkids will feel when they read about you in history books."

"An immense and prideful love, obviously."

They walked down the tree house stairs slowly, in no rush to make it to class before the bell rang. Other kids gathered their belongings and prepared for that last, brutal stretch of classes before the day broke free. Some were looking in Dave's direction, smiling, or whispering, or just staring for a moment before walking away. Dave wasn't sure he'd ever get used to eyes turning to look at him, but it no longer felt like it had never happened before.

When they reached the building, Dave put his hand on the door to open it for Gretchen, but hesitated for a second. He met her eyes and the words simply escaped him in a way he didn't fully understand, like the drops of rain suddenly becoming too heavy and breaking free from a cloud after staying together for so long. "Do you want to see my favorite bench in the world?"

Gretchen smiled but said nothing for a second, as if she wanted the words to soak in. Nicky Marquez passed between the two of them, looking at his phone and unaware of what he was stepping through. When he opened the door, Dave's eyes glanced into the hallway, and he saw Julia rubbing the sleep from her eyes, walking his direction. "Let's go, David Bro Bronofsky. Two more classes and then we're free."

"Friday," Dave added quietly. "We'll have some coffee on my favorite bench in the world."

"Yes," Gretchen said, nodding. "I'd like that."

DATE

DAVE CHECKED HIS phone and slid it back in his pocket for the tenth time in the last thirty seconds or so. He was sitting on his bench at Morro Bay, trying to avoid looking around frantically for any sight of Gretchen. When she showed up, he wanted her to see him first, sitting calmly with his legs stretched out in front of him, his hands folded on his stomach, a content smile on his face that showed he saw joy in the world, even on this unusually gray day.

Though he was certainly happy, the problem was that Dave's relaxed pose melted away almost as soon as he'd settled into it. His hands would go to his phone to see if she had canceled. He'd hunch over and look at his feet nervously, check his shirt for stains.

This was a date. Maybe. His first ever, and in a place that he associated with Julia. It was her he usually looked for from this spot, those blue eyes across the distance, her bare feet. But today Julia was on her way to a wedding with her dads, and Dave was looking for Gretchen's blond waves and scuffed sneakers. Once that thought crossed his mind, he'd lean back into the bench, take a deep breath, put on a slight smile, only to have it quickly fall away again, his hand going to the back of his neck, or wiping at his forehead, the sweat dripping freely now that he had no hair. If anyone was watching, they'd probably think he was schizophrenic. Having dreamed all his life of romantic love did not make him any good at first dates.

She showed up a couple of minutes later, coming up from behind him and tapping him on the shoulder. He rose up quickly with a nervous "Oh, heya" that he'd be cringing about for at least several nights, if not the rest of his life. He'd wondered about adding a hug or a kiss on the cheek or a handshake, and when it came time to do it, he did one of those weird side hugs that his socially anxious uncle always gave him.

Gretchen took it in stride, smiling when they parted. She was wearing a red shirt with white polka dots and a tan sweater over it, the buttons undone. "You look nice," he said, because once Julia had mentioned offhand that he should always say it on a date.

"Thanks," she said. "You do, too." She reached out and touched the hem of his shirt, a baby-blue button-down that he'd borrowed from his dad. "I like this shirt."

Dave rubbed the back of his neck. Shit, he hadn't thought about what to say from there. He hadn't ever actually said something like that directly to a girl, and he certainly never heard a looks-related compliment directed his way, except from aunts and the school librarian, who said it to everyone. They both stood by the bench, sheepishly smiling.

"So, this is it, huh? Your favorite bench in the world?"

"This is it," Dave said, looking down at it. "I come here at least twice a week."

"What makes it your favorite?"

"It reminds me of my mom," he said. "We used to come here when I was little, eating ice cream and people watching." He looked around the harbor, which wasn't as busy as it usually was on Fridays. There were a few fishermen coming back from the pier, their iceboxes dripping pink fluid. A couple of homeless guys were on the bench across the way, drinking from paper bags. One of them was reading a newspaper, the other scratched his beard in between sips. When Dave first started hanging out at the harbor on his own, in between missing his mom and falling in love with Julia, he'd get the homeless guys cups of water and sit with them, figuring they were probably just as lonely as he was. "Plus, it's so comfortable, I'm pretty sure it's made from angel feathers and the love of a thousand puppies."

"Oh man, puppy love is hard to get ahold of these days," Gretchen said, again unable to hide a smile. She handed Dave the purse she'd brought with her and then slowly sank onto the bench. It was curious how much he wanted her to find the bench comfortable, as if her not seeing the beauty of this spot might diminish the bench's value, or hers.

But then she smiled and said, "I think I feel a golden retriever," and stayed where she was, even lying back into the position that Dave had imagined for himself, her hands folded across her stomach, her feet out and crossed at the ankles. She looked out at the harbor slightly nodding to herself, looking perfectly content.

"What do you want from the coffee shop? I'll go get us a drink."

"I'll come with," Gretchen said, starting to rise.

"You sure? You look too comfortable," Dave said. "You'll save us our spot; I'll come back in a sec."

The sun peeked through from a break in the clouds, causing Gretchen to squint up at him, her hair turning completely golden in the light. "There aren't a lot of people around," she said, getting up completely and grabbing her purse from

Dave. "I'll come with. We just barely said hi; I don't wanna say good-bye already."

Dave laughed and they headed in the direction of the coffee shop. "It wouldn't have been a good-bye, just a 'be right back.'"

"Well, yeah," Gretchen said, and already Dave could hear that little warble in her tone that meant she was about to make a joke. "But I have huge abandonment issues."

"Have you ever in your life successfully lied?"

"God, am I really that bad?"

"There are worse things to be bad at," Dave said.

"Like what?" Gretchen responded, faking disbelief.

"What if you were really bad at eating?" Dave opened the coffee shop door and let Gretchen pass through. "Say you had really bad aim with forks. You would be hungry all the time, plus imagine all the scarring."

"But, Dave, I have so many jokes that I've missed out on delivering well. Do you know how much emotional scarring that's left behind? I may seem normal to you, but my soul is completely wrecked."

As they talked, they kept doing the eye-contact dance. Their eyes flitted around the room, at each other's foreheads or lips or feet. How did anyone maintain eye contact throughout a conversation?

They ordered hot chocolates and took them back to the bench. On the walk there, Dave discovered that she had a tattoo on the back of her neck. He caught a glimpse of it when she swept her hair over one shoulder right before they sat down.

"What's your tattoo say?"

Gretchen took a sip from her hot chocolate and self-consciously brushed her hair back to cover her neck. "It's from a book. It says, 'a little better than you found it.'"

"What's it mean?"

"Well, it's part of a longer quote, this really beautiful passage about how the best you can ever do is to leave the world a little better than you found it. It doesn't matter how you do it. Invent a new toaster or reach out a helping hand; just, you know, leave it a little better than you found it."

Dave noticed that their knees were touching. Amazing what kind of warmth could come from such slight contact. "What book is it?"

"*Timbuktu* by Paul Auster," she said. "I know it's weird to say or even think this, but that book has made me who I am. Not entirely, obviously. It didn't help me at soccer, or make me so good at telling jokes with a straight face. But certain lines felt like they were thoughts I'd had my whole life that just hadn't taken shape yet until I read them. 'A little better than you found it' is how I see everything now. Not just the world, but everything. People, too. I want people I know to be a little better off than when I found them. God, that sounds pretentious, doesn't it?"

"It sounds like kindness to me," Dave said.

"Well, thanks. My ex always thought it was stupid. He hated the tattoo." She popped the lid off her hot chocolate and scooped a fingerful of whipped cream. "Want some?"

"Sure," Dave said. He hesitated. "It's okay if I dip my finger in?"

"I insist." Gretchen smiled, holding out the cup toward him.

"Why'd your ex hate the tattoo?"

"If I had to guess, it's because he doesn't care about other people." She popped the lid back on. "That's not true. He cares about some people. I'm just bitter—legitimately this time."

"Can I ask why?"

"He cheated on me," she said, not really sounding all that bitter, as if the statement had lost its heartbreak. Dave wasn't sure if he should ask more, but a couple of the homeless guys walked by the bench just then, saying hi to Dave and asking for change. Dave gave them the two singles that he had loose in his pocket.

"Those guys knew your name," Gretchen said, following their slow retreat back to the other side of the harbor.

"Like I said, I come here often." He put his finished drink on the ground, trying to ignore how it felt to have her look at him. Their knees were still touching.

"I've only really been here a couple of times," Gretchen said, looking out at the boats docked in the harbor. "My family wanted to check out the aquarium when we first moved here but never got around to it."

"You've never been to the famed Morro Bay Aquarium? That's a travesty." He stood up, grabbing their empty cups and tossing them in a nearby trash can. "Come on, you're missing out on easily the thirty-second best aquarium in the western hemisphere…or at least the thirty-second best aquarium of the West Coast."

"What about the bench? What if it loves you back and misses you terribly when you're gone?"

"It'll have plenty of warm, fuzzy memories of your butt to hold it over until I come back," he said without really thinking about what he was saying. He held his hand out for her so she could lift herself up.

Gretchen laughed; God, she had so many different kinds of cute laughs. "Wow, I wasn't even sure this was a date, but now that you've complimented my butt I think it might be." She took his hand and lifted herself up.

Dave felt himself blush. Her hand was still cupped in his as they walked across the harbor toward the aquarium. He could feel her turquoise ring pressing against his fingers, the cool touch of metal standing out against the warmth of their palms. It was hard to think of anything to say, and Dave worried that he might just stare at their hands the rest of the walk, so he unclasped his fingers from hers and pointed out the bubble tea stand. "If you go there, never get the blackberry flavor. It tastes like licorice that's been sitting in dirty laundry for a week."

"You've tasted laundry-marinated licorice?"

"My dad likes to experiment in the kitchen," Dave said, his eyes still on the bubble tea stand. Even as the feel of Gretchen's hand lingered on his, Julia was in the back of his mind, all those times he'd shared bubble tea with her, the ease with which they reached for each other's drinks, so comfortable in each other's presence that they didn't even have to acknowledge it was happening. He wondered if he'd ever reach that level of comfort with Gretchen, or with anyone else at all.

The aquarium was nearly empty. There was a young dad showing his daughter around, lifting her in his arms so she could press her nose against the glass and watch the sharks swim in their elegant way. A couple in their sixties sat on a bench eating sandwiches by the jellyfish. The bare lighting inside the aquarium made it seem like it was much later in the evening than it was, and in most of the rooms it was just Dave and Gretchen on their own, free to talk.

They talked about things that Dave imagined people on first (maybe?) dates always talked about, favorite this or that, a story here or there, following the conversations down their natural tangents. As they watched the fish and the sea otters, making jokes and interviewing each other, Dave learned the following: that she volunteered at a hospice one weekend a month solely because she wanted to live by the words she'd tattooed on her neck. That she always had to joke about death for weeks after she left or she wouldn't have the heart to return. That she had an eight-year-old brother with Asperger's. That she smelled like honey. That she had no idea what she wanted to study at school, and hadn't even made a decision on where she was going yet. That she didn't like apples, and didn't understand why she'd never met anyone else that shared her distaste for them in all their varieties. That she made soft little moans of appreciation when faced with brightly colored fish, and that her eyes would never stray from one she found particularly appealing, not until the fish disappeared into a little cove in the coral or until Dave put a hand on her back and gently moved them along to the next room. That she loved driving, and sometimes when she couldn't sleep, she'd drive around neighborhoods late at night, counting how many lights were left on, how many TVs still flashed bright and blue, how many other cars were on the road. That sometimes she did this without even listening to music, because she liked how the silence calmed her thoughts.

When Dave told her that he'd never learned to drive, she decided that it was the end of their aquarium tour. She grabbed his hand, effortlessly, as if it was the easiest thing in the world, and led him toward the exit.

They got into her car and drove to the mall's parking lot, which was the largest one around. The stores were all closing by then, the last of the shoppers straggling to their cars holding their bags wearily, keys in hand reflecting the orange glow of parking-lot lights. Gretchen parked the car at the edge of the lot and they switched spots.

"Are you sure about this? I don't want to wreck your car."

In the passenger seat, Gretchen buckled her seat belt. "That should answer your question."

"I'm not good at this."

"I happen to be a pretty good teacher. Just don't kill us."

Dave tensed his fingers against the steering wheel. "Okay, aiming for no deaths. Got it. What do I do now?"

"Shift into drive."

"You're losing me."

"The stick on your right," Gretchen said, "move it next to the letter *D*."

"Which one is *D*? Did I mention I'm illiterate?"

Gretchen laughed and shifted for him, causing the car to lurch forward. "You have to hit the brake!" she squealed.

Dave hit the brake the only way he knew how, by slamming both feet down on the pedal. The sudden stop caused his seat belt to lock up tight against his chest. "Gretchen, your car is trying to kill me." He yanked at the fabric, which only made it pull back tighter, as if he and the car were involved in some sort of tug-of-war.

"This is going to be the funniest day of my life," Gretchen said.

For an hour, Gretchen talked him calmly through, giving him little pointers until the car's movement felt natural. Every now and then she'd touch his shoulder or his forearm when offering her advice, and in those moments he was glad he'd waited until now to learn how to drive, glad that Julia had always been around to drive for him.

When they both decided he'd had enough practice for his first time, they switched back so that Gretchen could drive. But instead of putting the car in drive they sat quietly for a moment, and in the silence Dave could spot a mutual desire to stretch out their night, to not go home. Gretchen pulled a

GPS out of the glove compartment and smiled at him. “Wanna do something cool?”

“Almost always.”

“Check this out,” she said, and she started driving the car around in strange patterns, stopping to turn the GPS on or off, hiding the screen so he couldn’t see what was happening.

After a few minutes she parked the car and turned the screen toward him. The parking lot was a blank white space in the GPS, while the streets surrounding the mall were yellow. A blue line showed the path the car had taken.

“You drew a smiley face.”

“I drew a smiley face.”

“With the car.”

“And a satellite,” she added.

“Gretchen,” Dave said, admiring the GPS screen, “you are so cool.”

It was another hour of GPS-drawing—a stick figure, a cat, the word *fuzzy*—before they left the parking lot and Gretchen took Dave home. It was nearly midnight, but he didn’t want to step away from Gretchen, didn’t want the night to end. But now that it was going to, he wondered how, exactly, it would. It *was* a first date, he knew, because how they would say good-bye mattered.

They were parked in his driveway, no lights on in his house save for the blue glow of the television in Brett’s room. Gretchen had put the car in park, but for almost thirty seconds neither one of them had moved or said a thing.

There was no doubt in his mind that he wanted to kiss her. He could feel the desire for it like a ball of energy high up in his chest, but there seemed no way to move it from there, as if a part of him was against the whole idea and would not allow it. He couldn't help but think that Julia was somehow responsible.

Dave noticed her iPod sitting in the cup holder, a wire plugging it into the car. "Play me your favorite song," he said, picking it up.

The screen lit at his touch, casting Gretchen's face in a soft white light. She took it from him, her fingers touching his for what seemed like a deliberately long moment. "You won't make fun of me?"

"I've never made fun of anyone in my entire life."

She narrowed her eyes at him over the iPod, bringing it close to her as she scrolled through. "Seriously. Almost no one knows this song is my favorite, and if I choose to trust you and you think it's cheesy or something, then for the rest of my life, any time I listen to the song, there'll be a tinge of shame. You might forever ruin my favorite song."

Dave stole a glance at her lips, like he'd been doing all day. "I swear on the bench at the harbor that I won't laugh. If I do, I'll never sit on it again."

Then Gretchen hit play and Dave turned his attention to the music coming softly through the speakers. Just a few guitar notes rang out, clean and unaccompanied. The singer's voice came on sounding like Kermit the Frog mixed with a typical indie singer-songwriter.

Don't let hurricanes hold you back, raging rivers or shark attack, find love, and give it all away.

It was a simple song, and Dave could see Gretchen moving her lips along with the words. Brett had always made fun of his taste in music, so Dave knew what it was like to resist the urge to sing out your favorite lyrics. He wanted her to sing, but settled for the fact that she was sharing the song with him.

When the song faded away, Gretchen reached to turn the volume down. "If you hated it, don't say anything."

"I loved it," Dave said, wondering if this was it, the moment when the ball of energy finally made its way up and he would lean to kiss her. She was smiling at him and their eyes held each other for long enough that Dave thought there was no way a good-bye could happen *without* a kiss. But he had no idea how to accomplish such a thing. When the time came for a good-bye, he leaned across the shift stick and gave Gretchen a hug, which was quick, and warm, and stayed with him as he lay in bed awake all night.

NUTELLA & CUPCAKES

DAVE UNWRAPPED THE lunch his dad had packed for him: a chicken *torta*, the tomatoes, lettuce, and chipotle salsa on the side to keep the bread from getting soggy. He was in the tree house, looking out at the blacktop. There'd been a test in class and he'd finished early, so he was the first one out for lunch. It was April. AP tests, finals, and graduation were within reach.

The bell rang and within a few seconds the doors to the building broke out into a stream of people. Everyone headed for the cafeteria, or for their usual lunch spots. A table had been set up near the blacktop to collect votes for who would go on the prom ballot, and though Dave had avoided it, a steady flow of people came by, dropping their folded ballots into a wooden box with the world's flimsiest lock on it.

He spotted Julia as soon as she was outside, her pink hair acting like a beacon, in case her attractiveness wasn't enough. It'd be convenient if he could forget his best friend was so pretty, if the attraction just kind of melted away as soon as he'd decided to see her the way she saw him, as soon as Gretchen started taking up his thoughts. But, clearly, life wasn't so convenient. Dave took a bite from his torta and chewed slowly, struggling with the fact that an attraction to Julia and a desire to keep her as a friend could coexist. It reminded him of how grief had made his dad both more quiet and more loving. The father he remembered before his mom died sometimes seemed like a whole other person, always laughing and teasing, encouraging roughhousing between his two sons. Now he was quieter, seemingly more distant, though his affection showed through more often. Things overlapping, contradictions; Dave knew these were common, that they were everywhere and he'd have to get used to them.

Julia joined him in the tree house, taking the stool next to him and jolting him out of his ruminations. "Hey, goof. Sorry I missed you in homeroom today. The dads are so hungover from the weekend that I think it spread to me. I'll tell you all about it, but first, I've got the best story of all time."

"Ugh, the hyperbole."

Julia picked a tomato that had fallen onto Dave's napkin and popped it into her mouth. "No hyperbole here, I promise. I was in Marroney's class..."

"He still lets you attend class? You haven't been served legal papers of some sort yet?"

"The looks the man gives me, I'm surprised we haven't made sweet, sweet love and eloped. But shush, let me tell you this story. It's actually a metastory, because he's the one who told it."

Dave's phone buzzed in his pocket as Julia started her story, and he had to fight to ignore it.

"So, a few years ago, this guy gets assigned as the ambassador to a small African country. He and his wife are thrilled. They've been going there for years for charity work or to in some other way assuage their white guilt."

"Is this in Marroney's words or are you adding your own commentary?"

"He didn't have to say it, Dave. We're so connected, I caught all the subtext." She mockingly rolled her eyes, pulling out pizza in tinfoil from her Ecuadorean bag. "Anyway, once this ambassador and his wife arrive in the country, they want to establish a good relationship with the local tribe. They reach out to the chief, who invites them to a feast at his house, asking only that they bring a dish to share.

"But this couple hasn't spent enough time in the country to learn about the local cuisine, and this happens before the time of Google, so it's hard for them to just look up what would be an appropriate dish to bring. At a loss, the wife spots some Nutella at the supermarket and she decides that she'll plate it all fancy-like with a bunch of cookies and that'll be that."

"Marroney did not say 'all fancy-like.'"

"Dave, will you please?"

"Sorry." Dave pulled his phone out of his pocket and glanced at it. There was a text message from Gretchen. *Want to help me study for AP Chem tomorrow night?* If the power of words was ever in doubt, a text message like this was all the proof Dave needed.

"So the night of the feast comes, and the ambassador and his wife bring this huge platter of Nutella that looks like something the Food Network would show to make you feel inadequate." Julia was talking excitedly now, getting into the story. Dave put the phone facedown on the counter he'd helped build so he wouldn't be tempted to text Gretchen back while Julia was still talking. "The chief accepts the platter and puts it on the table with all the other dishes, and then the feast begins. There's stewed goat and a million different vegetable and rice dishes and a handful of items that the ambassador and his wife can't recognize in the least. But the Nutella goes untouched. For the entire meal, no one reaches to scoop some on their plate. They don't even grab a cracker that surrounds the Nutella. The ambassador starts to worry that maybe he's somehow offended local customs, or that he's insulted the chief by bringing something that comes in a jar. He's so nervous he can barely eat. Dave, you listening?"

"Yeah," Dave said, "just trying to picture Marroney actually telling this story."

"He told it so much better than I could." She took a bite of her leftover pizza, dipping it in the Tupperware of Dave's chipotle salsa. "Then, when most of the food has been eaten, the feast spontaneously quiets down, and everyone turns their attention to the chief, who's standing up over the Nutella platter. The ambassador and his wife are shitting bricks. Then the chief very deliberately"—Julia imitated Marroney imitating the chief—"sticks his hand into the platter so that his fingers are covered in Nutella to the second knuckle. And then"—she mimicked the chief bringing his hand into his mouth and tasting the Nutella—"he spits it out!"

She started laughing hysterically, cackling so that everyone at the tree house was giving them weird looks. Tears were actually coming out of her eyes, and it took a while for her to notice that Dave was not laughing along with her. She wiped her eyes and sat up straight.

"That was it? That was the end of the story?"

"You don't get it," Julia said disappointed. "He spits it out!" She widened her eyes and leaned forward, as if repeating the punch line would help the story make more sense.

Dave shrugged and looked at his phone again, opening the text message to respond to Gretchen. "Sorry, Julia, but that guy is as bizarre as that story was."

"He's not bizarre! He's a romantic. That whole story was a metaphor."

"For what?"

Julia just shook her head and picked up her pizza again. "It doesn't matter." She chewed for a while, looking dejected.

Then she brushed the pizza crumbs from her hands. "We're going to his house tonight, by the way."

"His house? There's a weird feeling in my stomach that tells me you're not referring to me in the third person."

"You have such good instincts. We're going to Marroney's house. This courtship is a little too slow and Jane Austen for me. I'm a woman of action, and it's time to put myself out there."

"Reciting erotic slam poetry to his face doesn't count as putting yourself out there?"

"That was all innuendo. It was too indirect," Julia said, pouring out the rest of the salsa on her second slice. "I'm going to woo him with baked goods. We're going to his house tonight."

Dave looked down at his phone and back at Julia, who was now finishing his torta. He picked up his phone. Only if we can go GPS drawing after, Dave responded to Gretchen, slipping the phone back into his pocket. "I knew at some point in our friendship you were going to get me arrested."

"You've been saying that for years, and it hasn't happened yet," Julia said, throwing away her napkin into a trash can that the school had placed inside the tree house. Administration had turned a surprisingly blind eye to the structure that had suddenly appeared on school grounds. "You should probably wear black, though. Just in case."

o o o

They made the cupcakes at Julia's house. Though Dave had been texting back and forth with Gretchen throughout the day, watching Julia make cupcakes again—Nutella, this time—it almost felt like nothing had changed. He kept his phone in his pocket and forgot about it, as if his world still belonged to Julia entirely.

"How can I help?"

"Clean up after my mess?" She motioned toward the obscene pile of dirty dishes scattered around the counter. "The dads will kill me if they come back home to that."

"What if I'm a hit man and this was all part of my plan when I befriended you?"

"Who the hell would hire the world's nicest thirteen-year-old as an assassin?"

"A criminal mastermind," Dave answered. "Plus, how do you know I was nice before I met you? Maybe it was all an act."

"Dave, you are the best-hearted person in the world. Even if you were a murderer, you'd still be introducing yourself to homeless people and getting them cups of water from the coffee shop. Maybe you've been plotting my doom all these years. But the niceness is not an act."

"Well, shit. Now I feel bad about fooling your dads into murdering you." Dave turned on the faucet, taking his time with the soiled mixing bowls, shutting the water off while he scrubbed to avoid wasting water, to listen to Julia's movements.

"David Beth Kacinski, are you blushing?"

"What? No. It's all the steam from the water."

"I made you blush!" She set down the tray of unbaked cupcakes and came over to where he stood by the sink, wrapping him up in a hug, her face pressed against his back. "No hit man blushes when he gets called nice."

"You don't know that...." Dave said, the water from the faucet momentarily forgotten, little lumps of flour and sugar clinging to the lips of the bowls. He wondered why it was that his mind kept going to whichever girl was not with him.

Once they'd packed the cupcakes into a baking tray covered in foil, they climbed into Julia's car and headed to Marroney's house. For the first time in his life, he felt like driving. But there was too much to explain in asking Julia if he could drive, since they'd forgotten to recount their weekends. Or maybe he hadn't so much forgotten as chosen not to bring it up. He still didn't know how to explain to Julia what was happening between him and Gretchen. It was unknown territory, dreams meeting reality but with a different set of characters, and so he didn't even know how to explain it to himself.

Which isn't to say he didn't try. "You remember Gretchen," Dave said, knowing immediately that the non sequitur would sound weird. Julia was driving, following her phone's GPS directions. "I saw her this weekend. Slash ran into her. Though not literally ran into her. There were plans involved, I guess I should say."

"Cool beans. Keep working that popularity angle. I think even numbers are on your side," Julia said, clearly too wrapped up in turn-by-turn instructions to tune into Dave's rambling.

"Do I want to know how you got his address?" Dave asked, happy to divert the conversation elsewhere. "I kind of feel like asking just to find out a new euphemism for stalking."

"Oh, no euphemisms this time," Julia said, turning down a street and looking at the house numbers. "Just flat-out stalking."

Dave had thought she was kidding about dressing in black, but she was in full stalking regalia, the only parts of her that would be visible in the dark were her bare feet and hands, the pink hair poking out the side of her hoodie. "All right, so, what's the plan here?"

"The plan? We walk up to the front door, ring the doorbell, and hand him the cupcakes." Julia parked the car in front of a nondescript house, the kind that half of San Luis Obispo residents lived in: single story, white garage door, perfectly triangular roof like the kind children always drew in pictures.

"So what's with the ninja outfit?"

Julia looked down at her attire, as if noticing it for the first time. "Oh. Right. I don't know. I guess I'm just in stalker mode."

Dave laughed, and out of habit put his hand on her head and shook lightly, trying to determine if he could do this one gesture of affection he had with her and separate it from the feelings he no longer wanted to have. "I worry about you," he said, pulling his hand away and unbuckling his seat belt. "So, am I coming with?"

Exactly half of him wanted her to say no, so he could avoid getting sucked up in her craziness, wonderful though it may be. Three text messages to and from Gretchen. He could stay in the car and text Gretchen back and forth for a while until Julia came back. That was exactly what he should do.

"Yeah, I need you for moral support. But if things are going well I may need you to run to the drugstore to buy condoms."

"That's it. I'm throwing up."

"I'm kidding," Julia said with a grin. "I'll want to work up to that. Tonight we'll just make out and cuddle." She poked his stomach, then took off her hoodie, revealing a gray tank top with a band logo on it. And, of course, she looked fantastic, and of course, at that same moment his phone buzzed in his pocket, undoubtedly a text from Gretchen.

They got out of the car and walked up the driveway to the front door, Dave crinkling the foil on the cupcakes because crinkling foil was something small and simple to focus on as opposed to the turmoil of his contradicting desires. Julia had a bounce to her step as they reached the door, and she took a deep breath before ringing the bell. "You think I should have attached some sort of letter? Something cute?"

Dave shrugged. "I think if he doesn't get the picture by now, a love letter won't help." He thought about the love letter he'd written Julia sophomore year, how he'd thought that he couldn't handle it anymore. The fever with which he'd written the letter. How he didn't have the heart to reread it for fear he'd never be happy enough with the words and what they conveyed. He'd carried it around in his backpack for weeks, each day convinced that this was it, this was the day he finally came clean, so nervous he couldn't eat all day, his palms actually sweating, his hands shaking when taking notes in class. Every day he decided against it, or rather wasn't able to reach into the pocket in his backpack and hand it over to her, unable to imagine standing there as she read it, equally unable to imagine walking away before she could. The fear that it would irrevocably change things overruled anything else. He'd moved it to a drawer in his bedroom, then hidden it in the pocket of a jacket he never wore, then finally torn it into unreadable bits and let them flutter into the trash can thinking, *Let that be the end of it.*

Julia walked over to the window and put her face up to the glass, cupping her hands to block out the reflection. "I don't see any lights on," she said, then rang the doorbell again. About a minute later, when they were still standing outside and Dave was about to suggest heading back to the car, Julia started walking around the house.

"I don't like where this is going," Dave said when Julia tried to push open the window she'd glanced into.

"Don't worry, I'm not going to break a window. I'll only enter if there's one open." She crept past some rosemary bushes and turned the corner of the house.

"Jules—" Dave started to call out to her that this was not okay, but thought better of attracting attention by being loud. He followed behind her, just as she was lifting the kitchen window open.

"Success!" she whisper-yelled.

"Julia, don't you think you're overdoing the crazy? Just a bit?"

"Methinks the lady doth protest too much," she said, hoisting herself up on the windowsill, the blinds that were half-drawn bumping into her head. "We're just delivering these, and we're exceptionally committed to that task. If UPS did the same thing people would be thrilled."

"Thrilled to call the cops, maybe."

Julia stopped halfway through her climb and shot Dave a look over her shoulder that was at once challenging and kind, and so cute it might just haunt him for the rest of his life. "David Foster Wallace. If you're feeling nervous about getting arrested, all you have to do is stand by the window and pass me the cupcakes. I promise I will still love you as only a best friend can."

Dave crinkled the tinfoil, then walked over to the window as she continued to climb into Marroney's kitchen. "That's never been in question," he said, managing a smile.

CHEMISTRY

THE NEXT DAY, having miraculously avoided getting caught and/or arrested, Dave was sitting in AP Chem class, sneaking glances at Gretchen. She was sitting across the room, since Mr. Kahn had split them up into groups for the last lab of the year before they focused entirely on studying for the final. Dave had been grouped together with Doh Young, the smartest kid in class, who would have a much higher GPA than a 4.0 if only the administration was smart enough to figure out how to give him the grade he deserved, and so Dave allowed his mind to wander, knowing that an *A* was pretty much guaranteed. He allowed his eyes to wander, too, not just to Gretchen's pretty face, but to her little in-class habits that he'd only recently started paying attention to.

He was starting to remember her outfits, how she looked so great when wearing her hair a certain way, sexy in those scuffed sneakers of all things. How every now and then she'd stare off into the distance, or chew on her pen, or examine her split ends, then slowly come to again.

When Gretchen caught him looking, she smiled and he smiled back, embarrassed, looking away for a while. He studied the secret life of legs beneath the desks. The jittering and stretching, the rearranging for comfort, laps used as support for hidden devices and hidden books. He wondered what people were thinking about as the end of the year approached, if they had little to-do lists of their own, if they had love lives punctuated by ellipses, by question marks, if they had any love lives at all. Then his eyes would slowly return to Gretchen's scuffed sneakers and it was hard not follow them up. It made him happy just to look at her, and he had the urge to text her that message from across the room, but for some reason, he held back.

She was a constant snacker, on quartered oranges and potato chips and little Tupperware containers full of salad or trail mix. She didn't seem to know everyone's name, which was probably why Dave used to think of her as somehow elitist. But the more he took note, the more he came to the conclusion that she was simply less focused, dreamier than he'd realized.

The turn of her head, how she met people's eyes, her constant smile. Her neighbors were often flirting with her, no matter their social circle. Guys would try to steal her sunglasses or her notebook and she would take it in stride, hiding her annoyance. At one point she got bored and puffed her cheeks out, playing with them as her group members argued about something or another. It was adorable, and Dave wondered how he'd failed to notice that little habit before. One of his biggest pet peeves was people who were shitty whisperers, and it was a strange satisfaction when Gretchen whispered something and he couldn't hear it at all. And this girl was coming over to his house that night.

The PA system buzzed, snapping Dave from his reverie. It was the garbled voice of Leslie Winters, the senior class president. "Good morning, SLO High!" she called out. "I've got some exciting news for this year's senior class. The ballots for prom king and queen have been tallied up, and I'm happy to announce the contenders. For prom queen…" She started listing the candidates, and Dave caught Gretchen flashing a smile at him. On their date, they'd talked a little bit about the tree house, since Gretchen had seen the video like everyone else. Dave hadn't gone much into the details, but he had mentioned the Nevers to her, the fact that the prom king campaign was sort of like Julia's tree house idea. "And for prom king, the ballot will list: Carl Alvarez, Hugh Corners, James Everett, David Gutierrez, and Paul Rott. Congratulations, candidates, and see you at prom!"

o o o

After school, Julia was waiting for Dave by her car, one fist raised in the air.

"How long have you been holding that pose?" he asked as he approached.

"Since the moment you won," Julia said.

"Dork."

"You mispronounced *champion*, badass." She lowered her arm, smile beaming. The Nevers list was in her hand. "Time to cross another one off!"

"Six to go," Dave said, tossing his backpack into her car.

"I don't know about you, but I'm feeling invincible."

"What did Marroney say about the cupcakes?"

"Oh, we had a sub today," Julia said. She lowered the top on her car and slid into the driver's seat, plugging in her phone to play some music. "Turns out he's in Arizona for some sort of conference. It might send some mixed signals when he returns home to a plate of rotting, ant-infested cupcakes, but nothing's getting me down today."

"That man is going to get nightmares because of you."

"Sexy nightmares, maybe." Julia looked at her phone. "Ooh, perfect celebration music." She hit play and the opening chords of "Blister in the Sun" came on. Julia started dancing in her seat. "Harbor?" she asked between lyrics.

"Just for a bit. I've got an AP Chem group-study thing," Dave said. Then, feeling guilty about his word choice, he added, "That girl Gretchen is coming over at seven."

"Plenty of time," Julia said, taking the admission without a hint of suspicion. She turned up the music and shifted the car into drive, taking them down Highway 1 toward the coast, shouting the lyrics out at the top of her lungs. Instead of going to the harbor, though, Julia kept driving north along the Pacific Ocean, the mood too celebratory to stop the car. It was a beautiful drive, and Dave would never tire of it. That highway made you feel like no matter how much time you spent with it, it was not enough. An hour passed by without Dave really noticing. The fog reached across the highway like arms looking for an embrace, then it would slowly pull away and reveal the glimmer of the ocean, the brown-green facade of the cliffs. Just as the air was turning colder, Julia turned down the music, looking over at Dave with a raised eyebrow.

"What do you say about crossing another Never off the list?" She looked ahead at the curving highway.

She was talking about number nine, the epic road trip. He pictured them skipping class the rest of the week, going up as far as Seattle, returning down the coastline slowly, sleeping on the beach, hiking through Big Sur, roaming the streets of San Francisco and Portland, enjoying the many aesthetic beauties of their part of the world while everyone else was stuck at school. He thought about Gretchen ringing the doorbell at his house and his dad telling her that Dave wasn't home.

"Not yet," he said. "This chemistry project is pretty important and it's not the best week for a life-changing road trip."

"I like how you said, 'yet.' But I wasn't thinking road trip. I was thinking I'll host a 'BEER' party in celebration of your prom king campaign success. The dads are out of town next weekend and I feel like being irresponsible. What do you say?"

Dave stuck his hand out the window, making waves in the air, pretending to think it over. "I don't know, maybe. I *am* a prom king candidate now; I've got a lot on my plate. Press junkets, galas, charity balls."

Julia reached over and poked him in the stomach. "Goof."

They drove on for another half hour before turning back around. Julia turned down the music for their return journey as they planned out the party, most of it jokingly, lots of talk of explosions and celebrity DJs. The closer they got to San Luis Obispo, the more butterflies Dave was feeling in his stomach. He kept looking at his cell phone for the time, calculating how long it would take them to get back.

Julia dropped him off at home at a quarter to seven. Dave thought he might take a shower, then worried Gretchen would show up as he was in the bathroom, or that it would seem too obvious that he showered just for her arrival. Maybe that wasn't a bad thing, showering specifically for her. It pointed to a certain thoughtfulness. Or maybe it showed he was trying too hard. Or maybe it would just point to him being insecure about his body odor, which wasn't attractive. Or maybe it implied he thought she would get close enough to smell him, and what if she didn't actually want to get close to him at all? In the end, Dave stood by his bathroom door, lost in thought, vacillating between lines of reasoning until the moment the doorbell put an end to the debate in his head.

He yelled out, "I've got it!" then ran down the stairs, taking a deep breath at the foot of the stairs to settle his breathing, simultaneously realizing that he'd just lived out the girl-coming-over-to-study cliché he'd seen in countless sitcoms. He laughed, caught his breath again, then opened the door.

"Oh, you look nice," were the first words out of his mouth. He hadn't planned for that, not this time. They'd just kind of slipped out, like a liquid spilling out of a bottle.

Gretchen blushed and turned her eyes down, smiling. "Hi," she said after a while.

"Sorry," Dave said. "I just…sorry." He opened the door and stepped aside to let her in. "Hi."

She entered the house, her backpack slung over her shoulder, the smell of honey in her wake. "It's okay," she said. "I haven't showered today, so the compliment feels especially good." She took a quick look around, poking her head into the living room, where Dave's dad was watching a basketball game. "Hi," she called out. "I'm Gretchen."

Dave's dad looked away from the TV and then stood up quickly, surprised by Gretchen's presence. Dave expected him to shake her hand and mumble a hello before returning to his spot on the couch, but instead he introduced himself warmly, lingering by the entrance to the living room, not looking like he wanted to escape back to the TV. He was polite and smiley, just like Dave remembered him being years ago. Dave had thought that part of his dad had disappeared. But maybe he was different when he wasn't around Dave and Brett. Maybe at work, with friends, he'd gone back to being himself, able to escape the quiet grief he couldn't seem to shake around his sons.

"Well, I'll let you kids get to studying," he said, and Dave's head almost exploded when his dad winked at him slyly before turning away.

They took the stairs up to Dave's room. When he pushed open the door, he wished he'd spent those fifteen minutes tidying up instead of wondering whether or not to shower. Gretchen plopped her backpack down by Dave's desk, which was set against the wall by the door and mostly bare, save for his laptop and about six or seven pairs of tangled earphones. His bed was unmade, thanks to his dad's very lax policy on bed making. His laundry was mostly contained to the hamper in the corner, though a few shirts and socks hung on the edge like prisoners making a break for it.

"Sorry for the mess," Dave said, brushing the nest of headphones into his drawer, instead of into the trash can, like he should have done months ago.

"My room's worse." Gretchen looked around, her hands on her hips. "You don't do the whole hot babe and sports posters on your wall," she said. "That's refreshing."

One wall was blank, painted the same dull green it had been since Dave was a kid. Another two walls were technically blank, too, but one had the window that faced out at the big, pretty jacaranda tree in their yard, and the other was mounted with Dave's TV, so they didn't feel blank. The fourth wall had a whiteboard hanging above his desk, and it wasn't until now that Dave remembered he'd written *a little better than you found it* on his whiteboard after their date at the harbor. Gretchen sat herself on the edge of Dave's bed, her hands clasped between her thighs, staring at the board.

Dave wanted to smack himself for not erasing it. New to this whole pursuing-girls thing, he had no idea how to play it cool. He did know that writing a girl's life motto down on your whiteboard after only one date was not playing it cool. On the spectrum of coolness, it was way too close to building a shrine in her honor, which was way too close to collecting a bag of her hair. How had Dave so quickly turned into a hair collector?

"That's really cute," Gretchen said, then she lay back on Dave's bed, her hair and arms sprawled out beside her. Dave let out a sigh of relief. "I have a confession. I have very little interest in studying AP Chem tonight."

Was it weird to burp out of excitement? That was his first instinct, but he managed to suppress the burp, thankfully. Add that one to life's long list of mysteries. "You don't?"

"No. I've had very little interest in doing any studying at all, actually."

"Ah, you have it, too. Senioritis."

"Guilty," Gretchen said. She sat up, and Dave caught a flash of cleavage that he felt simultaneously guilty and blessed for having seen. "I have an idea."

"Is it a prank?"

"Not this time." She propped herself up on his bed, her elbows locked, the plunging V-neck T-shirt making it impossible to not at least glance in her direction. "Could we maybe watch a movie instead? Will your academic life survive if we do that? I want to watch a movie with you, but I don't want to be responsible for your downfall."

"You know," Dave said, getting up from his desk chair, "since it seems like tonight's one of those nights where I can't stop certain things from spilling out of my mouth"—he walked around to the far side of the bed, grabbing his remote off the nightstand, not entirely believing that he was allowing himself to say what he was saying, that he even had the ability to speak like this—"I don't think I'd mind if you *were* my downfall. Not one bit. A movie with you sounds perfect."

Gretchen smiled and kicked her shoes off and adjusted one of Dave's pillows so she could lie back comfortably. Dave had had daydreams a lot like this. Since when did real life act this way? "You get to choose the movie," Gretchen said, "but it has to fall within one of two categories: cute, or ridiculously bad."

"You don't happen to know of any that fall in the 'both' category, do you?"

"Too many, actually."

They chose a B-list horror movie about sharks in the woods and turned off the lights. Gretchen's foot lay against his before the opening credits had even finished.

"Who do you think is going to die first?" Dave asked, leaning just a little bit in her direction.

"The smartest character," Gretchen said with no hesitation.

"Really? Why?"

"You can't have smart people lingering around for too long in horror movies. Otherwise they come up with solutions and not enough people die."

"Good point," Dave said. The movie's run time was ninety-four minutes, and he felt a rush of gratitude knowing that he would spend every single one of those with Gretchen nearby. "I can't wait for all the shark puns."

"Ooh, you think there'll be shark puns?" Gretchen smiled. The stud in her ear glinted green, reflecting the light from the TV.

"I would be willing to bet five hundred points on my SAT score that someone is going to say, 'We're fin-ished.'"

Gretchen snorted, smacking him slightly across the ribs. "I can't believe how quickly you came up with one."

Dave shrugged, folding his hands over his stomach and maybe sticking his elbows out a little more than was comfortable so that they would brush against Gretchen's side.

As the movie ran on, Dave noticed that he and Gretchen talked almost as much as the characters on the screen did. With every comment or joke, they scooched closer to each other, Dave pretending not to notice the diminishing space between them, wondering if Gretchen was pretending, too. He laughed at the movie, and at Gretchen's jokes, and in their laughter he found little excuses to touch, to lean into her.

When Gretchen would lean into him, Dave could smell her breath (honey, too). He would think about kissing her but laugh instead, or he would shift so that his leg was touching more of hers. The closer he got to her, the more he wanted to kiss her, the more insane it felt that he wasn't already kissing her.

On the screen, a shark swam in the creek near where the characters had set up camp. The ditzy redhead and the bro-y one who kept saying he knew kung fu were making out in a tent.

"Do you think it's a good way to go or a bad way to go?" Gretchen asked, her knee bent and resting on Dave's thigh.

"Eaten by a shark in a forest? Pretty bad."

"No," Gretchen said, "while making out."

Dave thought about it for a while. Or, rather, he tried to actually come up with an answer, rather than picture kissing Gretchen. "There are worse ways to go," he said finally.

"I agree. If you're going to die via shark, it may as well come as a surprise, in the middle of doing something that feels as nice as kissing does."

Now, every fiber of his being screamed. *Now.* But Dave kept his eyes on the screen. The fingers on his left hand, out of sight from Gretchen, tensed into a fist. "Yeah," he said simply, still thinking, *Now now now.* Still thinking, despite it all, about Julia.

For five perfect minutes as the credits rolled, Dave's and Gretchen's hands clasped together. Dave didn't know how it had happened, if he had initiated the contact or if it had been her. He only knew their fingers were interlocked. They cracked a joke or two about how awful and great the movie had been, neither of them acknowledging the moist warmth of each other's skin, the lack of a kiss.

What Dave could acknowledge, though, was this: Julia. Julia in the back of his mind the whole time, restraining his movements. Every way he touched Gretchen, every place he touched Gretchen, he thought of how he'd failed to touch Julia. The movie made them both laugh, and Dave thought about all the Friday night movies he'd watched with Julia. He thought about how long he'd loved Julia, how recently he'd become interested in Gretchen. How Julia didn't even know that he loved her, after all this time. And so even after those five finger-clasped minutes, even after they looked at each other with smiles still plastered on their faces, smiles practically lingering all over the room, smiles clinging off his hamper, smiles perched on the corner of the TV and the whiteboard, even after Dave walked Gretchen downstairs with his hand against her lower back, even after he opened her car door for her, Dave felt too much like he was cheating on Julia to kiss Gretchen. He knew it was crazy. It was ridiculous. It was dumb. Everything told him he should be kissing her, everything except Julia in his head (even though Julia, if she were actually present, would probably tell him he was an idiot for not kissing Gretchen). In the end he could only touch Gretchen in just the way he'd been touching Julia for years: He hugged her, warm and friendly but nothing more, and said good night.

NEVERTHELESS BELONG

"WHAT THE HELL is going on with you guys?" Brett said as he delivered the three kegs to Julia's house. "Now you're *hosting* parties? And Dave's on the ballot for prom king?"

"Thanks to your video," Julia offered.

"Of course it was thanks to my video. But I'm still confused about your whole new we-actually-hang-out-with-other-people thing. It's not like you. What happened to thinking you're better than everybody else?"

"We never thought we were better than anyone," Julia said with a sigh, like she'd tried to explain this to him dozens of times before. "Like you said, we're just coming out of our shells a little bit. Just because we did different things than other people didn't mean we thought we were better than anyone."

"Sure," Brett said. "Now you're just slummin' it with us common folk for a while to see what it's like."

Julia blushed. "Don't go back to being mean."

"You mean calling you on your shit?"

"That's exactly what I mean," Julia said, smiling.

They were in Julia's backyard, the three kegs set strategically in three different corners to spread out the crowd. Dave was lounging in the grass, trying to get a nap in before the party started. He hadn't been sleeping all week. Every time he was about to nod off, the thought of not kissing Gretchen popped in his head, as insistent as a mosquito buzzing past his ear. He'd texted Gretchen the next morning about what a great time he'd had, and they still sat together in Chem when they could, and walked in the halls together whenever he wasn't walking with Julia. But he hadn't touched her since Tuesday night, hadn't even brushed her knee with his. The lack of a kiss lingered like a sore muscle.

It was a hot day. Dave looked up at the clouds and watched the smallest white wisps evaporate before his eyes, little by little. His lower back was sweaty, his T-shirt sticking to him and making the grass beneath him itchy. His cell phone was resting on his stomach. He felt like a failure, like someone who would never experience love because he couldn't bring himself to do anything about it. A mopey thought, sure, but it felt true.

"Dave, come help me get stuff ready inside. I need to hide all the dads' valuables."

"But I'm sleepy," Dave said, trying to sink further into the grass. "I'll need all my energy to schmooze with the crowd tonight."

"You've been a zombie all week," Julia said, handing Brett the money for the kegs. "Fine, sleep. But I'm waking you up an hour before the party so we can have you fitted for your prom king sash and tiara."

"You know so little about prom," Brett said, taking a seat on the patio furniture and pulling a cigarette from his shirt pocket.

"You know so little about humor," Julia said grabbing his cigarette and tossing it in the bushes. "And that's gross."

"You're gonna have so much more gross than that to clean up."

Julia sighed and called Brett a jerk, then the two of them disappeared into the house, teasing each other. Dave still had the urge to watch her leave. He checked his cell phone, as if a message might show up at any moment that could change everything for him, Gretchen telling him she was going to take matters into her own hands. Or maybe something from his dad, some little nugget of wisdom he'd kept to himself until now, knowing Dave needed it. But his phone showed nothing but the time, and Dave set it back down on his stomach, not surprised.

o o o

At seven Julia walked over to Dave and squatted by him, flicking the tip of his nose. "I'm awake," he said.

"Yes. And I am flicking your nose. Shall we continue to update one another on our activities?"

"As long as you promise to exclude any Marroney-related updates," Dave said, taking off the sunglasses he'd been wearing.

"Deal," she said. "I'm gonna go shower. I left out a towel for you in case you want to use the dads' bathroom to shower, too." She flicked his nose again. "You ready to celebrate your unlikeliest of victories?"

"I was conceived ready."

She stood up and looked around the yard as if assessing it, then turned toward the house. "If anyone shows up while I'm upstairs, tell them they're unfashionably early and then mock them until they feel ostracized."

"Will do," Dave said.

The sky was starting to darken into purple, the few clouds that had survived the heat of the afternoon took on shades of gold. Dave stayed on the grass, watching the sky, unable to muster the inertia to move until night had finally settled in. He tried not to think about Gretchen but that inertia was hard to overcome, too, so he went into the house and changed into the shirt he'd brought with him for the party.

Julia had hung a banner in the kitchen that read, IN HONOR OF THE GREAT AND VENERABLE POTENTIAL PROM KING, DAVE "THAT'S NOT MY NAME" GUTIERREZ. Cans of beer were strategically placed throughout the house for drunk people to stumble into as the night progressed. "We may be embracing clichés, but we're allowed to make them ours," Julia said with that mischievous smile. Some were on the bookshelves, one on top of each blade of the fan in the living room, in drawers and the microwave and in between the couch cushions. Julia had set out bowls of chips surrounded by assorted dips. Some of the dips weren't actual dips, another experiment Julia had been dying to try for years. She had set out hot sauces and butter and soy sauce and a little melted puddle of vanilla ice cream, just to see how many people would dip their chips into anything that was nearby.

By the time people started showing up, Dave and Julia had crossed off another Never and toasted with a minibottle of champagne Julia had nabbed from the wedding she'd gone to the weekend before. They argued for about twenty minutes over what kind of music to play, since Julia insisted that she had good party music, and Dave insisted that people would not enjoy listening to Fiona Apple, no matter how brilliant her lyrics were. Julia texted some photos of the setup to her mom and was checking her phone constantly for a response when the doorbell rang.

"Welcome!" Julia said to the first group that arrived, three somewhat nerdy juniors with copycat shaggy hair. "Beer!"

"Uh, thanks," the taller of them said, though they didn't enter until Dave waved them in. As soon as Julia shut the door, Dave could hear voices on the other side. Dave went back to the door as Julia led the shaggy juniors to the kitchen, rambling in a fake Victorian English accent about the glory of the night.

Within an hour, the house was packed. Because it kept him from looking at the entrance awaiting Gretchen's arrival, Dave tried to clean up after people, collecting the empty beer cans and the red plastic cups that Julia had purchased entirely too many of. Then Julia scolded him, telling him that making a mess of her parents' place was part of the idea, and that he was robbing her of a typical high school experience.

"Mingle with your people," she said, snatching the garbage bag away from his hand and hanging it off the corner of a picture frame, which instantly tipped and came crashing to the ground. "These people came for you."

"They came for the beer."

"You can't prove that. Your face on the flyer was just as big as the word *beer* was."

"True. Have I told you how uncomfortable that made me?"

"Oh, being loved by the masses is so hard," Julia said, frowning exaggeratedly. "I'm gonna go make sure Debbie is still mostly white and green and pink and alive." She headed for the stairs, sidestepping the pillow fort that they'd built at the foot to keep people from venturing upstairs. Almost as soon as she'd turned down the hallway, Dave felt a tap on his shoulder.

"Gretchen! Hi." He leaned in to give her a hug, and somehow his lips ended up on her cheek, close to her mouth, way more sensual than he'd meant to. It took them both a little by surprise, and nothing was said for a while. Someone took hold of the music and switched it over to rap, the bass booming through the house.

"Hi," she said, her hand going to the spot he'd awkwardly

kissed. She'd done her hair in a braid that hung over her shoulder, exposing her neck on the opposite side. A trace of collarbone poked out from her blouse. It was so different picturing someone's face all day and then being up close to it. It was like the difference between seeing a picture of a beach and stepping onto the sand. "This is insane; there are so many people here."

"Oh, Julia and I hired a bunch of desperate actors from L.A. None of these people are actually teenagers."

Gretchen bit her bottom lip and looked down at her scuffed sneakers for a second. When she didn't say anything for a while, he said that it was too crowded inside and that they should go to the backyard. He led her through the crowd, slowly squeezing between random, isolated dance-offs and couples already making out. At the kitchen table, Joey Planko was sitting in just his underwear, organizing some sort of drinking game that involved a deck of cards and a beer mug in the middle of the table. Girls were sitting two to a chair to join in on the game.

Outside, someone had started a bonfire in the middle of the yard. Which was impressive and a little worrying, considering that Julia's house had neither a fire pit nor firewood. Someone standing by the fire finished his beer and tossed the can into the fire, where it immediately crumpled in on itself. Dave and Gretchen caught up to Vince at one of the kegs. He'd just finished pouring a cup, and when he noticed the two of them he immediately handed it off to Gretchen and poured another two.

"Congrats on getting on the ballot, man," Vince said. "That was pretty badass what you guys did. Just the idea to build a tree house on school property is ballsy. Were you high?"

"Nope," Dave laughed.

"The tree house is so great," Gretchen said, nodding. She

sipped shyly from her beer and looked around the party. She looked so lovely, and he wished they were elsewhere, some place they could be alone.

"Well, all the more credit to you. I don't know why you've been hiding these past four years of high school, but I wish you'd shown yourself earlier. It's a shame everyone's figuring out how cool you are this late."

"I can't imagine how many cool things you and Julia have done," Gretchen said. She was holding her cup with both hands and smiling, but she didn't meet Dave's eyes. "Be honest, how many times have you saved the world from imminent destruction?"

"Once or twice," Dave said, mustering a smile. He spotted Julia coming outside, yelling, "All right, which of you bastards fed my cat cheese puffs?" She made her way around the party, checking people's hands for evidence, finally stopping to chat with the Kapoor triplets, who were wearing different shades of the same pastel polo shirt, the collars, of course, popped.

Dave, Gretchen, and Vince stood in their little circle. Gretchen and Vince started talking about some project for their French class. Dave took constant, tiny sips of his beer, the mild bitterness coating his tongue. He looked up at the sky, where clouds were rolling in to cover up the stars. It felt like all he could do was stand there, and that even if it started to rain he wouldn't be able to move. He was tired of inaction, tired of not having learned a thing from years of sitting still. It built up in him, like the desire to kiss Gretchen had on their date, but this time more powerful, more urgent. As if this was his last chance, a momentous fork in the road. If he chose inaction now, inaction it would be for the rest of his life.

"Hey, Vince, you mind if I talk to Gretchen for a sec?"

Vince stopped talking midsentence. "Uh, sure, man." He gave Gretchen a look and then made his way toward the house.

"Sorry if I interrupted that," Dave said. He picked a leaf that had fallen into his beer and flicked it onto the grass. "I've been meaning to talk to you about the other night."

Gretchen shifted her weight from one foot to another. She looked down at the grass, too. If there was one thing Dave would ask of adults at that moment it was why people his age were constantly looking down at the ground, and if they would ever grow out of it. "You don't have to, Dave, it's okay. I get it." She shrugged and smiled, a smile that felt somehow rehearsed, like the way he'd kept it in mind on their date at the harbor to compliment her looks.

"What do you mean?"

"It's okay; I get that you're with Julia. I'm sorry if I came on too strong." Her smile faded to more of a lopsided grin. The hand not holding her beer reached across to her elbow, the turquoise ring catching a glint from the backyard lights. "I still like spending time with you, so—"

"I'm not with Julia," Dave said. Across the party, Julia was trying to unpop the Kapoors' collars, yelling something. "It's not like that."

Gretchen looked up at him just for a second. Her expression gave nothing away. Or it did, and he simply wasn't familiar enough with her face to catch its subtle changes; he couldn't read her silences the way he could read Julia's. "You kind of act like you're together," Gretchen said with another shrug that spilled a blob of foamy beer down to the grass. "You don't have to feel sorry for me. It's okay. I'll learn how to pull pranks some other way."

Dave had never seen someone who smiled this often, in such a variety of ways. She looked sad and embarrassed and still managed an honest smile. It felt insane, all of a sudden, how long he'd been reaching for Julia. And if not insane, then too long by exactly four days. Tuesday night, watching a movie with Gretchen, that was the exact moment he should have let go for good. "I'm not with Julia," he said again.

"Dave, it's okay—" she said, but he didn't let her continue. He dropped his beer to the ground, ignoring the way it splashed at his feet and soaked his legs, and he finally kissed Gretchen.

She tasted like honey, too. Her lips were warm and soft and wet, all the descriptions he'd read and heard and imagined a thousand times, sure. But they were so much more than that. They were real, and wonderful.

AGAINST THE CURRENT

WHEN THE PARTY had mostly cleared out—excepting the few people passed out on couches or in the pillow fort at the foot of the stairs, plus a couple making out in the yard—Dave and Julia started going about the task of making the house somewhat presentable before the dads returned from Napa in the morning.

"I'd say that was a success," Julia said, grabbing cans and tossing them into a garbage bag. Dave was searching the house for cups that people had tossed aside, the taste of Gretchen's kiss still on his lips, a warmth inside him that loomed much larger than the buzzed, in-love-with-the-world feeling from the Kapoor party. That had been a flame, and this was a fire.

"Yeah, pretty great turnout. Maybe we've been wrong all this time about what makes someone a good beer host. I thought being from Bangladesh and having hundreds of siblings was a requirement, but it turns out you have what it takes, too."

"I think the only real requirement is vast quantities of alcohol and a house to put it all in. And the attendance of a man on the cusp of celebrity such as yourself to lure in the masses, of course." Julia kicked at the charred remains of the bonfire, then used a log that hadn't been burned to scoop some of the cans into her bag. "The dads are going to empty my college fund when they see this. Good thing they already emptied it out for their restaurant venture! Student loans here I come."

When Dave didn't say anything—he was still recalling how he'd kissed Gretchen good night at the front door before she left, the smile on her face—Julia said, "Just kidding, I'm a little drunk. I'm sure they were always planning on making me get student loans."

Dave took their garbage bags to the curb, then came back and grabbed new ones from beneath the sink. Julia was already in the kitchen, examining the remains of the chips and dips. "Gnarly, someone ate all of the butter." She brought the bowls to the sink and dropped them in with a clatter. Whoever it was that had fallen asleep on the couch moaned in complaint at the sound. "Never mind, it's all right here on the carpet."

Dave rustled his fresh garbage bag to get it to open up. He slid in some crumbs and a couple of cups from the kitchen table, then took a seat on one of the chairs, staring off into the distance. "Hey, did you notice that Gretchen was here?"

"Yeah," Julia said, picking with a fingernail at something on the kitchen counter. "I saw you two being chummy. You running for student council, too? Prom queen? Mayor? You're running for mayor? I've created an ambitious, power-hungry monster. Forgive me, world!" She giggled, then walked toward the living room. "Well, shit. Maybe the beers on the ceiling fan were not a good idea."

Dave followed her gaze to a beer can that had lodged itself in the drywall. "Yikes."

Julia walked up to the beer in the wall, studying it, as if afraid that if she tried to pull it out the whole house would come crumbling down. "There's a joke here about how alcohol kills; I just don't have it yet."

Dave took a deep breath. "I like Gretchen," he said.

"Don't drink and fan? No, that doesn't make sense," Julia said. She scrunched her mouth to one side of her face, thoughtful. "Can-cer. Beer. Something about holes?" Julia's arms dropped to her sides. "Eh, I've got nothing." She turned back toward Dave. "What were you saying about Gretchen?"

"Nothing. I just think she's cool," Dave said, suddenly feeling tired.

"Cool as a cardboard cutout." Julia chuckled.

Dave hid the scowl that he could feel forming by fiddling with the trash bag in his hand. Julia was drunk; he should take what she was saying with a grain of salt.

"You know, at the Kapoors', I was pretty entertained by how lame everyone was. Tonight it just seemed sad. I had the exact same conversation with three people. Whole sentences were repeated. It's like the same person is writing all their dialogue."

"I'm sure that's an exaggeration."

"Dave, you know I swore off hyperbole a thousand years ago." Julia grabbed a nearby beer can and walked over to the kitchen, pouring out the contents into the sink. "So, what did you and cool-as-a-cutout Gretchen talk about? Let me guess," she called out from behind him. "Summer plans and how great college is going to be and how she totally prefers the shitty beer we had tonight to other kinds of shitty beer."

Dave forced a laugh. "Clearly, you've never had a conversation with her."

"Why would I want to?" Julia came back into the living room holding a cup of water, which she drank from in great big gulps.

He thought about every wonderful thing he'd learned about Gretchen. About her favorite song by Clem Snide, how she took care of her brother, how she actually tried to live by what she believed in, leaving the world a little better than she found it. If Julia knew that, she'd appreciate her, Dave knew. He just had to say it the right way to make her see. "Gretchen and I..." Dave started. "I've seen her a couple of times outside of school now, and I really like her. A lot. I thought you should know."

Julia was quiet for a few moments, her back to him, finishing her glass of water. She turned around slowly, smirking. "Oh, Dave, seriously? I mean, I know we're embracing clichés, but Gretchen Powers?"

He grabbed a plastic cup that was under the chair he was sitting on and dropped it into his trash bag. "She's not a cliché, Julia."

"The blond chick who's on the soccer team and dates older guys with tattoos and smiles at everyone like she's best friends with the whole fucking world? Ha!" Julia turned back to the wall and pulled the beer can out of the drywall, which crumbled and now had a gaping hole. She wiped off the top of the can with her shirt and popped it open, foam rising with a hiss over her hand and spilling on the carpet. "I bet she volunteers somewhere really snappy to get her college application super shiny."

"There's more to her than meets the eye," Dave said quietly. "There's more to most of these people than you realize; you're just too busy making fun of everyone to see it."

"Whoa there, defender of the popular." She went back to picking up trash from around the living room, reaching for a cup that was tucked under the head of the guy passed out on the love seat. "So, when did the other side win you over?"

"It's not about that." Dave sighed. "Seriously, Gretchen is great. You'd like her if you made the effort."

"Okay, next student council meeting I'll sit next to her."

"What's so wrong about student council?"

"Yikes. What's so great about this girl that you'll stand up for student council on her behalf?"

Dave leaned back in the chair, running a hand through the little that remained of his hair. "Look, I kissed her. We've had a couple of dates. And yeah, she's great. You'd think so, too, if you spent a little time with her instead of judging her from afar."

"By great, do you mean pretty? 'Cause I'll give you that, the girl's pretty."

"No, I mean great."

"Wonderful. You made out with one of the cool kids; I'm happy for you."

"Just stop, Julia. I'm trying to tell you for the first time in our friendship that I'm into someone."

"You're right," Julia said. "Would you like a high five?"

"You can be such an asshole," Dave snapped. "It's just never been directed at me before, so I couldn't see it."

"Wow, you're taking this personally."

"No shit, Julia. I like the girl." Dave stood from the chair. He had to stand up, unload some of the sudden energy he was feeling. He tensed his fingers into a fist. It was so unfair. He'd loved Julia for so long, and he'd always managed to be happy for her when she was with other guys, however fleetingly. And now that he finally liked someone else, she couldn't return that simple favor. Julia had taken a seat on the arm of the couch, her arms crossed in front of her chest, still holding on to the garbage bag full of beer cans, which clinked against each other like the world's worst wind chime. "You know what? I don't think you have any idea what people are really like. Your mom put this idea in your head about a life less ordinary, and I let you drag me along with it because..." He exhaled, trailing off and turning his back to her.

Then he turned back around, tried to soften his voice. "We separated ourselves from all these people, and we thought we knew who they are. But we don't, not at all."

"I know who they are," Julia said. "I just didn't know you preferred them over me."

"Jesus Christ, will you listen to yourself?" He leaned against the wall near the couch. "I'm not renouncing our friendship, you crazy person. I'm just saying they're not all as awful as we thought."

Dave could see Julia's lips form another smirk. "Speak for yourself," she said loudly, as if daring her voice to break. "These people are clichés, even more so than I'd imagined. I just thought you were different."

"You know what? You're not different either!" Dave yelled. He saw Julia flinch, and felt a strange satisfaction that he'd caught her off guard. When he moved, he accidentally flipped on the switch for the ceiling fan, and it started whirring noisily, spinning shakily, like it'd been knocked off its usual axis. In any other situation the two of them would have burst out laughing at the timing, at how wobbly it moved. But now they were quiet, and the fan was the only sound in the room, save for the light snoring coming from the couch. "You think forcing yourself—forcing *us*—to become outsiders makes us unique? It doesn't. Rebellious teenage girl swims against the current? You know what that sounds like to me? You're a cliché, Julia."

The words felt right up until the moment he spoke them, right even as he spit them out across the room. The venom felt righteous, a lesson Julia had to learn.

But when her face crumpled up, when the hurt rippled

across that beautiful face he'd all but memorized, Dave wished that there was some way to undo it all, to skip back a few chapters and rewrite the scene, find a different way to approach the subject, of Gretchen, some way to make Julia understand.

"Please leave," Julia said simply.

He didn't dare to move. It felt like they were in some other universe, and if he left her house, the real world wouldn't ever come back. He feared that leaving would make this permanent, but he didn't know how to do anything but stand there. He wondered how he could be so mad at her now, how things could take such a turn so quickly. Julia said again, "Get out," like she was already writing it into their history.

So he left.

PART 2
JULIA

WITHOUT KNOWING

HOW JULIA HAD felt something so deeply for so long without knowing it herself was a mystery. As if love was a fugitive harboring in an attic, hidden even from the people residing in the house. Dave liked Gretchen? Well, Julia loved him. *She loved him.*

If it didn't hurt so much, she might have marveled at the way the mind/heart/psyche/whatever worked. How she'd known without a doubt that she was in love with Dave and had been for a very long time only when he told her he'd kissed someone else. How the words *I love you* had popped into her head so loud and so clear that she'd wondered if she'd really never said them before. How the realization seemed to unwind backward through time, suffusing every moment they'd had together with a love she'd simply failed to notice before. Of course she loved Dave. His humor, his—and she hated to even think the expression, but, trite as it was, it rang completely true—heart of gold, the selfless way he did everything he could for her. His sheepish smile. His hands, big and gentle. How had she loved his hands this entire time and not known it?

Julia was still in the living room when the front door closed softly. She'd been expecting Dave to slam it. She stared at the beer in her hand, didn't want another sip of it but finished it anyway. Dave didn't feel like slamming any doors? That was fine. She did.

She walked to front of the house and opened the door only to throw it back against its frame, the windows giving a satisfying rumble. Julia smiled to herself and did it again. There was a crazy freedom in knowing she could blame anyone else if something actually broke. She looked around the house, the stains on the carpet, the faint smell of vomit coming from somewhere not yet discovered, the hole in the drywall. The party's damage was done, and nothing she could do would hide it. Her smile spread wider.

There was no hesitation when she chucked the beer can through the back window. She thought of this newly discovered love for Dave, her awful, stupid timing in realizing it, and then her anger basically did all the work for her. Breaking glass looked beautiful in the hazy light of drunkenness. The crash scared the couple making out in the backyard and they scurried away. Julia felt a savage pleasure in interrupting them.

Next, Julia tried punching a hole in the wall. The first attempt went horribly and sent a wave of pain through her knuckles, which coincided with a fit of laughter at how satisfying it was to drunkenly punch a wall in anger. She did it a second time, too in love with the thought of it not to try again. The pain was too bad for a third attempt. She hurled a bowl of chip crumbles across the yard, and it soared like a broken Frisbee. She broke the chair Joey Planko had sat in against the lawn, leaving wooden splinters sticking out of the scorched grass at dangerous angles.

She pictured Dave—her Dave, the funniest guy she knew, her best friend, the only person she could even imagine spending her days with—side by side with cookie-cutter Gretchen and her perfect blond waves and Julia broke into laughter so uncontrollable she had to lie down and let it tear through her. She ripped out a patch of grass and ripped the blades to shreds, throwing them in the air like confetti. As the bits of green rained down on her, she thought about waking up the guy on the couch and kissing him as an act of revenge, but she settled on going to the kitchen and finding more beer. Whether to drink or throw she hadn't yet decided.

Julia loved Dave. And she would tear her house apart to prove it.

o o o

Julia woke up to the sound of the garage door rumbling open. Sunlight streamed into her room. She'd forgotten to close the blinds last night, and she hadn't bothered to change out of her clothes. She was on top of her bedding, sweating slightly from the heat, her head pounding, a pain in her hand. In the far corner of her room, her phone lay facedown on the carpet, she didn't know why. It looked like it'd been thrown against the wall, but she couldn't remember doing that. Ugh, alcohol.

The garage door rumbled shut, and she heard the muffled voices of her dads getting out of the car. Julia wondered if her dads would wait to ambush her downstairs or if they'd come barging in. Then, in a flash, she remembered the love seat that she'd drunkenly dragged into the bathroom. Looping this image into the memory of last night, she knew it had happened after Dave had left, though it felt like something they would have done together. She laughed into her pillow, as pieces of the night started coming back, knowing for a fact now that the dads would be running in at any moment. She was so hungover that laughing hurt; she felt like a desert floor with cracks running through it. Looking over at her empty nightstand, she wished her drunken self had been smart enough to get a glass of water for this exact moment.

The dads started stomping their way up the stairs. They knocked twice, loud and hard, like a couple of gunshots. Tom came in first, his face bright red, the way it looked when he had even a sip of wine. Ethan, in poorer shape, lagged behind, huffing from the hurried climb up the stairs.

"Julia," Tom said, arms crossed in front of his chest, "care to explain why the hell my house looks the way that it does?"

Julia decided she was going to lie in bed and take the yelling barrage without comment for a while. She tried to remember getting into bed last night, but all that came to her was a fuzzy memory of a bonfire, which felt more like something out of a dream. Why did her hand hurt? And why hadn't Dave slept over, sprawled out next to her bed in that musky sleeping bag like he usually did?

"There's a hole in my wall, ash all over my carpet, and a crusty puddle of puke on my suede couch," Tom was yelling, that vein in his neck starting to pop out. Ethan was standing by the door, biting his thumb, looking like he was the one in trouble. "There's trash all over the place, and that doesn't even come close to mattering compared to the fact that you had underage kids drinking here. The whole school judging by how many empty beer cans are around. Do you realize how irresponsible that is?"

The memory of a fight with Dave appeared suddenly, her on the verge of tears after he'd left. Wait. Had she drunkenly decided that she was in love with Dave? Julia almost laughed in the middle of her dad's tirade. Of all the stupid ideas people get when under the influence; Julia shook her head at the thought. It couldn't have actually happened. And even if it did, Julia would plead temporary beer-induced insanity. But it didn't happen. "What if the cops had been called? What if someone had been hurt?" Tom was leaning over her now, gesticulating wildly with his hands as he yelled, like some conductor in the midst of a crescendo. "Hell, maybe someone was; we haven't had time to really check."

Ethan stepped away from the door and put his hands on Tom's shoulder, whispering something into his ear that Julia couldn't hear. Julia strained to remember more about the end of the night, and what had happened with Dave. She hoped she hadn't done anything as embarrassing as tell Dave she loved him. A distinct memory of climbing onto the roof and throwing eggs out the window, watching them disappear into the night, popped into her head. That would have been great to do with Dave, but his presence wasn't there in the memory, even though she couldn't remember them ever saying goodbye. He should have been there for that.

"It's unacceptable," Tom was saying, still in conference with Ethan, who spoke calmly, quietly enough that Julia could only hear the breath of his words, and not the words themselves. "No, there is no side to her story. What, she accidentally threw a party?"

"Ooh, yes!" Julia said. "It was an accident. Peer pressure and the aching desire to be accepted by my peers."

Tom got even redder and Ethan shook his head. "Now's not the time for jokes."

Julia tried to get up, but the movement made her head feel like it was about to explode, so she sank back into the comfort of lying down. "Sheesh, okay. Just trying to lighten the mood a little. I know I messed up. Can we skip the lecture and just get to the repercussions? I plead guilty."

"No, you don't get off that light," Tom said, still yelling. "The lecture is part of the punishment."

Julia sighed and slowly slipped out of the blazer she'd fallen asleep in. She gave it a whiff, then immediately regretting doing so. She tossed it across the room toward her laundry pile. "Trust me, what I just smelled was punishment enough."

"You're paying for that to get dry-cleaned," Ethan said. True businessman that he was, the only punishments he could ever think of were financial. Disciplining did not come easily to him.

"I understand that I am financially responsible for the mayhem below. I wouldn't have thrown the party if I weren't ready to face some consequences. So can we just call this my one big teenage fuckup and move on? I could use some coffee and a greasy breakfast."

Ethan sighed and took a seat on the foot of her bed. He looked up at Tom with a smile and a shrug. "She's tougher than I am. You're gonna have to do all the lecturing." Then he turned back to Julia. "To be clear, I'm not okay with any of what happened."

"Unbelievable," Tom said. He shook his head and recrossed his arms. "What was going through your head?"

"Honestly? I was hoping to get laid."

"Julia!"

"I'm kidding! When did you guys lose your sense of humor?"

"No father would ever laugh at that joke." Ethan scooted up the bed to sit beside Julia, his back to the headboard and his legs stretched out in front of him.

"What do you want me to say?" Julia said to Tom. "High school is wrapping up, Dave got voted onto the prom king ballot, you guys were out of town. It was on the Nevers list, so I took advantage. I'm eighteen. I'm allowed the rare burst of immaturity."

"If only it were rare."

Julia held her hands to her heart. "Ouch, Dad." Another

piece of the night came to her: an image of her yelling at Dave. Something to do with that soccer-playing blonde he'd been chummy with all night. She nestled into her dad for comfort, not wanting to believe that she could have ever been so dramatic. "Look, I'm sorry. Can I blame this one on my genes?"

Tom raised his hands in surrender, palms out. "I can't handle this right now. I'm going for a drive." He pointed at Ethan. "You, stop facilitating." Then he pointed at Julia. "And you, go clean my house. The couch smells like an orgy."

"Eww." Julia laughed. "I love you, too, Dad!"

Tom grumbled a response as he made his way downstairs.

"Next time you have a party, I'd like to be invited," Ethan said. "Just, you know, not for a few years."

"No promises." She nuzzled her nose into his side, the hangover getting worse. "Have you talked to my mom at all? Did she get tickets yet?"

"Do me a favor, don't bring her up while Dad's around. We told her she can stay with us, but if he starts thinking you're acting out because of her visit, he could change his mind."

"I'm not acting out 'cause she's coming," Julia mumbled. "I'm acting out 'cause I'm a teenage cliché."

Ethan chuckled and put an arm around her, rubbing at her back the way he'd done so many times when she was little. "Wanting to party does not make you a cliché." Julia smiled and sank further into his side, comforted by his warmth and the relief that came with closing her eyes. It was tempting to keep them closed the rest of the day, let the details remain fuzzy. Whatever she'd said to Dave, he would forgive her. Whatever had taken them apart at the end of the party would be forgotten.

APOLOGIES

Julia and Dave hadn't talked all weekend. She'd of course been grounded, though the dads had let her keep her phone. It wasn't completely without precedent for them to go all weekend without even texting each other, just a little weird. But if they didn't talk, it was usually Julia's fault, and radio silence from Dave made Julia realize that maybe their fight had been worse than she remembered.

Monday morning, Julia went to school, happy to get out of the house and to not have to clean up anymore. Her phone was full of pictures of the mayhem so she could show Dave. On another weekend she probably would have messaged them to him, but the thought of Dave with the soccer girl made her pull away. She remembered his confession now, the fact that he liked Gretchen, though she still didn't know quite what to make of the two of them being together. Whatever she thought of Gretchen, though, she had to go apologize. For the fight, and whatever it was she may have said. Her friendship with Dave hadn't changed in four years, and it wasn't about to now. The first thing she was going to do was find Dave and tell him that she was happy for him, no matter who his little love interest was. She definitely wasn't going to phrase it like that, though. But on her way to homeroom, Dr. Hill intercepted her in the hallway. "Julia," he said. "Come with me."

Julia followed absently, her mind still on the fight with

Dave, trying to phrase an apology, brush it all away. Then she saw Marroney sitting in the chair behind the desk and her head cleared.

"Please, have a seat." Dr. Hill pointed at one of the twin chairs that faced his desk.

She did as he asked, moving slowly, wondering how much Marroney had accused her of. Marroney looked like a smaller version of himself. When she took a seat, she could have sworn she saw him push himself farther away. This was going to be great.

Dr. Hill moved around her so he was standing to the side of the desk, in between her and Marroney. He crossed his arms in front of his chest. The dads always talked about how attractive Dr. Hill was, often joking that they were going to leave each other for him. "I'm sure you've already figured out why you're here." He leaned forward and put his fingertips on the desk in front of her. "It has to stop, Julia. I'm going to assume for propriety's sake and to save myself a headache that you're just having some fun at Mr. Marroney's expense. But following him around town? Breaking into his house? Unwanted physical assault? Even you have to see how inappropriate that is."

Marroney practically flinched at the euphemistic reminder of the tickling incident. With all that had happened, she'd almost forgotten about that ill-conceived initial flirtation in the Chili's bathroom. How the hell had she let Dave talk her into that one? Marroney looked downright scared to be in front of her, and Julia felt a little sorry for what she'd put him through. She poked fun a lot, but she genuinely liked the oddball. "Sir, in my defense, the cupcakes were a gift for Teacher Appreciation Day."

"That's in May."

"I'm so appreciative, I couldn't wait that long."

"That's enough," Dr. Hill said. "Mr. Marroney would be within his rights to press charges against you and file a restraining order, but he was considerate enough to come to us first and ask us to intervene. You should be thankful he did, because a police record could jeopardize your graduation, not to mention your collegiate future."

Julia wished she could record the conversation so Dave could laugh with her about it. He'd joked about her getting a restraining order. That she'd come close to actually getting one was, in her opinion, a smashing success, and maybe even better than hooking up with a teacher. Julia's mom would have a good laugh about this. It wasn't exactly playing keep-away with a security guard's lunch in Singapore, but it was tinged with just the right distaste for authority.

"You've clearly crossed the line, and I need your word that it stops now. I want you to apologize to Mr. Marroney for the discomfort you've caused."

Julia raised her hands up. "No, you're right. Mr. Marroney, I am so sorry for all the discomfort I've caused. I never meant for it. Quite the opposite, really."

"Ms. Stokes."

Marroney was looking down, a thin sheen of sweat visible on his forehead. Maybe it was her imagination, but she thought she saw his lip quivering beneath his mustache. He rubbed his hands over each other like he was trying to calm himself.

"That time it legitimately just came out wrong. I never meant to make you uncomfortable, truly. I was having a bit of fun, and I'm sorry I took it so far. I was mostly kidding." Dr. Hill raised his eyebrows at her. "Entirely kidding," she corrected, even though deep down, there was something she found appealing about Marroney. It wasn't a physical attraction like she'd joked about with Dave, but something had made her pick him over every other teacher. "I promise to no longer cross any sort of lines or give you any baked goods or recite any kind of poetry in your honor."

"Mr. Marroney, is that enough of an apology for you?"

"Let's just put the matter behind us." He tried to sigh, but it came out more like a wheeze. Julia fought the urge to settle things with a hug. He really looked like he was near tears.

"Wonderful," Dr. Hill said, clapping his hands together. "Julia, first period's about to begin, you can go straight there."

Julia stood from her chair, a little sad that she'd have to back off. She wanted to run straight to Dave to tell him what happened, but homeroom was over and her English teacher was way too intense about tardiness, so it would have to wait. Julia went to her locker to grab her copy of *Heart of Darkness*, which she'd read exactly zero percent of. She rummaged around until she found a half-filled crossword puzzle she could entertain herself with, then shut her locker and turned down the hall to get to class. Halfway there, eyes already searching the crossword clues, she ran right into Dave.

"Hey," he said, his arm on her shoulder to steady her from the impact. He pulled it away slowly. "I saw you walk out of Hill's office. What was all that about?"

The hallway filled with the sound of people talking, making their way to their classes. Julia didn't know how anyone could be so chatty and loud that early in the morning. People pushed past them, their backpacks hanging off their shoulders, phones in their hands. Dave looked so great in the morning. She wondered how he did that, how he always seemed ready for the day as soon as it arrived. Maybe it had something to do with sleep cycles, or it was just the softness of the morning light that worked with his features. He was probably having completely normal thoughts, and here she was trying to figure out why her best friend looked good in the morning. Maybe she was still hungover. She shook the thought away, wanting to get to the apology, to make sure he knew she stood right where she always had. "Marroney finally ratted me out. *Never hook up with a teacher* might officially be off the docket."

"That's too bad." He shifted the weight of his backpack and put his hand on the back of his neck like he always did when he was nervous. Were things awkward? Had the fight been that bad? "Are we going to talk about the other night?" Dave said.

"God, yes, please. Sorry I didn't text. The dads had me spit-shine the whole house, which I probably deserved. Also, sorry about our fight. I guess I was a little drunk. I remember you telling me about Gretchen and that's about it. Was I a bitch about it?"

Dave smiled in that cute, sheepish way he often did and shrugged. "Maybe a little bit."

"Well, that sucks." Julia stepped out of her shoes, feeling the comfort of the floor on her bare feet. "Whatever I said, I'm sorry I said it. Did you yell back at me?"

"There was some yelling."

"David Daniel Davis, get the hell out of here! You yelled? I'm so proud of you. Tell me more."

Dave blushed. "I was mean."

"Wow, I brought the mean out of you? I've never seen you be mean. What did I say?"

"You made fun of me for liking Gretchen." Dave's hand was still clutching the back of his neck and she chuckled as she pulled it down for him. The mention of Gretchen made Julia's heart sink for some reason, but the touch of his skin on her fingers was solid and reassuring.

Julia grimaced. "I'm sorry I was a drunken asshole. That was very cliché of me. I remember that part, and you're completely right. It'll never happen again. Except for the five or six times I still have to be a cliché to live out the Nevers. I'm happy for you, Dave. Now Marroney and I have someone to go on double dates with!"

Dave laughed and shoved his hands into his pockets. "I'm sorry about what I said, too. Every time I think about it I feel sick. Things were heated. I didn't mean it."

"Water under the proverbial bridge," Julia said, feeling that peculiar urge to poke him. But when her finger touched his stomach, it didn't just pull away like it always did. It lingered there as if it had its own agenda, and Julia had to take a step backward to keep from making the moment awkward. What the hell was going on with her? "I'm going to try to get to know Gretchen better," she said. "With the exception of your gross underappreciation for a certain faculty member at this school, you're the best judge of character I know. If you say she's cool, she's cool."

"Thanks, Julia," he said, smiling sheepishly like he was wont to do.

"No worries." The hallway was quieter now, just a few stragglers shutting their lockers and rushing to class, the sound of their sneakers slapping against the linoleum floor. Teachers reached to shut their doors so latecomers couldn't sneak in. "I gotta get going or else Ms. T is gonna smack me around for being late. See ya!" Julia said, forcing cheerfulness.

They parted ways with a smile and Julia took a seat in class, happy that the tension had been put to rest so easily. That she was having strange thoughts and buzzing at his touch could be chalked up to it still being so early in the morning. Cringing when she thought of Gretchen, that was just because of what she knew about Gretchen, nothing to do with Dave liking her. Maybe the buzzing was just relief that everything was still right between Julia and Dave, relief that her ominous recollection of their fight had been a case of overworrying. This was all normal.

CUE THE MONTAGE

Julia had been the one to suggest the three of them hang out together. She wanted to see in Gretchen whatever it was Dave saw in her. She really did, even if she had her doubts about it.

Julia parked her car at Morro Bay, running late as usual. She stepped out of her car, avoiding a beer bottle that lay shattered nearby. When Dave's bench came into view, it was strange to see a second body on it next to his. Julia had always loved this moment, the slow, watchful approach before Dave saw her.

Now there was a head of blond waves next to him, and Julia could hear them laughing. The sound actually slowed her down. She felt like she was about to interrupt, which was bullshit. This was Julia's bench to share with Dave. If anyone should feel like she was interrupting, it was Gretchen.

This was not normal. Gretchen being there, and Julia's reaction to it.

She took a breath, forced herself to move at a normal speed, to approach casually. "Hi, guys," she called out, waving.

"Hi," Dave said. "You guys know each other, right?"

"Yeah, of course," Gretchen said, waving her hand once across her body, "we had world history together last year."

"And we have a standing appointment every Tuesday to talk about you behind your back," Julia said. "Nothing too judgmental. Just what color you should dye your hair, how you're super conceited for running for prom king. That kind of thing."

"Oh my God, teach me to keep a straight face like you do," Gretchen said. "That was so good. You didn't even flinch."

Julia smiled and went to Dave's side of the bench, scooting him toward the middle, feeling bittersweet that he'd be closer to both her and Gretchen. "Sorry I'm late. What'd I miss?"

"Well, Dave was telling me he's never mall-ratted before, and I was having trouble believing him."

"Mall-ratting? That's a thing? I thought that was a made-up term from that nineties movie."

"Apparently it exists," Dave says. "People go to the mall. To hang out. For hours."

"Surely, you mean they go to indulge in the great tradition of consumerism before returning home to enjoy their recently purchased products," Julia said.

"No. Just...to spend time at the mall."

"Spend money, you mean."

"I can't tell if you guys are kidding," Gretchen said. "You've seriously never hung out at the mall? You're going to get your teenager licenses revoked."

"I don't think we were ever issued any," Dave said. "We're eighteen and going on sixty-five."

"Look, having better taste than most people our age doesn't excuse you from missing out on a major part of adolescence."

"Wasting time in a symbol of capitalism is a major part of adolescence?"

"You're goddamn right," Gretchen said, her voice giving away her desire to laugh, and damn if Julia didn't find that charming. Julia suddenly felt nauseous. Gretchen stood up, pulling out a set of car keys from the pocket of her jeans. "Come on, I'll drive. We're going to the mall."

"I feel like she's not going to let this go," Julia said, getting up and standing by Gretchen. They were similarly built, Julia noticed. Almost the exact same height, though Julia wasn't wearing shoes, and Gretchen's hair gave her an extra quarter inch. Julia had no idea why that would matter, why she would suddenly start measuring herself against this girl who was nothing like her. "You and I are rebels. We should rebel against capitalism by defacing it with the refusal to spend money. Plus, it wasn't on the list, but it may as well have been. We're looking for ordinary high school experiences, and if Gretchen says this one's worth doing, well then, let's give it a shot."

"Thank you, Julia," Gretchen said, and Julia watched as she reached over and grabbed Dave by the wrist, pulling him up to his feet, her fingers lingering on his skin like they were used to touching him, like they belonged on him.

o o o

On the drive to the mall, Julia discovered backseats are a kind of hell when you are there on your own. She'd sat behind Gretchen, giving her a clear view of Dave and how often he looked toward the driver's side. She could barely hear the conversation, and had to stick her face in between theirs to not feel like she was on a deserted island.

"I have to hand it to you, Gretchen," Julia said at the first opportunity she could. "You are rocking this minivan so well that I can't tell if you're doing it ironically or not."

"Oh, you mean Vantastic? No irony here; I love this thing. It's been in the family for about twenty years. I couldn't wait to drive it, even though half the time I'm in it I am actively fearing death."

Dave glanced over his shoulder at Julia, giving her a smile that she understood immediately: *Isn't she so much more than you thought?* Julia stuck her tongue out at Dave, the move feeling too middle school even as she did it, like a girl desperate to be cute.

When they walked in through the glass doors of the mall, Julia instinctively cringed. "Dave, tell Gretchen what the look on my face means."

"She's going to throw up."

"You guys are ridiculous."

They were walking in the direction of the food court, the three of them in a row, Dave in the middle. Julia spotted the kid who'd fallen asleep on her couch after the party, but he was a bit too far away to yell at.

"So," Dave said, "how, exactly, does one mall-rat?"

"Technically, we've started." Gretchen extended her arms outward, as if presenting them with a new world. "Yaaaay," she said, poking just enough fun at herself for Julia to feel a shift starting to take place. Julia was starting to like Gretchen, and it shouldn't have been a problem. It should have been great, all the more reason to be happy for Dave. But it *was* a problem, one that caused her throat to dry up. "Actually, I know the best way to break you guys into this," Gretchen said. "And I'll admit, this isn't exactly within the normal mall-ratting activity. But it's my favorite thing to do, especially on days when I'm feeling a little down."

She took them to the food court and ordered a single ice-cream cone, not allowing them to get their own. Then she led them toward the escalators down to the first floor, only licking away the drops that threatened to drip onto her hand. A little kid in front of them dangled his shoelaces near the gap at the edge of the escalator stairs while his mom stared at her phone, her free hand gripping his like that was all there was to parenting. Julia caught Gretchen shaking her head. They walked past what seemed to be the same exact athletic shoe store replicated in three different spots, then entered the pet store that was tucked away in the corner.

It was a sad place, puppies in glass cages, frolicking as much as they could, trying to avoid little puddles of pee they'd left behind. Some yipped happily, some whimpered, some looked defeated and just stared through the glass as if they'd given up. A mutt with short brown fur lay on its front paws, looking up at Julia with big, sad eyes that reminded her of Dave's. She looked over at Dave peering into the dog's cage and felt the urge to throw her arms around his neck, which was silly.

An employee came by, a tall and lanky guy with a slouch and a pronounced Adam's apple. Gretchen asked him if she could pet a dog. The guy shrugged, probably bored, his mind rotting away inside the depressing pet store all day.

"This one!" Julia said, pointing at the scruffy brown puppy, desperate for the dog's warmth, for something to touch. "If I'd known puppy-holding was involved in mall-ratting I might have been more receptive," she said, taking the dog in her arms.

"Just you wait," Gretchen said, stepping up to Julia. "This might feel weird at first. Just trust me." She reached out and dipped the ice-cream cone against Julia's nose.

"What the hell?" Julia forced a laugh. Dave stood behind Gretchen, his head tilted.

Gretchen just smiled, and within a second or two the mutt had sniffed out the ice cream and was licking Julia's nose enthusiastically. Julia laughed, which resulted in the dog trying to slip her some tongue, so she turned her head to the side a little to avoid the kisses but keep the whole nose-licking thing going. "I'm so happy right now," Julia said, feeling better, though there was nothing she should have been feeling better from.

"Just looking at what's happening is making me happier than I've been in years," Dave said. "Seriously, years."

Even the lanky employee cracked a smile. The three of them took turns passing the dog to each other, then touching the increasingly melting ice-cream cone to their noses. To keep the dog from getting sick from all the ice cream, and because the other locked-up dogs seemed to be in ravenous fits of jealousy, the employee took away the Dave-looking mutt and brought a few other ones: twin golden retrievers, a spotted pit bull, something that looked less like a dog and more like a gremlin. They kept going until the ice cream was nothing but a puddle dripping through the bottom of the soggy cone.

They left the pet store mildly dazed, smiles still plastered on their faces. "Touché," Julia said. "I'm going to do that from now on. Always. Every day of my life."

Dave, standing close to Gretchen, gave her a little shoulder bump. "What else you got?"

"Cue the montage," Julia said, a bit too sarcastically, that unexpected jealousy almost giving rise to anger.

Gretchen laughed. "You're so right. That would have definitely been the movie cue for a montage."

They went to the department store and made Dave try on clothes, simply because that was exactly what would happen in the montage. They sat by the dressing room on a bench as the clerk gave them strange looks. "You are the slowest dresser on the planet," Julia called out, trying to hide the annoyance in her voice, or transfer it over to something she should have been annoyed by. "You're slowing down our montage. Did you notice the happy pop music stopped playing? That's your fault."

"I don't understand vests," he called out from the dressing room.

"They go on your chest," Gretchen called back.

"Har har. And do I really have to wear the hat?"

"Yes!" they said in unison.

He stepped out of the dressing room, looking uncomfortable in his clothes, but undoubtedly handsome. Julia paused, swirling that thought around her head like a beverage she was savoring. Dave was handsome. That wasn't new information to her; she'd always thought it strange that a great guy like him with his looks had never pursued anyone, had never even accidentally stumbled into a fleeting romance. But had Julia ever thought it in those terms before?

"You look so cute," Gretchen said, and almost immediately Julia felt like punching her.

Julia had a quick flash of what this could turn into: her and Gretchen becoming friends, Dave and Gretchen touching more and more, little stolen glances between them that Julia wouldn't be able to avoid intercepting. Julia would be the third wheel in a friendship that had never needed more than two people.

Suddenly flushed, Julia went off to find a bathroom to calm herself down. What the fuck was going on? Ridiculing others was her usual coping mechanism, not this mad jealousy. If anything, Julia had expected to make fun of Gretchen today. She thought back to the night of the party, how it had felt when she'd started tearing apart her house. She'd been lying on the grass, telling herself she was in love with Dave. And drunk as she may have been, maybe it was true. Maybe she was in love with Dave.

Julia found the department store's bathroom, which was small and clean with a large plant in the corner, lavender in the air. She went up to the sink and splashed some water on her face, letting it drip-dry as she shook her head at the little mantra now running through her head, taking root. No, Julia told herself. It's not true.

When she'd managed to convince herself, Julia returned to the dressing area and saw Gretchen and Dave standing close to each other, their fingers interlaced. Julia stared at the sight for a while, scrunching her mouth over to one corner. Fuck. It *was* true.

She was in love with Dave.

JUST LIKE THIS

Julia watched the clock tick. It was a stupid thing to do, she knew, the seconds bleeding out slower when observed. But now that flirting with Marroney was apparently frowned upon, she had nothing else to do in class.

Her phone buzzed in her pocket, and she pulled it out to read a text from Dave. I just got the best idea of all time. Or of the past four minutes. Hard to tell. Meet me by your locker.

Julia texted back, Hyperbole foul.

You're a hyperbole foul.

Yeah, she loved Dave. And life had gotten a little bit suckier since the realization sunk in. But in many ways, things were still exactly the same. Sure, every now and then she'd buy a bag of chips just to stomp on it and watch the crumbs explode out. But that was kind of a cool thing that she could envision herself doing for the rest of her life, even when ecstatic and in mutual love with some unknown, future person. Everything else was normal. Dave was her best friend. She was his best friend. Nothing had changed.

She wasn't about to spend her class periods lamenting the fact that Dave was dating someone else. Most of the time, she barely even noticed. It was weird that Dave could drive now, because Dave never drove. Aside from that, the bag of chips thing, and the occasional passing bout of sadness or desire to punch Gretchen, Julia was dealing with it pretty damn well.

"Julia, would you like to come up and solve this equation?"

Julia looked up to see the class's eyes on her. Marroney was holding up a piece of chalk like an offering. She considered going up and reciting her slam poem, but thought better of it. "Eh, not really. I wasn't paying attention and wouldn't want to embarrass myself."

A few people snickered and Marroney sighed. "I guess I'll thank you for your honesty."

"Anytime," Julia said, resisting the urge to wink.

Marroney called on someone else and Julia sank back into her chair, fiddling with her phone. A small crack ran along the side of the screen from when she'd thrown it at her bedroom wall the night of the party. She couldn't help but think of Dave when she saw that sliver of broken glass, so fine it didn't even sting her finger.

A few classes later, when the clock finally reached 2:30 and the clanging bell released her from her seat, Julia grabbed her bag and shot out of the classroom. School was starting to weigh more than she could bear. Expecting Dave to be a little late, off smooching with Gretchen, Julia slipped in her earbuds, stepped out of her mocs, and leaned against her locker, watching everyone pass by. When music was playing, Julia felt not as critical of people. At the moment, she couldn't stand the sight of couples, but everyone else seemed a little less offensive, a little closer to her when, say, Conor Oberst was singing.

Dave appeared earlier than she'd expected him to, on his own. She kept her earbuds in as he made his way toward her, trying not to think of the light in his eyes, trying not to look at his hands. When he started speaking she couldn't hear a word of it. Then he plucked out the earbuds.

"Oww, dude, I hate that feeling," Julia said, rubbing at her ear and curling the white cord around her phone.

"Sorry. You feel like scheming?"

She slipped her phone in her bag. "I don't know if I've got another tree house in me. I nearly hammered my finger off last time."

"No, this doesn't involve any construction. It's a promposal."

Julia stared at him blankly.

"Get it? It's the words prom and proposal combined into one. Prom-posal. A proposal for prom."

"I understood, I'm just having trouble, you know"—she gestured with her hands—"understanding."

"It's another cliché."

"I'm well aware."

"It wasn't on the Nevers, but only because when we were freshmen we couldn't really envision anyone dating us." They started walking down the hall toward the parking lot, the habit long ago ingrained into their end of school ritual. "But if we'd had the foresight and the self-esteem, it totally would have been."

"Speak for yourself, I've always known I'm awesome. People date me all the time."

"That's not that point." Dave held open the door for her and a few other people. "I'm gonna ask Gretchen to prom and I need your help to make it as over-the-top as possible."

"Oh, right, you and Gretchen."

Dave laughed. "Who'd you think I was talking about?"

"I don't know. You and Vince Staffert would be cute together. He seems really into you."

"You know, I do like being little spoon and he seems like a great big spoon. But that's a whole other conversation. Are you gonna help me?"

Julia popped her trunk and they both tossed their bags inside. "Help you? I barely know you." She reached for her sunglasses in the car's cup holder, slipping them on even though it was grayer than usual today. Prom was supposed to be the last item crossed off the list, *never date your best friend*, and maybe it was dumb, but Julia hadn't really thought about how Gretchen would affect that.

"Come on. I'll buy you pizza if you help me scheme."

"You think I'm going to whore out my brain for a few slices of pizza?"

"I absolutely do."

"I hate how well you know me," Julia said. Then she smiled at him, not even forcing it. That much. "Fine. Let's plan ourselves a promposal."

○ ○ ○

Julia and Dave sat side by side at a booth at Fratelli's, a sheet of paper in front of them. It looked a little like the Nevers list, the same generic ruled notebook paper, both of their handwriting filling up the page, not necessarily sticking to the lines. The last slice of pizza sat uneaten on its tray, the cheese congealing to the stainless steel surface. The restaurant was starting to fill up, and a group by the door was eyeing the four-person booth they had been taking up for over an hour.

"I really don't think I can afford that many rose petals," Dave said.

"Fine. Then we buy however many you can afford and we stick them in a paper shredder."

"That sounds like an awful idea."

"How is rose-petal confetti an awful idea?"

"When you put it that way, it actually doesn't sound bad."

Julia loved this so much that she'd managed to ignore the fact that everything they were planning was for Gretchen. She got to be with Dave, sit with him, laugh, touch his wrist like she meant nothing by it. Moments like these could carry her until it was no longer necessary.

"What else can we do? This seems a little too low-key."

Julia looked at their plan. "We've got the scavenger-hunt-esque buildup, the perfect location, the rose-petal confetti. I'm assuming if I try to suggest explosions you're just gonna shoot me down again?"

"You know me so well."

"What about music? No cheesy moment is complete without the swelling of an orchestra."

Dave thought for a while. "I mean, Brett's got a pretty solid set of speakers I could borrow."

"You bring Brett's crappy Best Buy speakers to this beautiful promposal I've planned out and I'll never speak to you again. That'd be like bringing nail clippers to a gun fight."

"Fine, what do you suggest, then? It's not like I'm personally acquainted with an orchestra."

They both turned to look at each other at the same time. She could love him just like this. It was enough for her, to be this close.

"Are we really?" Dave said, but his eyes weren't wide with surprise. They were smiling, like he already knew the answer.

"We absolutely are," Julia said.

"How?"

"What do you mean, how? You're Dave the tree house builder, boyfriend of cute soccer girl with the blond waves. People at the school would give up their firstborns for you." Julia took her phone out of her pocket for effect. "Oh, look, there's a text from Christa Howards, renowned flutist and teen mom. She says she's in and please don't change her baby's name."

Dave laughed and looked off into the distance, his mind clearly on Gretchen, on how the night he was planning for her would play out. Julia grabbed the pen they'd been using and squeezed in the word *orchestra* in between two lines, then drew an arrow to show when the music would start to play, right after Gretchen saw Julia's car, right before the kiss. *Never pine silently*, she thought to herself and smiled, because she was doing exactly what they were supposed to be doing. Not doing. Sometimes doing.

"You know," she said, "I think we can add more to this list. There are a few clichés we haven't touched on yet. How do you feel about showing up in a whipped-cream bikini?"

"That might be a little too over-the-top."

"What if the orchestra members are all in whipped-cream bikinis?"

She could do this the whole day, plan something out with him, pretend that, like the snow fort they'd designed freshman year, it would never come to fruition. It was just her and Dave at the pizza place. No matter how many families crowded nearby, how many kids from school waved to them from other tables, no matter how many times Gretchen's name was scrawled on the sheet of paper in front of them, it was just her and Dave, like it always had been.

THE PROMPOSAL

A WEEK OF planning later, Julia was outside the school with Brett, waiting for the bell to ring. She was clenching a section of white string in her hand, and she stared at it sloping upward from the gray asphalt of the parking lot, swaying slightly in the breeze. She was incredibly proud of this string, despite all the clichés it would lead to, or rather, because of them. Because her tongue was planted firmly in her cheek, because her mom would approve of this, because she'd done all of it for Dave and none of it for Gretchen.

"It is stupid hot in here," Brett said from inside the teddy bear costume they'd rented for him.

"Don't you dare take off that mask," Julia said, snapping a few pictures of him on her phone for later blackmail use. "You remember your lines?"

"How dumb do you think I am? It's a sentence."

"You've never really been good with words, Brett."

"And you've never been good at interacting with humans other than my brother. People change."

"I don't know. I'm still pretty iffy about how to talk to non-Daveians. 'Iffy,' by the way, means unsure, suspect."

The school bell interrupted Brett's comeback. "Okay, get in position." She called Dave's cell phone as she pulled the string taut. One end was tied to Gretchen's car door, the other led to a tree at the park down the hill. Julia had skipped her last two periods to set it up, and now she was hiding behind Brett's truck to make sure Gretchen would follow it. Dave's handwritten signs hung along the length of the string. Meanwhile, Brett waddled in his bear suit to the halfway marker, a single rose in his hand.

"I still think we should have gone for the walkie-talkies," Julia said as soon as Dave answered. "It feels lame this way."

"Walkie-talkies are expensive, shitty, two-way cell phones. You guys all set?"

"Yup," Julia said, eyeing the crowd just now coming through the double doors of the school for Gretchen's blond waves.

"Okay, I'll see you at the harbor. You sure it's okay for me to take the car?"

Julia looked across the lot at her formerly white Mazda. She'd joked about Dave's newfound popularity, but it was incredible what a couple of text messages had achieved, how quickly the word spread, the number of people that had shown up to write on her car. She didn't credit herself, or the tree house. This was all Dave. As much as she wanted to keep him to herself, Julia loved knowing that this was for him. He deserved to be liked this much, this widely. "If you don't take it, the three thousand 'you should go to prom with Dave' messages will be kind of pointless."

Dave laughed. "This is so ridiculous. We are outdoing ourselves."

"We are outcliché-ing ourselves. Ooh, I see her." Julia hung up without another word, and pulled the string up higher. Paper arrows pointing down the line dangled, and kids—those not involved in the plan—were starting to point. Gretchen was reading a book as she walked, and part of Julia kind of wished that she would get in her car without noticing and drive off, dragging the string behind her. Then Gretchen looked up and noticed the string and the first sign, which read, FOLLOW ME!

Julia never thought she'd want to be in Gretchen the soccer girl's shoes. Or cleats, whatever. But that's exactly what she wanted: to be acting out this cliché-riddled promposal that would eventually lead to Dave. Swallowing down the thought that she was doing all of this for him, not Gretchen, Julia waited for her to take the string in her hand. When it was clear Gretchen would follow, Julia turned to go into the high school, where the band kids would be waiting to load their instruments into Brett's truck. Jealousy would have to wait.

THE FIRST ROSE

Brett in the teddy bear suit sitting motionless, the rose in his hand. If Julia were being honest with herself, the bear suit was not really crucial to the whole operation. It just made it a little cheesier, and therefore better. And how many chances was she going to get to convince Brett to pretend he was a teddy bear? She didn't know what she was planning to do with the pictures of him in it, especially now that Brett felt like more of a friend than like Dave's meathead brother. At the very least, she could jokingly torture him for a few months. Once Gretchen approached, Brett would hand her the rose and tell her that there were eleven more waiting for her around town, then go back to being motionless until she was out of sight. After that, he'd run back to the school and help load his truck.

THE SECOND ROSE

At the park, after following the arrows and Dave's signs, which were sweet to the point that they'd made Julia want to buy a bag of chips for stomping, Gretchen would find that the string disappeared into the branches of a tree. Maybe out of a twisted desire to pretend they were for her, or maybe simply out of masochism, Julia had insisted on having Dave share whatever inside jokes he had with Gretchen, to repeat whatever small details they could use for the promposal. It'd been strange to hear all that he already knew about the girl, strange to see how he'd smiled when he related the simplest things, like the fact that she loved climbing trees. Yeah, no shit, anyone with a halfway decent childhood loved climbing trees.

Julia pictured Gretchen deftly maneuvering her way up the branches, and despite herself, she wanted the rose to still be there, with the tiny message still tucked into the folds of its petals, the cryptic clue easy enough to be understood, hard enough to be thoughtful. They'd placed the rose on one of the highest climbable branches, high enough that Gretchen would be able to poke her head above the leaves and look out at San Luis Obispo stretching out below her. What a strange kind of love it was, to be rooting against yourself.

THE THIRD ROSE

"We've got a problem," Brett said. "The cellist is demanding to ride with her cello, but I've got sixteen other instruments and music stands to take, and there's no way I'm letting her ride back there. I can't get any more tickets. Endangering the life of a cellist is, like, six points off your license."

Right now, if she'd figured out the clue, Gretchen would be arriving to the ice cream shop owned by a friend of Dave's dad. The flavor of the week was rose. When Julia had come up with that part of the plan, she'd been simultaneously proud of herself and deeply ashamed that her brain could even think in such cheesy terms. Though how happy Dave had looked made her lean on the side of the former.

"Shit." Julia had no time to deal with finicky cellists. "Tell her she can ride in the truck, but she has to lie down flat with the cello on top."

Brett's hair was mussed with sweat from the bear mask, and he was still wearing the rest of the costume. "That's insane."

"Just do it, Brett. I have to get the cupcake."

"Wait, Julia. Before you go?"

"What?"

Brett started to say something, then ran the back of his hand across his forehead, his forearm coming away slick with sweat. He smiled wide, then stared at the ground, a move that felt strangely Dave-like. "You're really freaking good at this."

THE FOURTH ROSE

"Dave? How's it going over there?"

"The second string is in place, and Gretchen's about to finish her ice cream."

"Damn." Julia was watching a YouTube clip of how to draw a rose petal made out of frosting for the fiftieth time. She'd messed up eleven times already and only one cupcake remained, which was to be the sixth rose. Where the hell was Chef Mike when she needed him? Gretchen would follow the new string to the library, where it would lead her to a rose tucked in between her two favorite books. Julia didn't have much more time. "You didn't tell me she was a fast ice-cream eater."

"I had no idea."

"David Moneybags Gutierrez, how are you dating someone without knowing how fast they eat their ice cream?"

"Ha! You used my actual last name."

"This frosting thing is impossible," Julia said. "Pastry chefs are severely underpaid."

"She's done. I gotta go."

THE FIFTH ROSE

It'd been a hard rose to leave behind, and Julia kind of hated that it had been up to her to do it. Dave had chosen the first place he and Gretchen had kissed as a spot, and since that had happened at Julia's house, it only made sense for her to be the one to do it. After she had finally succeeded in drawing a rose made out of freaking sugar on a cupcake, she went downstairs and set up the string. She tied it to her mailbox and then took it around the side of her house toward the backyard. Dave had walked around a few days before, looking at the lawn, trying to remember exactly where it had happened, and Julia had felt like screaming that she didn't want to know, begging to be spared the details. Now she tied the string to the stem of the rose and stuck it in the grass. Inside the mailbox, she left Dave's note. Hopefully it would take Gretchen long enough to find so Julia could get the cupcake to the next location.

THE SIXTH ROSE

Julia made it back to school, where Gretchen's car was one of the only ones still in the lot. Marroney's car was still there, and for a crazy moment she considered leaving him a note, just for fun, just to let him know she wasn't *completely* over him. Instead, she left the cupcake on the hood of Gretchen's car, with the next clue tucked into the windshield wiper. It'd be so easy to leave it a little too close to the edge of the rubber, where the wind would blow it away and put a stop to the whole thing. Then her phone chimed. In position. Again. Have I mentioned this is ridiculous? You are a mastermind.

Julia smiled. We*, she wrote back.

THE SEVENTH ROSE

The rose hanging from the top post of the goal felt too cheesy even for the promposal, but Julia made sure it was centered and that the knot was nice and tight. Attached to it was a treasure map that would lead Gretchen on a very specific route to the next rose. It was a gorgeous day, the breeze just as Julia liked it, the sun just as she liked it, the sky so blue it was as if someone had gathered a week's worth of skies and jammed them all together. Love was people creating memories for each other, and Julia knew that today would be memorable not just for Dave and Gretchen.

THE EIGHTH ROSE

Courtesy of one of Brett's friends, a beautiful rose was graffitied on the side of the abandoned warehouse near the highway. Black and white and every imaginable shade of gray, the clue in Dave's handwriting beside it. Too nervous to do it during the day, Dave had done it at two in the morning, and Julia could picture the stain of black paint on his index finger, Brett making fun of Dave for being nervous. She could almost picture Dave starting and stopping, looking over his shoulder. She wished she had gone with them. She drove past the warehouse just to take a look at it again when another phone call came through.

THE NINTH ROSE

It'd been strangely easy to find an a cappella group on such short notice. The Internet did wonderful things. "La Vie en Rose" was even in their repertoire, and they were open to the idea of performing just one song, at a stoplight in the middle of town, for an audience of one.

THE TENTH ROSE

Julia had really pushed for skywriting or fireworks on this one. Dave could argue all he wanted, Julia couldn't see anything else that would match the over-the-top glory of roses in the sky. In the end, logistics had put a stop to the discussion. The alternative wasn't half-bad: Evan Royster, a junior, had recently been written up in the local newspaper for his "fire art," elaborate drawings of lighter fluid that blazed for a few minutes before disappearing forever.

He was dressed in the bear suit, waiting with his lighter in the far corner of the mall's parking lot where Dave and Gretchen had gone GPS-drawing.

THE ELEVENTH ROSE

Julia could not believe their luck when they went to the costume shop to find the bear suit and they'd found a giant rose costume.

"You know that's going to be you inside, right?"

"Absolutely," Dave said, already grabbing it off the rack. "I can't believe rose costumes exist."

"Never underestimate people's cheesiness," Julia said, poking Dave in the stomach, wishing it would elicit his usual head-shaking response.

THE TWELFTH ROSE

Julia arrived at the harbor right as Dave texted her that he was about to meet up with Gretchen at the mall. Julia's Mazda was parked in the harbor's lot. The orchestra kids were set up in a semicircle around the car. They were in their little band tuxedos, practicing their sections. The sun had already dipped behind the ocean, and twilight was growing darker.

"They're on their way!" Julia cried out, and the orchestra

fell quiet. "Remember, start playing once she sees the car, and crescendo right before they kiss."

"How will we know when they're going to kiss?" one of the violinists called out.

"Seriously? Have you never seen two people kissing?"

"I don't know..." the shy voice said, trailing off in a way that made Julia feel bad.

"Just. You know. Take a guess. When their faces are about to touch would be a good time." She looked around for Brett. "Did you get a confetti shooter?"

"Get the fuck out of here."

"I'm kidding. You have the rose petals?"

"Right here." He pointed at two buckets on either side of the car, filled to the brim.

"Perfect. You get one; I'll get the other. Wait until they kiss."

They stood at opposite sides of the car, looking out in the direction of the mall. The band kids were quiet, too, used to remaining silent until their cue. For a long time, Julia could only see the lights of the mall, the faint green of trees that lined the road to it from the harbor. She could hear the ocean, and the sound of cars on the highway. Her knuckles hurt from how hard she was gripping the bucket, and for a second she closed her eyes and wished for this whole thing to fail, for Gretchen to admit that she was not interested in Dave in the least, that she'd been faking it, just like Julia and Dave had faked their way through most of the Nevers.

Then Dave and Gretchen stepped out from the shadows, smiles plastered on both of their faces. Julia turned and motioned for the orchestra to begin playing. Even Julia couldn't help but smile as the couple came closer. She could see exactly when Gretchen read the writing on Julia's car, and she hoped that the happiness in her eyes was real, because that's what Dave deserved.

"Ha!" Gretchen cried out, beaming at the sound of the string section getting louder. "Guns N' Roses!" She turned to face Dave and threw her arms around his neck. "You are insane. A crazy rose serenading me with clichés."

"I had help." Dave shrugged, glancing at Julia, tearing her heart apart just like that, then wrapping his arms around Gretchen's waist. "Is that a yes?"

"I would have said yes at the first rose."

As the music crescendoed, Julia threw fistfuls of shredded rose petals into the air, using the shower of red and white as an excuse to avert her eyes. This was how she could love Dave. From exactly this distance. Within sight but apart. Cheering him on, providing whatever happiness she could provide for him. As his best friend.

ROAD TRIPPOSAL

HOMEROOM, AS USUAL, was more or less a shit show. Ms. Romero was checking her Facebook when Julia walked in with her tardy slip in hand. Dave was on his feet with a smile on his face, chatting with Jenny Owens and that guy that always smelled like cheese. Julia waved and kept her earbuds in, but Dave still sidestepped backpacks and chairs to come over and give her a wordless high five before returning to whatever conversation he was having.

Julia laid her head on her desk, trying to sleep but mostly watching Dave. She hadn't managed to fall asleep the night before. At first it'd been the adrenaline of executing the plan so well. But even after her eyelids felt swollen with tiredness, her mind was a flurry of thoughts. Nothing too obvious like being heartbroken. More like a bunch of little things, debris caught in a tree after a storm. What her mom was like in high school, whether she would have done something as cliché as love her best friend silently, whether she was finally going to come. Whether anyone would ever know about all the Nevers, or if in a few months her college friends would have no idea that this period of her life had ever existed. She wondered if there was some sort of expiration date to her friendship with Dave as she knew it, if it was possible that it had already passed.

The bell rang out and everyone gathered their belongings and took their conversations to the hallways, where girls were taking selfies and a couple of jock types were throwing granola bars at each other, picking them up only to reload and shoot again. When the game lost its fun, they left the crumbled remains on the ground like spent ammunition. Julia followed Dave and they wordlessly tossed the mess in the trash. Then they went to his locker, where he replaced one of the binders in his backpack with a different binder that was hidden under piles of loose-leaf paper.

"Hey, I've got a surprise for you."

"Thanks for softening the blow by announcing that a surprise will be coming."

"Why do I even talk to you in the mornings?"

"Because despite your new position as the center of attention, you still crave the intimacy of someone who really gets you, and only I fill that role?"

"Deep."

Julia laid her head against the row of lockers. "These should be lined with pillows."

Dave rummaged through his binder, flipping through plastic folders and dividers covered in pencil-scratched band names and lyrics. After what felt like a long time, he pulled out a sheet of paper, handing it to her.

"What's this?"

"Neko Case is playing tonight. I know San Francisco isn't exactly a life-changing trip, but we're gonna make it feel as epic as possible."

His words didn't really sink in right away, nor did her eyes focus on the page. It was a printout receipt for concert tickets in San Francisco. For eight o'clock that night. "It's a thank-you. For the promposal and how awesome you were."

"Dave. These are Neko Case tickets."

"We leave right after school. I had exactly enough money left over to buy the tickets, so you're paying for gas."

"These are Neko Case tickets for tonight."

"Did you have a stroke or something?" He laughed.

"What did you tell Gretchen?"

Dave furrowed his brow, a confused smile tugging at the corner of his mouth. "About tonight? That I'm taking my best friend on a Nevers road trip. What else would I say? She says you're a genius for planning yesterday."

"Oh." Julia was still holding the printout in her hand. "Well, this is pretty cool, then."

"Understatement foul. I know it's not cross-country or Holy Grail epic, but we'll make it as epic as possible. We'll blast music and pick up hitchhikers and have epiphanies. If they don't come naturally, we'll find a bunch of peyote and wander the desert. We might have to find a desert. Plus, check this out." He stowed the binder back into his bag and reached into his pocket.

"You have a driver's license?"

"Yeah, Gretchen took me over the weekend."

Julia grabbed the license out of his hand, just to get Gretchen's name out of the conversation. "You look like a murderer."

"Isn't that the point of picture IDs? That way if you become a murderer they can flash your picture on the news and everyone will be like, 'Yup, that guy totally kills people.'"

"How did you even get your eyes to do that?"

"I'd love to take all the credit, but that, dear friend, was good fortune smiling down upon me." She handed him back his license and he shut his locker. "As I am the official driver of our Nevers-breaking road trip, I'm bestowing upon you the role of Snack Master. I know you'll take your duties seriously."

"Prunes and warm milk, got it," Julia said, more out of a

habit to always keep the joke going than anything. They were at the hallway where they would split in different directions until lunch.

"I'm thinking we'll take the One the whole way there, and after the concert we'll have late-night Thai food somewhere in the city. Maybe even do a bit of stargazing on one of those little beaches on the way back? If the fog isn't too bad. We'll pull an all-nighter, make it back to school in the morning exhausted and hating life. It'll be great. You've always wanted to see Neko live."

"Yeah," Julia said. "I have."

"If you're nice, we can even play the boxers or briefs game."

"That sounds sketchy. What's the boxers or briefs game?"

"That's where the passenger holds up a paper to cars passing by that tells them to honk once if they're wearing briefs and twice if they're wearing boxers. If they don't honk, you assume they're free as a bird."

"Gross."

"It's important sociological research, Julia. It's supposed to be gross."

o o o

Julia and Dave stood in front of her car in the parking lot. Her once-white car was now everything but white. Markers in every color of the rainbow had been used to ask Gretchen out to prom, most of them not the washable kind. Julia had been more than okay with that, wanting to go all out. Now, in the light of the afternoon, knowing she'd be driving somewhere other than the SLO High parking lot, something inside her cringed.

"I think I was hoping this would disappear overnight," Julia said, arms crossed in front of her.

"No such luck. Now quit stalling and hand me the keys."

"You're serious about this? I thought that license you showed me was a fake. Are men even allowed to drive?"

"The times they are a-changin'." Dave stuck his hand out.

"This feels so weird." She placed the keys in his hand but refused to let go. "My whole world is falling apart. Up is down, black is white, the Cretaceous period came before the Jurassic era."

"That was so nerdy."

"David Goffrey Pickleback, you're really downplaying how big of a moment this is for me. I feel the very fabric of reality unwinding." Julia could feel the warmth of his palm beneath the keys, and it was strange what a specific desire she suddenly felt to have him wrap his fingers around hers.

"An entire list's worth of activities we would never have thought to do in a million years, sure, why not? But letting your best friend of over four years drive, and you start having a panic attack?"

"You say that like it's unreasonable!"

Dave laughed and snatched the keys fully away from her grip. "You goof. Get in the car. I promise things will be exactly as they've always been."

First, they went to a gas station and loaded up on snacks, lowered the top on the Miata and headed for the coast. They began the road trip like all road trips should begin, with music blaring, hearts pumping. Julia stuck her hand out the window and made those stupid waves in the air that people were always doing in car commercials, admitting out loud that it actually felt really great. She removed her hair tie so that her hair flurried in the wind, and she leaned in toward Dave so that the pink strands would sting his face, too. "You're going to kill us!" he cried out over the music as the wind rushed all around.

She immediately switched the song over to The Smiths'

"There Is a Light That Never Goes Out," singing along to the chorus directly in Dave's face.

To die by your side is such a heavenly way to die.

"Are we going to play clichéd music the whole way there?"

"You call The Smiths clichéd one more time and I'm going to put this song on repeat, then run us off the cliff so that people think we died in some teenage suicide death pact. Then everyone at school will be sad and they'll do a big teary gesture by making you win prom king, then you'll be that guy that gets memorialized by a candlelight vigil by people who didn't know him all that well. You'll get voted into the cliché hall of fame."

"I would throw up inside my grave."

"You have a very poor grasp on the science of death."

Dave laughed and grabbed her head again, pushing her gently away from him. She wouldn't have minded if his hand never left, if it somehow slipped down to her bare shoulder, to her fingers. It was an absolutely gorgeous drive up the shore and into Big Sur, where the slow and winding roads among redwoods and cliffs changed the mood in the car from blasting music to something mellower. They switched over to Neko Case to prepare for the concert. There was not a trace of fog, so the ocean shimmered brightly for much of the ride. Dave borrowed a pair of old sunglasses Julia kept in her car, and he looked cute in them, though Julia bit her tongue to keep from saying so.

They kept getting stuck behind RVs going thirty-five miles an hour, cars slowing down to pull into scenic overlooks to snap pictures. They weren't making great time, but if they subsisted off the junk food in the car and didn't stop for a meal or too many bathroom breaks, they'd even arrive in time for the opening act. Of course, they did stop and take a few pictures on some of the more beautiful curves, because what life-changing trip was complete without photographic evidence to rub in people's faces?

They drove past the Bixby Canyon Bridge and Monterey, the sun starting to dip lower toward the ocean. The haze by the horizon weakened its rays, and it turned into a perfect orange sphere, like some strange cookie being dunked in slow motion. In Half Moon Bay they stopped to watch it set all the way, Dave reasoning that the rest of the drive was less curvy and would go by quicker. Since the landscape got significantly less impressive in the dark, they could speed and still make it to San Francisco in time.

Dave parked at a roadside convenience store and they walked down to the seaside, taking a seat at a bench that was remarkably like Dave's bench at Morro Bay.

"Can we play the *Before Midnight* game?" Julia asked.

"Wow, usually you don't ask, you just tell me we're doing it."

Julia sighed. "See? Letting you drive was a mistake. I don't even know who I am anymore."

"Still there." Dave held his hand out in front of him, his fingers parallel to the horizon, a trick they'd learned to know when the sun would be setting. Each finger equaled about fifteen minutes.

The sun was the color of a perfect orange, and the ocean below it had turned to something resembling steel, shimmering a line to where they were sitting, a yellow brick road cutting straight across the water.

"Still there," Julia said after a moment. The game was a little silly and completely unoriginal, but it never failed to make Julia feel somewhat cathartic, regardless of whether or not she'd had anything resembling a catharsis. "Are we gonna make it there on time?"

"We should be fine. I'll take the 101 and it'll be a bit faster." The sky around the sun was hazy and soaking up the color, so that it looked like someone had poked a hole in the sun and it was slowly bleeding out. "Still there."

A thin cloud turned bright red and both of them *ooh*ed at it at the same time. "Definitely still there."

Out of the corner of her eye, she could see Dave look away from the sun, swiveling his head to take in the whole scene. He was the only person she knew who actively reminded himself to look around, to enjoy everything about a given moment. They'd never actually spoken about it, but she'd been watching it happen for years. "This is pretty great," Dave said. "On a school night. Two hundred miles from home. Going to see Neko in San Francisco."

Julia turned to look at him. The sun was golden on his skin, a bead of sweat was hiding at the very edge of his hairline. "Still there." She smiled.

"Still there," Dave repeated.

When the last orange-red sliver of the sun completely dipped beneath the ocean, they both said, "Gone."

This time, Julia could feel a very specific epiphany, bittersweet though it may have been: She and Dave could still be friends. Nothing had changed.

THAT TEENAGE FEELING

FROM THE FIRST note Neko Case sang, chills ran down Julia's arms. It was a tiny venue, with a bar in the back that never fully quieted down, even during the quiet songs. It was hot, too, Julia's shirt sticking to her back almost from the start. The crowd was sparse enough that Julia wasn't pressed up against a bunch of sweaty strangers, but she and Dave were up near the stage, where people kept jockeying for position, and every now and then the crowd would move in waves and Dave would put a hand on her shoulders to steady her. As much as she loved Neko's lyrics, Julia's mind wandered during the concert, especially when Dave's arm brushed against hers, when he leaned into her ear to comment about how her voice sounded even bigger live.

When she recognized the opening of "That Teenage Feeling," Julia felt everything but her, Neko, and Dave melt away. She'd looked up the lyrics before and thought them somewhat twee, but what a colossal difference there was between a line on paper and a line sung with the entirety of someone's heart to a rapt audience. What a strange, wonderful feeling it was to know that Julia was right in the midst of what Neko Case was singing about. She cast a glance at Dave, who was smiling slightly, trying to sing along to lyrics he clearly didn't know.

The concert was over at nearly midnight, and though they'd assumed there'd be tons of Thai places open late at night, it turned out that San Francisco was not New York and very much enjoyed its sleep. Julia searched for nearby restaurants on her phone as Dave called Gretchen to say good night and that he would see her at school in the morning. She heard the sweet tone in his voice, and she decided that she was thrilled by it. Her best friend was an overwhelmingly good person, and if she wasn't receiving his romantic affection, at least someone was.

When he hung up, they started walking back toward where they'd parked the car. "No luck on Thai food," she said. "How's Gretchen?"

"Half-asleep. She says hi." Dave twirled the car keys around his finger. They passed by a group of teens in ragged clothing hanging out in front of a coffee shop. One of them had faded green hair poking out from beneath his beanie, a metal chain swinging from his belt loop to his back pocket. He was holding a cardboard sign that read, WHY LIE, I NEED BEER? The smell of weed and body odor lingered around them. "So, more junk food for the drive back?"

"I've got another idea," Julia said.

o o o

They finally found a suitable spot a bit south of Carmel. It was a perfect isolated stretch of sandy beach hidden from the road by a little hill. Passing cops wouldn't be able to see the illegal fire they were going to build. They'd bought a Quick Start chemically coated log, a bundle of firewood, skewers, a package of gourmet sausages stuffed with mozzarella and sundried tomatoes, a can of pineapple, ingredients for s'mores, and a flimsy beach towel. Julia wished they had a bottle of wine to share, but since neither of them had a fake ID, a jug of their favorite iced tea would do.

Julia, the much more seasoned camper between the two of them, dug a little hole and assembled the logs into a tepee, running back to the car for some paper to help the starter log catch fire quickly. Dave set their purchases around the towel to keep it from flapping around and collecting sand in the breeze.

Within a few minutes Julia had the fire going and they'd impaled sausages and pineapple squares on the skewers, digging them into the sand around the fire so that they would roast hands-free. They sat with their legs crossed, the ocean's constant roar like a song of approval, their faces lit up in tiny orange flickers of flames reflecting in their eyes.

"Well, this was a fantastic idea," Dave said, twisting the cap off the jug of iced tea and raising it to his lips.

"Wait!" Julia lowered the bottle before he could take a drink. "We need a toast first."

Dave gestured out to the scene in front of them. "This on a Tuesday night? Do we really need a toast?"

Julia grabbed the jug out of his hands. "That's too long. Toasts have to be short and wise. Like Hemingway." She thought for a second, then raised it up. "To the fire in our hearts," she said, a line she remembered from one of her mom's postcards. Then she took a long pull, wincing as if it were whiskey. She handed Dave the bottle, conscious of how their fingers brushed against each other. Her ears were ringing from the concert, and the slight chill in the air was completely canceled out by the warmth of the blaze. Dave set the bottle in the sand in front of them, smacking his lips from the sweetness. A car drove past them on the highway behind, just a whirr of tires on pavement. Not even the headlights reached them. They let the sound of the ocean rule for a while, and exchanged swigs from the bottle while giving the skewered sausages quarter turns so that they'd cook the whole way through. Every time one of them raised the bottle, the other would come up with a new toast that would fit Julia's criteria of being Hemingway-esque.

Dave: "To another numbered night."

Julia: "To small differences."

Dave: "To being really thankful this isn't alcohol because I'd be plastered by now."

Julia: "To my friend's low alcohol tolerance. May his life be blessed with cheap bar tabs and designated drivers."

Within the hour, they were giggly from the sugar high. Skewers lay strewn about the beach, sand sticking to the pineapple juice that had run down their sides, little bits of sausage indistinguishable from the shadows cast by the fire. They were recovering from a laughing bout, though she couldn't quite recall what had set it off. She reached for another log from their dwindling stack and placed it diagonally into the fire. Julia leaned back, feeling herself start to sweat.

"I think this is officially a night of good ideas," Dave said, suddenly standing up. He was taking his shoes off, holding his arms out for balance. "We're already crossing off one Never tonight, right? Why not take it further?" He grabbed the bottom of his shirt with one hand and pulled it swiftly over his head.

"What are you doing?"

"Number six: *Never go skinny-dipping.*"

"Seriously?"

He shrugged. "No one can see us. No chance of it going viral, unless one of us is the culprit." He looked over at the ocean and unbuttoned his jeans. "I don't know about you, but nothing sounds better to me right now than getting in that ocean." A big grin spread across his face and he turned away from Julia, stepping out of his jeans and boxers as he ran out into the incoming tide, his ass pale, sticking out in the night.

Julia could barely breathe from the laughter, and with very

little hesitation she slipped out of her shorts, leaving a trail of T-shirt, bra, and panties as she joined Dave in the Pacific. "This is so fucking cold!"

"The fire in our hearts will keep us warm," Dave said, though his teeth were already chattering.

"The shivering brought on by hypothermia might do a better job." They kept close to the shore, crouching on their knees so that the water would wash over them completely. Julia dunked her head under the water, feeling her lungs shout for air and warmth.

"Julia! Look."

She wiped the salt water from her eyes and oriented herself until she spotted Dave pointing out toward the horizon. She followed his gaze and saw the moon, a duller replica of the orange ball the sun had been when it dipped below the surface a few hours ago. It wasn't completely full, but it was bigger than she'd ever seen it, and, like the sun they'd watched just a few hours earlier, the moon was the exact shade of the oranges people sold on the side of the road. "Wow," was all she could manage.

They floated side by side for a while, watching the spectacle before them, the sound of their chattering teeth and the waves crashing behind them filling Julia simultaneously with adrenaline and a sense of peace.

A few seconds later, overtaken by the cold, they ran back to shore, headed straight for the fire. Julia covered herself up more for the warmth of her arms than propriety. She sat on the towel, leaning in close to the fire, though now that she was next to it, it didn't seem all that necessary; adrenaline was doing plenty. She left a space for Dave, but he grabbed what remained of the towel and draped it over her. He sat right next to her, their sides touching, his jeans on and soaking up the Pacific off his legs. They breathed heavily, staring at the fire instead of the moon rising, which was getting more ordinary as it climbed up the night sky, their smiles refusing to die down. Julia knew that there were moments in your life that meant something but passed by unnoticed, and she knew that this was not one of them.

Another car passed by behind them, this one heading north. Julia could barely hear it over the sound of the ocean and the crackle of the fire, not to mention her fluttering chest. Dave held her gaze, and Julia felt everything that she'd pushed down on the drive start to bubble back up. She thought about doing it again, about swallowing the love and hanging on to just this. Loving him just like this, or from farther away.

Then Dave, head still cocked to the side like a confused puppy, reached over and brushed a wet strand of hair away from her forehead, tucking it behind her ear and giving her a smile. Without meaning to, Julia grabbed his hand before he pulled it away, interlacing her fingers with his. Warmed by the fire and the towel, Julia no longer felt cold. But a shiver ran through her when she understood that she would not be able to keep the words inside her anymore.

"Dave," she said, feeling a sort of release in knowing that it was coming and there was nothing she could do to stop it. He looked down at their hands together but didn't make a move to let go. She waited until those kind eyes of his met hers, and then as if it was the easiest thing in the world, she told him she loved him.

PART 3
DAVE & JULIA

BECAUSE I'M DUMB

LIKE SO MANY times before, Dave knew what Julia was about to say before she said it. He could see it in her beautiful blue eyes, eyes he'd dreamed about for the past five years, even when awake. He'd imagined that look in them enough times to recognize it exactly for what it was before Julia confirmed it with her words.

His heart was already pounding from the swim in the ocean, the ridiculous and beautiful timing of the moon rising as they bathed in the frigid waters. He'd tried not to stare, but the sight of her running back to the shore had been funny and yet also a dream come true, the way she looked in the darkness, pale and shapely, the curves and folds of her flesh reflecting moonlight.

Now she was loosely draped in the towel they'd bought at the grocery store in Carmel. Water dripped down her face, down her collarbone, which disappeared into the darkness beneath the towel. The fire brought out her eyes, the tint in her lips, her cheeks flushed from the cold. He could think of nothing else but how beautiful she looked just then, how long he'd been dreaming of exactly this moment. Although this was better than dreaming. Then her words were out. "I love you," she said, the way he'd been keeping himself from saying. Dave immediately leaned into Julia, getting closer to the person he'd always been closest to.

It felt so right to kiss her.

After so long of dreaming about it, it should have been a disappointment. His expectations, never reined in, had climbed so high that reality should not have been able to live up to the moment. The mind got carried away and life's job was to show it how things really were. Dave knew that's how these things often went for romantics. People longed for something for years, and when they got it, they couldn't help but feel cheated.

This wasn't like that at all. Kissing Julia was exactly as great as kissing Julia should have been. Their mouths fit each other. He couldn't think of it any other way. It wasn't all that long of a kiss, and the world didn't go into slow motion or anything like that. He felt her lips, the sweet tea on her breath, a quick flick of their tongues meeting. They pulled away rather quickly, though their hands remained on each other, their sides pressed together, the cheap towel slipping down from around Julia's shoulder just an inch.

"You have no idea how long I've wanted to do that," Dave said, unable to keep himself from whispering.

"Really?"

"Years," Dave said, nodding, leaning in for a repeat.

The second kiss was longer, hungrier. Julia turned herself over and sat on his lap, wrapping them both up inside the towel. "Why didn't you say anything?"

"Because I'm dumb." He kissed her again, one hand on the side of her face, the other holding the towel up around them. The fire had dwindled down, and he grabbed one of the last remaining logs and tossed it at Julia's impromptu pit, not wanting the whole thing to turn to ash. It had already been one of those nights that felt significant even before the kissing—the drive, the concert, this perfectly isolated beach—and he didn't want it to end. He wished they'd bought more firewood. "I can't believe we could have been doing this the whole time."

Julia laughed through her kisses, as if she didn't want to pull away from his lips for even a second. "I guess we have to make up for lost time."

She laid herself heavy against him until he was lying down on the sand, the weight of her a wonder. It was strange that of all the things he could be marveling at, Julia's hair falling across his face, her lips on his, the sheer nakedness of her as the towel slipped away, it was weight that he was focusing on. She raised herself slightly to kiss his neck and he instantly pulled her closer, wanting the weight of her to remain.

"Easy, Dave. I'm not going anywhere."

"I know," he said. "You just feel great."

"I hate to be crass, but I bet I can make you feel better."

"You do not hate to be crass," Dave said, laughing a little and brushing the hair away from her face—uselessly, since it only fell back down.

"True. I'd much rather be crass than touchy about this."

"About what?"

"Boning my best friend on a beach," she said, grabbing his hands and holding them down, smirking even as she moved to kiss him again, to more than kiss him.

When the moon had turned into something a little less spectacular, a little more itself, Julia and Dave were lying together on the towel, the last of the logs dropped into the fire along with the skewers, the charred remains of marshmallows that hadn't made it into s'mores. Sand was absolutely everywhere.

"This is such a cliché," Dave said, offering dozens of little pecks all over her face, beneath her ears, those three freckles on her neck, which he could have devoted his attention to for the rest of the night.

"What is?" Julia's eyes were closed, her arms on his bare back.

"Sex on a beach." He kissed his way across her throat, down to her collarbone. "The fire, the moon. Virginities lost amidst romance. We are so cheesy."

She pulled him up and kissed him firmly, wrapping her legs around his, pulling him as close as they could get. "No complaints here."

Sand continued to get everywhere, and every now and then a car would pass by unseen on the highway, sometimes with music blasting from open windows. Mostly it was the sound of the ocean and their kisses that filled the night, the occasional murmured *I love you*, or a joke that would make them both break out into laughter, burrowing their faces into the nooks in each other's necks until the laughter subsided and was once again replaced by kissing.

This, Dave thought to himself as Julia's hands ran down his back, as he kissed her over and over again, this was perfect.

PERFECT

THIS, JULIA THOUGHT to herself as Dave ran his hands down her sides, as she kissed him over and over again, this was perfect.

SUNRISE

DAVE WOKE UP—like he'd imagined so many times—with Julia in his arms. The sun had just barely risen behind them. Fog tinted the sky a light yellow and made the water look gray. Julia's head was resting on his chest, her arm draped around him, their bodies keeping each other warm in the briskness of dawn. A few strands of her hair moved in the ocean breeze, clearing away to show her peacefully sleeping face. It was still perfect, except Gretchen was on his mind.

She'd never seen the sunrise. Well, maybe in passing, on the way to school or the airport to catch an early flight. But she'd never woken up specifically to see it, never taken the time to watch the sky lighten from complete darkness to unquestioned day. She'd told him that on their date at the harbor, and Dave had promised to take her someday. He'd already picked out the spot where they would go—Brett knew a way to get to the roof of the school, which gave an unobstructed view clear to the mountains in the east—but he'd been putting together a playlist for them to listen to and it wasn't yet long enough.

Dave looked around their impromptu campsite. Their clothes were strewn about, one of Dave's shoes dangerously close to where the fire had been. A forgotten marshmallow lay in the sand, half-buried next to the jug of iced tea, which had tipped over on its side. The sound of cars on the freeway was not yet constant, but Dave knew it would be soon.

Gretchen would be waking up right about now. He'd watched her wake up before, though they hadn't gone as far as he and Julia had. She'd probably be on her side, curled into a ball, her hands reaching out to her cell phone as soon as she opened her eyes. He could picture the glow of the screen reflected on her face, in the big brown eyes that he'd been looking into so often the last couple of weeks, on those cheekbones. A sick feeling took root in his stomach.

He looked down at Julia, who kept sleeping peacefully, her breath steady as a metronome. He couldn't completely see her mouth, but he imagined that she'd fallen asleep with a smile on her face and that it was still there. Unlike him, she would wake up with no one on her mind but Dave himself.

Dave remembered their countless movie nights, how he'd long for the loll of her head, which meant the movie was losing her and she'd soon rest her cheek against his shoulder. Once, they'd both drifted off, and Dave had woken up in the middle of the night to the movie playing over again, Julia's arm looped through his. He'd kept his eyes closed and pretended to still be sleeping, the joy so simple that he didn't dare disturb it. At one point, Julia had stirred, then nestled back into him, as if the same thing was on her mind. Strange now to think that it might have been, that everything he'd wanted had been well within reach.

He undoubtedly loved her. It had been an incredible night, extraordinary despite the clichés that were peppered in the details. It was a dream come true, literally and metaphorically, except that dream was now tangled up with the dream of Gretchen.

Dave shifted a little, bringing his hand to Julia's temple and rubbing it in slight circles to gently wake her up. He wished he could just focus on this, let her sleep. He wanted to be overjoyed, rather than happy and wrecked by guilt.

Gretchen was going to be hurt, and angry. She might never talk to him again. The thought brought a panic in Dave's chest that made him want to get up that instant, shake Julia awake, as if leaving could undo it all. But he'd been hoping for exactly this to happen for so long that it was impossible to walk away from it. "Julia," he said softly, not knowing what else there was to say.

She stirred, but only pressed herself closer against him, planting a kiss on his chest before resuming her rhythmic breathing. A seagull suddenly appeared near them, stepping cautiously toward him. It peered at Dave suspiciously, its eyes little black marbles that saw him only as a threat. Dave nodded, as if to confirm that he dealt out harm all the time. The sun climbed higher through the fog. The seagull made away with the marshmallow. Emptied out by guilt, the shame rising from his stomach and exuding through his pores, Dave let Julia sleep a little longer, delaying what was to come for as long as he could.

RIDICULOUS

THE ONLY WORD Julia could use to describe herself when she woke up was ridiculous. It was ridiculous to wake up feeling so happy. She was like the cartoon of someone in love. Any second now animated bluebirds were going to land on her shoulder and start harmonizing. She felt like a Jack White guitar riff.

She kissed Dave again as soon as she woke up, laughed at how much sand there was everywhere. Sitting up, she looked around at the detritus of their little picnic: the half-empty jug of tea on its side as if it had passed out, the pile of ash in the fire pit, their clothes surrounding the towel like a blast radius. There were bird tracks in the sand, and Julia, amused, pictured those animated bluebirds singing around the two of them as they slept. The sun was already burning the fog away, and by the time they would get back to San Luis Obispo, it would probably be a perfectly clear day, the sky a deep shade of blue. Ridiculous.

Dave was quiet as they picked up the mess they had made and got dressed. Julia figured he was worried about getting caught by the cops, worried about getting to school on time, which there was no way they were going to do. It was his nature, and she tried taking his mind off those small worries by joking around. "By the way, there's a video of you running naked into the ocean all over the Internet now."

"Liar," Dave said, kicking sand into the fire pit, bending over to grab the cap for the jug of tea.

"I was very sneaky about it. Don't get me wrong, I felt awful doing it and e-mailing it to the entire school but it is explicitly mentioned in the Nevers, so I figured recording the event was kind of a must. I probably shouldn't have added your grandparents to the e-mail, though."

Dave chuckled, then picked up the towel and whipped the sand off it a few times before draping it over his arm. "Ready to go?"

"You mean we have to go back? I thought we might stay here for a few more days. Live off the land. Grow beards." Dave was not laughing nearly as much as he should have been. This was golden material. "We could have really beardy sex. That'd be hot. Actually, can you even grow a beard? You can be honest. I'll still be attracted to you. I would just prefer to know if I'll be the more bearded one in our relationship. For logistics."

Dave didn't respond, and there was a brief flutter in her stomach, like something was wrong, though what could possibly be wrong? She went up to him and wrapped her arms around his waist, pressing herself to his back. "You know the joking around isn't all I'm feeling, right?"

His arms went over hers and he gave her hand a squeeze. "I know."

"Good." She kissed him through his shirt, sincerely hoping they might not leave at all. "You wanna, like, talk about it? Us...you know...sleeping together. And how we're feeling about that?" She burrowed her nose into his back, thrilled and a little weirded out by what she'd just said.

Dave chuckled, then turned around to face Julia, wrapping her up in a hug. The ocean breeze blew by, the morning sun weak against it, sending chills down Julia's spine. Held tightly in Dave's arms, sensing the tenderness in his embrace, she'd bet that he was feeling the same, reluctant to leave. After a few moments, Dave loosened and pulled back, kissing Julia quickly on the lips.

Julia followed behind Dave, a little slow because she'd woken up about six minutes ago and the sand felt nothing short of magical between her toes. The whole world should have been filled with sand. Dave was already up by the highway shoulder, walking a little too quickly. Julia glanced back at the spot, because the day could survive another cliché. She took note of the surroundings, the trees on the other side of the road, the wooden fence that must have belonged to some unseen property. Oh, how trite it was to be a girl memorizing the details of her first time.

She turned back and saw Dave was already in the car, which they'd parked behind some boulders to avoid being spotted. He was in the driver's seat with the engine started, squinting though the sun wasn't completely on his face. They were a bit more than a couple of hours outside of San Luis Obispo, and Julia was going to relish every mile of the drive back home.

She put her feet up on the dashboard, undid her hair tie, and let the wind whip away the sand as they pulled onto the freeway. She grabbed her sunglasses from the center console but didn't put them on, not wanting to lessen the brightness of the day. "I wish we'd brought some breakfast snacks," Julia said, plugging her phone into the car for music. "You wanna stop at a diner somewhere?"

Dave leaned his elbow on the car door, looking worried. "We should probably get back soonish."

"So cute, still worried about school." Julia reached over and poked him in the stomach. "All right, no diner. But we need some road-trip food. I want Flamin' Hot Cheetos for breakfast."

"Gross."

"David Babycakes Howard, you start bad mouthing hot Cheetos and I'm gonna take away your Mexican passport."

Dave smiled at that, but he was squinting like the sun was in his eyes, worried. He reached over to turn the music up a bit, which was weird because a dance song was playing and Dave didn't like dance music. Julia sat back and sang along, shoulder-shimmying in her seat, her hand out the window. It was cold enough outside to get goose bumps from the wind, but Julia was too happy to care.

They pulled into a gas station. "What are you having for breakfast?" Julia said, climbing out of the car. Dave didn't make a move to get out. "Want me to grab you anything? Skittles? Red Bull? Hot Cheetos?"

"A barf bag," Dave said with a groan.

When Julia came back out from the store with a bag full of junk food, Dave was resting his head back with his eyes closed. She stood and stared for a second, thankful she couldn't see the look on her own face, how wide she was grinning. Dave, on the other hand, was not grinning very much. Quite the contrary, actually. He looked stressed. She was about to make a joke about postcoital vulnerability, when she was struck by a realization that she was surprised hadn't come sooner. Gretchen was on his mind. His heart was too big not to think about her.

"You want me to drive?"

Dave opened one eye. "You're never getting these keys back. I'm the driver now."

"That was your plan all along, wasn't it? Sneaky." She reached into the bag and tossed the Cheetos at Dave, then slid back into the passenger seat. Before he could turn the car back on, Julia reached for his hand, lacing their fingers together. "This is kind of cool, isn't it?" She smiled, holding their hands up together, then bringing them up to her mouth and planting a long kiss on the knuckle of his middle finger.

Dave nodded, then did the same thing to her hand, though his kiss was short. Then he peeled away his fingers and turned on the ignition. Was it more than guilt causing him to be quiet? Was it doubt?

For two hours, Julia switched songs. She stared out at the ocean, which was as beautiful as she'd ever seen it. She laid her hand on Dave's thigh, and when she saw his face turn tense she pulled the hand away, switched songs, made a joke. She tried not to think of Dave with Gretchen, but it wasn't as if she was imagining things. He *had* been with her. Just yesterday, he'd kissed her, ran his hands through her blond hair.

"Would you rather..." Julia started without knowing how she was going to finish, just wanting the silence to go away, "have to sit through eight years' worth of Marroney classes or get lobotomized without anesthetic?"

"That's dumb, of course I'd choose Marroney's classes."

"Err! Trick question. They're the same thing."

Dave laughed. "You are so in love with that guy."

"No, you goof." Julia sat up, reaching out for his hand again, looking out at Highway 1 curve away from the ocean as they approached San Luis Obispo. "I'm in love with you."

"I didn't say the two were mutually exclusive." He chuckled, squeezing her fingers. Now it was Julia who reached to turn up the music. She wished they would have just stayed behind on that beach in Carmel. They should have kept their trip going, at least for the day. Julia watched the familiar surroundings of San Luis Obispo pass by her window. The chain restaurants in those strip malls, Laundromats and nail salons that wouldn't have survived without a restaurant to draw traffic in. The farmland stretching from the edges of the city to the distant hills. The high school, which would be releasing into lunch any moment now, the seniors scurrying away in their cars to get slices at Fratelli's down the street.

"You're just gonna go ahead and drive past school, right?" Julia said. "It's almost noon."

"Yeah," Dave said, trailing off. She could hear Gretchen on his voice.

"Can I come over to your place? Watch a movie? The last few movie dates we had I've been dying to cuddle with you."

"Julia Battlefield Gunteski, I had no idea you were so sentimental."

"Shut the fuck up. Cuddling is not about sentimentality. It's about the immense pleasure of skin on skin, especially when that skin contains someone you feel more or less strongly about."

Dave was quiet as they arrived at a stoplight. He gripped the steering wheel, rubbed the back of his neck. She tried hard not to remember what the a cappella group had looked like as they got ready to sing on the far corner.

"Seriously? This is the first red light we get in town?"

Dave broke out in a smile. "I don't know about a movie. But I am definitely not going to school right now."

They pulled into Dave's driveway, which was empty, Brett and his dad off at work. As soon as the car was stopped, Julia unbuckled her seat belt, leaned across the console, put her hand on the back of his neck and pulled him in for a kiss.

His lips were not stiff or unwelcoming. There was no sign of his mind being on Gretchen. Far from it, actually. They fit as wonderfully as they had last night, and for one blissful moment she knew that there were many of these on the way.

Then Dave put a gentle stop to it with that signature smack of lips ending a kiss. His hand was on the side of her face, his eyes set on hers. She smiled at him and was about to move back in when his eyes flitted to something in the rearview mirror.

"Shit," Dave said, like the wind had just been knocked out of him. Julia looked behind and saw Gretchen's van behind them. The door was half-open, Gretchen's face already in tears. She was wearing her hair in this side-ponytail thing that should have looked ridiculous but somehow worked.

The sound of the van door slamming shut rang out in the stillness of the afternoon. Dave quickly pulled away from Julia, one hand already on the door handle. "I'm sorry," he said, although Julia wasn't sure who that was meant for. She remained frozen in the car as Dave tried to chase after Gretchen, who'd already started her car.

Julia watched it all through the tiny slit of a back windshield in her Miata. Gretchen crying, Dave looking miserable, trying to explain himself. It was only a few moments until Gretchen peeled away, but for Julia it had felt like a very long time, like some uncomfortably extensive scene from a soap opera, all close-ups and faces stretched into exaggerated misery. When Gretchen was gone, Dave lingered for a long moment at the edge of his driveway, hands dropped at his sides, his face hidden from view. It felt like a moment in limbo, like the slightest breeze would either send Dave chasing after Gretchen or pull him back to Julia. Julia held her breath, as if that was all it would take to sway him.

"Please," she found herself whispering. "Please."

A car drove past, the driver switching radio stations, casting furtive glances at the road ahead, oblivious of what Julia was about to lose or gain. "Please," she said again. It took Dave a while, a hesitation she would allow him as long as he got back in the car. His arms were at his sides, his head hanging low. It felt like his decision would be based on something slight, the flapping of butterfly wings somewhere far off sending Dave away from her. When he turned around and slowly slid back in, Julia felt herself ease.

Dave smacked his head back and hit the car seat, his eyes closed, his face entirely stress again. "Fuck."

Julia froze, not knowing what to say or do, until she remembered that this was still Dave. She was still herself. Gretchen might be heartbroken right now, and Julia wouldn't wish that on anyone. But she'd just kissed Dave, not for the first time, and definitely not for the last. After all, he was here. He'd chosen Julia.

"You know," Julia said. "My instinct right now is to be a supportive girlfriend. But I have no idea what that would entail, in this specific situation. So I'm gonna be a supportive best friend and say this: You wanna go get mac 'n' cheese?"

She didn't get as much of a reaction as she'd hoped, just Dave's little snort/laugh thing. Not overwhelmingly reassuring. Then Dave opened his eyes and smiled at her. "You know how wonderfully bizarre it is to hear you call yourself my girlfriend?"

"I think I do," she said, and leaned back into him.

LAZY

BEFORE, WHEN DAVE had dreamed about love, this is what it looked like:

It was lazy. Love was lazy as hell. Love laid around in bed, warm from the sheets and the sunlight pouring into the room. Love was too lazy to get up to close the blinds. Love was too comfortable to get up and go pee. Love took too many naps, it watched TV, but not really, because it was too busy kissing and napping. Love was also funny, which somehow made the bed more comfortable, the laughter warming the sheets, softening the mattress and the lovers' skin.

Dave was staring at Julia's face. He was lying beside her, his head a few inches above the warmth of her skin, the pink hair that he loved finding all over his room. Dave tilted his head to the side, his eyes open wide.

"You are such a weirdo."

Dave blinked, bobbed his neck.

"What are you even doing?" Julia laughed, flinching. Then he sprung on her, attacking her face with kisses, dozens of quick pecks that left her breathless from the laughter. She put her hands on his face and moved him toward her mouth.

This was exactly like everything he'd dreamed about. True, it had felt close to this with Gretchen, too. True, he still found long blond hairs on his carpet, on his clothes. Sometimes, he caught himself about to compliment Julia in the same way he'd complimented Gretchen before. But he imagined that love often looked similar, regardless of who was involved. He tried to think of a compliment he'd never said and when nothing came, he buried his face into her neck. They hadn't done a thing for hours. The TV was on, but God knew what it was playing. Homework had not left their backpacks in days.

Dave fell back onto his pillow. "I need to pee."

"If you get up, you have to pee for me."

"Why haven't scientists figured that one out yet? You should be able to transfer the need to pee."

Dave pulled back to fluff his pillow. He found the remote and turned to the TV to put on a movie. They hadn't even made it through a movie as a couple yet. Before the closing credits could roll, they'd both be asleep, or giggling, or...well. He got distracted halfway through scrolling to look down at Julia. Brushing her pink hair behind her ear, he wondered why it often looked like she was tearing up. The first few times he'd asked if everything was okay, she'd looked at him like he was crazy. So he'd stopped asking. Every time he saw that glint, though, he wondered what was on her mind. Maybe nothing was, and it was just him imagining things.

He placed his hand on her shoulder as he turned his attention back to the TV. It was hard to have her nearby and not touch her. At school, their legs were constantly shifting under their desks, always leaning against each other.

"What's that one?" Julia had turned to look at the TV.

"That's, uh," Dave said, stammering, not wanting to bring up the fact that the movie she was talking about was the one he'd watched with Gretchen, "I watched that already. Not great."

"But is it not great in a great way?"

"Not really."

"Ah. Lame."

Dave kept scrolling through the options, and Julia scooched closer, resting her head on his chest. Downstairs, he could hear Brett and his dad watching sports on TV, nothing said between them. He finally chose some political drama series that he'd heard good things about. It didn't take long for Julia to fall asleep, and the feel of her breathing made him want to join her. Then his phone buzzed on the nightstand, and despite the comfort and the warmth, his arm jolted for it.

Gretchen's name was on his screen. It wasn't a text message, but an e-mail. The subject line was empty, only a few words from the body of the text appearing in the preview. Did you know...was all he could see. He stared at his phone for a second, then looked down at Julia. She was in a tank top and the shorts she'd borrowed from him every time she'd come over that week. The three freckles on her neck were right in his line of vision. He'd kissed every one of them over and over again.

Dave slid his thumb across the screen. He owed her that much. Even if the bliss of having Julia often distracted him from the fact, Dave felt awful about what he'd done to Gretchen. If she'd written an angry e-mail telling him what an awful person he was, then he deserved the discomfort of reading it. As the e-mail loaded, he planted a kiss on the top of Julia's head.

... that I almost told you that I love you? I know that's insane. But I've always been quick to love, and I'm actually surprised I held it in this long. I shouldn't even be writing this e-mail. If my friends knew I was writing it, they'd yell at me, and I'll probably yell at myself tomorrow. Unless I don't get any sleep, as has been the case, and my mental state is even worse than it is at this moment.

You hurt me, Dave. You're smart enough to know that. Part of me wants to rub it in your face, how much you hurt me. But the other part of me loves you enough to want to say this: It is not totally, completely, unequivocally your fault. Your heart is an asshole for choosing someone else. But I know that's not a choice that's yours to make.

Most days, most moments, I'm angry at you. But right now? This second? I hope you are happy. Even if it's with her. I really do.

Someone in the TV show was yelling. A sliver of sunlight broke through the blinds and landed across Julia, right where her tank top had bunched up to expose the skin of her lower back. Dave tried to stop rereading the e-mail but couldn't help himself. He'd take a look around the room, try to follow what was going on in the show, watch Julia. Then his thumb would slide across the screen of his phone again and he'd re-read Gretchen's words.

He fell asleep cuddled close to Julia, and when he woke up the room was no longer as warm, the day slept away. Julia was putting her shoes on, back in her school clothes. "The dads want me home for dinner," she said. "Sorry I'm boring and fell asleep for so long."

"Me too. I mean, I'm sorry I'm boring and fell asleep, too. Not that you're boring. I don't think sleeping with you is boring."

Julia kneeled by the side of the bed, running her hand over Dave's head. "I'm gonna let you keep rambling on until your foot is completely in your mouth."

"I'm done now."

"Tease." She leaned over and kissed him. "I like this. Spending time with you this way."

"Me too," Dave said, and he reached for her hand, rubbing his thumb over her knuckles, thinking about Gretchen's e-mail, knowing he'd reread it again as soon as Julia was gone.

o o o

Later that night, Dave was wide awake, having napped too long to be tired. A text came in from Julia, who was in the same predicament.

I bet if we were still in the same bed we could fall asleep, she wrote. After a certain act or two.

You mean eating sandwiches, right?

Yup.

Dave played the next episode in the political drama, which he'd gotten hooked on after Julia left, despite not actually following most of what was going on. Which would you say is the sexiest sandwich?

Grilled cheese, probably.

Pfft, Dave wrote. Grilled cheese is a sandwich you settle down with, a sandwich that you would want raising your kids. I'm talking the kind of sandwich you want to stay up all night eating. The kind of sandwich you wouldn't introduce to your dads but would tell all your friends about.

The three dots that meant Julia was typing stayed on for a while. He'd chosen her. That's what he kept thinking. That he'd *chosen* her.

That was kind of hot.

What? The sandwich?

You, you goof.

Dave typed out a few responses, but none of them felt right. He put the phone down and turned his attention back to the TV, waiting for something else to come to mind. Almost fifteen minutes later, his phone buzzed again.

doing anything?

For some reason, the lack of capitalization, the fact that she'd sent only two words, it made him wonder if she was upset, if he'd said something wrong. It was ridiculous to think so, and Dave shook his head at the thought that he'd become the kind of person who overanalyzed the grammar in a text message for subtext. But ever since the beach, he'd been having trouble reading her, as if being physically close to her had muddled up how well he knew her. In bed with her, he'd found himself struggling to come up with things to say, settling instead on making her laugh some other way. Not really. TV. Thinking about sandwiches in ways I've never thought before.

Another five minutes passed before he added, You?

Trying to think of a way to convince you to be in an open relationship so I can keep seeing Marroney on the side.

Jerk.

Monogamist, she responded, attaching a picture of herself sticking out her tongue. The lights were on in her room, her hair down, wearing a different tank top than before. Once, receiving a picture like this would be bittersweet, the joy of her face, the sadness of being without it.

Dave turned over onto his stomach. There was a crick in his shoulder from sleeping in awkward positions just to hold Julia close. He put his cell phone on the second pillow and closed his eyes, trying to force himself into tiredness. Then he caught a whiff of honey on his pillowcase. It made sense. He hadn't changed his sheets in a couple of weeks. He wondered if Julia had smelled it, if she'd known that's what Gretchen smelled like. If that's why Dave had thought he'd seen a flash of sadness pass through her eyes.

Before he fell asleep, Dave wondered why it wasn't just Julia in his head. Why he couldn't think of what to respond to her. Why that one line from Gretchen's e-mail was imbued in his thoughts. Your heart is an asshole for choosing someone else.

ENERGY

JULIA AND DAVE sat in the gym, watching kids play basketball. The tree house had silently been given up, no longer their lunch spot. No one had really said anything to keep them away, but Julia couldn't stand the way Gretchen's friends looked at her, as if Julia herself had set out to break Gretchen's heart.

"Any news from your mom? End of the year's getting close." Dave dipped a celery stick in hummus, the crunch loud despite the sound of sneakers squeaking on the hardwood.

"Not yet. I think she's waiting on ticket prices to go down," Julia said, though her mom had not told her anything close to that. She actually hadn't heard from her mom in a couple of weeks. But she was trying not to read anything into that. "Basketball would be more exciting with some rule changes," Julia said. "Like, multiple balls and secret tunnels that lead to bonus points."

"So, basically you want basketball to be more like pinball."

"That'd be perfect."

Another crunch from Dave's celery stick. Julia bit into her chicken salad sandwich. "You think she's actually gonna come?"

Julia chewed slowly, watching the kids run up and down the court, sweat clinging to their T-shirts. "Shit, Dave, I don't know. I hope so."

The days had started to feel much longer. Julia found herself yearning for the final bell to release her and Dave into their own little world. The time they spent together at school felt somehow lesser, as if now that they'd become a couple it was not acceptable for them to act like they had before. She constantly caught herself wondering how close to sit next to him, where to put her hands, how long to keep eye contact.

"Me too. Sorry."

Julia took another bite from her sandwich. She leaned her head on Dave's shoulder, chewing lethargically. "Is school over yet?"

"Like, for the day? Is your stroke coming back? It's only lunch."

"For the year, you goof. This week's been brutal. I catch myself gazing out the window for what feels like hours, only to find out that it's been two minutes and the class I'm in doesn't actually have any windows. One of those violinists in my Euro history class has ADD so bad, *I* can't pay attention."

Immediately after she said it, Julia realized that the violinist she'd referred to had been there the night of the promposal. Julia had invoked Gretchen's presence, and she could feel it in Dave's silence. The sound of the basketball dribbling up and down the court reverberated, an amateur bass line, rhythmless.

Julia straightened out, finished her sandwich, narrowly avoiding a glob of chicken salad that plopped onto the space between her and Dave. He kept crunching on celery sticks. "How's your day been?"

Julia hated the question. It had always felt to her like a question asked between people with nothing else to say. Her mom had once written to her that if she ever started her conversations with *How was your day?* to reexamine her choices in life. Like she always did with her mom's nuggets of wisdom, Julia thought back, trying to remember the exact details of when or how it had been delivered. Probably when she was sixteen, when her dads had started begging her to make it through her teenage years without getting pregnant. It'd been a postcard from Costa Rica, the one depicting a green volcano, the handwriting on the back carelessly sprawling, so that only a couple of sentences fit. She'd always wished her mom could fit more on each postcard.

"How about your day?" Dave said, popping the lid back on the Tupperware of hummus. Julia hadn't heard a word of his response.

"Enthralling, of course," she said. "You ever wonder why asking 'how's your day been?' seems so…desperate? I didn't mean it that way when I just asked it now. But, I mean, what a boring question, right?"

Dave shrugged. "I don't see anything wrong with it. I care about how your day's been."

"Yeah, but there are more interesting ways to ask."

"Such as?"

Julia paused, suddenly defensive. "I don't know. You could ask specific questions that'll give you a better feel for the other person's day. It's like asking strangers how they are when you don't actually care about the response."

"What would you ask instead?"

A sigh escaped Julia's lips and they both fell quiet. The basketball players started arguing about something, all in lingo Julia couldn't understand. Julia wondered what she and Dave were even doing still at school. They could have gone off campus on their lunch breaks, snuck away to the harbor, avoiding the gaze of all the people who'd helped at the promposal and now didn't understand why Dave was with the pink-haired girl instead of Gretchen. They could have been wrapped up in each other. Julia reached into her bag, found the side pocket where the Nevers list had been resting since they found it. She knew it by heart, knew that most of the items had been crossed off now. But she wanted something else to be on there, some new adventure to share with Dave.

"You could ask about erections," Dave said, his voice cracking at the end.

Julia folded up the list, laughing. "Really? Erections are the best way to measure the quality of a day?"

"Maybe not the best way. But it could paint a picture."

"That's a pretty gross picture." She looked over at Dave. When they were alone, she felt these uncontainable urges to touch him, not necessarily in sexual ways, just rub her face against his, lay a hand on his neck. At school, those urges fell away, and she sometimes found herself forcing the issue, throwing her arms around him as if to prove something to herself. "Plus, aside from the gross inherent sexism of that male-dominated question, are you really saying each erection carries with it the same exact ecstasy? Every day, every man, an erection carries with it the exact same shot of happiness, every time?"

"This is a bizarre conversation."

"Don't back away now, David Vas Deferens. You started the conversation."

Dave laughed, his hand going to the back of his neck. "Probably not the exact same, no."

"Absolutely not. I mean, if the desire men feel is anything like what I feel—and, I'll admit the flaw in this argument, since I don't really know a thing about male desire, if it's the same thing as female desire or a whole other beast—there are different grades of it. There's the longing to be with someone you love"—here she gave him a stomach poke—"there's the instinctive desire you feel for someone who you find attractive even though you have no intentions to pursue the desire. There's the slight desperation in thinking that particular desire wouldn't ever have the chance to live itself out. There's the kind of sad desire that comes along with loneliness, the mad desire from sexual frustration. If the sexist question of how many times you had an erection *had* a perfect female equivalent, it would still have the completely erroneous assumption that all boners are created equal."

Dave's eyebrows were raised, his jaw ever so slack with surprise. As if to punctuate her speech, the bell rang, which caused the basketball players to groan in complaint. "Next point wins," someone called out.

"Well, shit."

"Plus," Julia added, standing up and slinging her bag over her shoulder, "no erection could equal the amount of joy that a Marroney erection provides to the world."

Dave made a face. "Yup, gonna throw up."

"That got weird, didn't it?"

"I want to say 'massively weird,' but I'm now strangely put off by the word 'massive.'" They hopped off the bleachers and exited the gym, Julia leading them the long way around so they would avoid as many people as possible. It felt cruel that there was still an hour and a half left of school.

"Let's skip class," Julia said, pausing at the entrance to the hallway. "I can't go through those doors."

"I don't know, Jules."

"I promise to not bring up Marroney's erection ever again." She bumped him with her shoulder, suddenly desperate at the thought of going to class, of staying in a room, staring at all those home-printed quotations about knowledge on the wall, the same ones she'd reread millions of times throughout the year. "Come on, let's do something."

Dave's eyes flicked ahead, as if his desperation lay in the exact opposite direction. "I feel like I've been slacking in class, and finals are coming up."

"I can't do it, Dave. I can't sit in a classroom right now. My life can't handle it; I'll explode."

"How about after school?"

"Nope." Julia reached in her bag and found her car keys. She started to turn away, sure that Dave would follow. He'd always followed. She even made a big gesture of jangling the keys, motioning with her head toward the parking lot, the entire world outside of school that was waiting for them. "Right now. You, me, adventure. Erections optional."

Dave stood frozen, his eyes downcast. "I don't want my grades to drop too much, Jules. UCLA can pull my scholarship."

"They're not gonna drop, Dave." She took a few steps back toward him. A group of girls sneered at them as they walked by and though Julia had no idea who they were, she had that sudden rush of guilt that had been seizing her lately, that I-broke-up-Dave-and-Gretchen guilt. "Come on. Your grades are fine." She put a hand on his side and pulled herself to him, rising up on her toes to kiss him gently. "Your girlfriend wants to do stuff with you."

The second bell rang out, and the sound of doors shutting echoed down the hallway. Dave attempted a smile, but his eyes went over her shoulder, toward the one place she wanted to get away from. "I'm sorry. I think we have a quiz today." Now he initiated a kiss, but it had the distinct taste of a kiss good-bye.

Before, when Julia had dreamed about love, this is what it looked like:

Like two sprinters making their way around a track. Spurts of energy followed by collapsing into a heap on the ground. Sweaty arms laid across chests, big, gulping breaths of air. Love traveled, it ran, it covered ground, eager to see more, do more. It was two people keeping pace with each other.

OFF

DAVE SAT WITH Julia in homeroom, connected to her by the white cord of Julia's earphones. They hadn't said anything yet, though they'd smiled hello at each other, noticed the matching circles beneath their eyes. Dave was looking at the calendar on the wall, trying to recall exactly when things had happened. The day they'd found the Nevers, the hair dyeing fiasco, Julia's slam poem. It had felt like ages had gone by, but it had only been a matter of weeks.

Without warning, the Jell-O feeling had returned. Maybe because they'd crossed off almost all the Nevers. It was only 8:06 in the morning and there were six hours left watching that clock and silently begging teachers not to make him do too much. The second hand came into focus, and it moved glacially. There were still four weeks of school left, and the way it was going he had no idea if his life could handle that. Fourteen years of schooling, and the weight of every single day was suddenly compressed into this one homeroom period. He looked over at Julia, who was breathing softly, eyes closed. There was something keeping him from going over and unburdening the desperation with her, the way he'd always done. He didn't know how to behave around her at school anymore, like there was some sort of fuzz between the two of them that kept things from being exactly how they always had been.

Only a tick or two had gone by. Every second carried with

it an entire lifetime of academic obligations, even if at this particular moment he was just sitting there listening to music. There was so much of it still left, time in school, it never ended, never moved. Dave was going to die within four walls just like these, wasn't he?

Dave pulled out his earphone, whispered, "Bathroom," and walked out of class, trying to calm himself down. He reminded himself that there were only four weeks left of school, and right away he knew that this wasn't about school at all. This was about Julia. Something was wrong.

If he could put his finger on it he'd instantly flick the thing away, whatever it was. Because it was pesky and stupid and small. But things just didn't add up. They still laughed. The kissing was incredible. They'd always spent the majority of their time together, so it wasn't like it was weird to suddenly be in bed all afternoon with her.

Dave got himself a drink of water, lingered by the fountain for as long as he could, then went back to class. Julia's head was still on her desk, the earphone he'd pulled out dangling over the edge of the table. For once, Ms. Romero had the bulletin board up and the attention of a handful of kids. Taking his place beside Julia again, Dave made sure to keep his eyes off the clock. He took the earphone but kept it in his hand, fiddling with the cord as he pretended to listen to Ms. Romero go on about whatever. Then he looked down at Julia, whose eyes were open, fixed on him. He smiled and brought the earphone up, and when she simply closed her eyes again the feeling that something was wrong came back.

○ ○ ○

AP Chem, right before lunch. Ever since the beach, Dave had been sitting at the front of the class, keeping his back turned the entire period to make it easier on Gretchen, to avoid the awkwardness of eye contact. The class was restless, their interest waning as blood sugar levels plummeted. Mr. Kahn asked questions and was met with silence, no one even interested in cracking jokes. There was a lull, and Dave could feel everyone reaching for the end of the day.

"Bueller? Bueller?" Mr. Kahn was saying. He sighed. "Do you guys even catch that reference?"

"*Ferris Bueller's Day Off*," someone yelled back. "We're bored, not uncultured."

The class broke out into laughter. Mr. Kahn frowned, then went to his desk to collect a stack of papers. "All right, I guess lecturing is over. This is your homework. You can take the last ten minutes of class to get started."

Chairs instantly pushed back, the volume of chattering rising like a spark set to fuel.

"Quietly please!" Mr. Kahn said, and the chattering diminished but was not snuffed out. Then he walked over with the stack of papers and handed it to Dave. "Would you mind passing these out?"

Dave's heart sank. "Sure." He stood up, trying to keep his eyes from flitting in Gretchen's direction. Would he be able to see the heartbreak on her face? Would she be crying? Avoiding his gaze? Maybe there was an e-mail feature he didn't know about that told people how many times you'd reread their e-mail. Maybe she'd be able to see it on his face, no technology required.

When he handed her the packet, he tried to fix his eyes on something innocuous, the wooden desk, or the wall, or the floor. But on her desk was her forearm with its film of fine golden hairs, and on the wall was the clock, and on the floor were her scuffed sneakers. So his eyes in the end landed on her. She was looking at the paper already, uncapping her pen, her shoulders hunched over the desk, blond waves falling onto the papers. In a surprisingly sweet voice, she said, "Thanks, Dave."

"I'm sorry," he said, the words out of his mouth before he was conscious they'd been bubbling up. Gretchen tapped her pen against her desk a few times, biting her bottom lip. He hadn't apologized at all, he now realized. Even that morning when she'd seen him with Julia. He'd run after her, but he'd never said he was sorry. The shame caused him to look away, take in the sights of the classroom. There was a ballet of pens twirling around fingers, plenty of doodling going on, Jane Henley was eating an apple.

"Dude, the papers!" someone called out, and Dave handed the remaining stack to the girl sitting next to Gretchen. A second ago he couldn't imagine facing her, and now he couldn't step away. Julia would want him to apologize, right? He'd avoided bringing Gretchen up at all, and maybe that'd been what was off between them.

Gretchen finally looked up at Dave. She had bags under her eyes. Reaching back, she piled her hair together, sticking her pen through the bun to keep it in place. Then she leaned forward, putting her chin in her hand. "I was just saying thanks for the papers. You don't have to apologize."

"But I want to. I'm sorry."

Gretchen looked around the room. He found himself wishing he knew her a little better, well enough to guess at what she was thinking. "That's not enough," Gretchen said after a moment. "To be sorry you hurt me is not enough for me to forgive you."

Dave stuck his hands in his pockets, eyes on the ground. From years of watching Julia do it, he felt the impulse to kick his shoes off. He wondered in the silence that—regardless of the noise in the classroom—filled the space between him and Gretchen how Julia's barefoot obsession had started. "I know. I think I should say it again anyway. I'm sorry. For what it's worth, I hadn't planned on that happening. I thought it was just a friendly road—"

"Dave, stop." She shifted in her seat, pulling up one leg and tucking it beneath her. "Just 'cause there's a part of me that sends emotional e-mails doesn't mean I want the details." She grabbed the pen out of the bun, causing her hair to spill down. Then she lowered her gaze back to the papers in front of her. "You made your choice."

o o o

They'd spent the afternoon in bed again, Dave trying to interpret what the slightest touch meant. When Julia turned her back to him, he thought, *She feels it, too.* Then a second later she asked him to be the big spoon and he wondered what the hell was wrong with him, why he insisted that things weren't perfect. He pressed himself close and kissed the back of her neck.

The lull fell into place quickly, and what should have felt like lazy love now made Dave restless. "You wanna go grab some food? I realized I've been an awful boyfriend and haven't even taken you out on a date."

"We've been dating for years; we were just missing this part." She turned over to face him. "I don't need you to take me on dates. This is great."

"You're not hungry?"

"Yeah. Just order some pizza and shove it into my face. We can have saucy, not-beardy sex afterward."

"You know, one of these days I'm going to get really offended by the beard jokes and you're going to lose me."

"That's why I keep that sexy mathematician around. He's my backup."

"I'm sure I'm the backup." Dave kissed her forehead, then sat up. "Let's get out of the house. See the world. I feel like my muscles are atrophying."

"What muscles? I didn't know you had muscles."

"Wow, hurtful," Dave said, poking her stomach.

"Wow, sensitive," Julia said, burying her face into his stomach and wrapping her arms and legs around him like a vise. "Where was that spark the other day when I wanted to skip school? Now I'm feeling lazy."

"You're not gonna let me get out of bed, are you?"

Julia tightened her grip. "I don't know what you mean."

He tried to relax into her arms. He ran his hand along her side, then looked around his room. The jacaranda outside his window was swaying. Laundry was overflowing from his hamper. His whiteboard still had the quote from Gretchen's tattoo on it. He wondered if Julia had noticed it. He remembered seeing it on Gretchen's neck when they had cuddled, rubbing his finger over it.

He shook away the memory. Was this what it was always like with love? Memories wrapping themselves around acts, no chance of prying them apart? Or was this not normal at all? Was this not how it was supposed to be?

"You're so antsy," Julia said. She was still holding him close, but her grip had relaxed a little. She was looking up at him. "I had no idea you were the kind of guy that needed more than cuddling."

"Even sustenance?"

"You know how many calories there are in cuddling? And vitamins?"

Dave chuckled, his eyes still on the whiteboard. He wanted

Julia to keep joking, because when they were laughing everything felt exactly as it should be. But he couldn't keep the banter going, and soon the silence fell over the two of them. It was an uneasy silence, like a liquid on the verge of boiling.

"Hey. Everything okay?"

"Yeah, fine," Dave said.

Julia pulled back a little. "Don't do that. That whole, 'yeah I'm fine' thing. I know you too well for that shit." Her leg fell away from his.

Dave tried to meet her eyes, but when he saw those intense blue irises he was afraid every single one of his thoughts would be on display. He turned to look at the dust particles dancing in the light, trying to follow just one of them. "I don't know," Dave said. "I'm restless."

"Like, you wanna go jogging?"

"Not quite."

"Wanna play Ultimate Frisbee? Let a bunch of mice loose in the mall and then chase after them?"

"You're a crazy person," Dave said, squeezing her forearm. Then he let his head fall back and closed his eyes, as if this doubt were just some dizzy spell that would pass if he gave it a moment or two.

"Come on, don't get all quiet on me. Something's on your mind."

Dave took a deep breath, exhaling slowly with his lips pursed, as if he was trying to whistle. "Gretchen," he said, not believing he had said it.

"Oh."

Dave kept his eyes closed, so he couldn't tell what Julia was doing, just that less and less of her was making contact with his skin. Her weight shifted around the mattress until it felt like she was sitting on the corner of it. "In what way is she on your mind?"

"I don't know. She's just there."

"Do you feel bad for her?"

"Yeah."

Her hand landed on his thigh, soft and warm, reassuring. "You've got a good heart, Dave. It's okay if you feel bad." He felt her scoot back toward him, and he opened his eyes. She put her arms around his neck. "I wish it had happened some other way, too. But I'm glad you're with me." Leaning in, she kissed him. "You have a good heart, Dave. I wouldn't love you as much as I do if it weren't for that."

Dave managed a smile, but the feeling that something was off hadn't gone away. If anything, it was more acute, like he was just about to figure out exactly what it meant. "She wrote me an e-mail this week," he said. Julia pulled her arms back, and he folded his hands in his lap, not knowing what else to do with them. "And I've been thinking about something she said."

Julia got off from the bed and started to pace. She sat back against his desk, her hands leaning on it for support, her jaw clenched. "Yeah? What'd she say?"

"It was actually a nice e-mail. She said she wished I was happy even if it's not with her."

Julia relaxed, but she stayed away from the bed. "Okay."

"She also said that we can't choose who we love. The way she said it was, 'Your heart's an asshole for choosing someone else. But that's not really your choice to make.'" He sat up a little, crossing his legs in front of him. "What I've been wondering is..." He paused, trying to figure out the right way to phrase it. If there was a right way. If he even knew exactly what he wanted to say. The wind blew stronger outside, and the branches of the jacaranda scraped against his window with a squeak.

"Just say it, dammit."

"Calm down, I don't know what I'm trying to say."

"Oh, you don't know?" Julia rolled her eyes. "Where the hell is this coming from?"

"Where's what coming from? I haven't said anything."

"You're thinking you chose wrong, Dave. You can stammer all you want, but that's what you were going to say." Dave exhaled, wanting to deny it. Then he looked down at his tangled sheets, the dimples in the pillow where Julia's head had been just a moment ago. "Tell me it's not true. Tell me that's not what you've been thinking."

Dave couldn't say anything, though. He was trying to find the words, but they were like the earphones on his desk, a whole bunch of them tangled together. Even if he managed to unravel them, he didn't know how much use they could be.

Julia started pacing again. She turned the corner from his room and went into the bathroom, that signature pitter-patter of her bare feet on tile. When she came back he could see the tears forming in her eyes. He expected her to yell. To force him to say something. To force him to figure out what was going on. But she took a seat on the bed in front of him and she brought her knees up to her chest, wrapping her arms around them and tucking them close. She didn't look away from him.

"I don't think I chose wrong," Dave finally said, weakly. "I don't know if I *made* a choice at all."

"So, what, then? What are you saying?"

"It's not just Gretchen," Dave said. "Haven't things been a little...I don't know."

"Dave, you say you don't know one more time, I'm going to throw a dictionary at you."

"Sorry." He smoothed out a patch of bedsheets by his side. "Off," he said. "Things have been a little off. Haven't they felt that way to you?"

Julia leaned down so her forehead was touching her knees. She shook her head that way, slowly, and when she looked up over the ridge of her kneecaps, tears were on the brink of her eyelids, caught on her lashes like divers about to jump. She bit her lip, she put her forehead down again, she shook her head. "I don't know," she said finally, managing a smile. "Maybe a little. But this is still new."

"Julia, we've been best friends for five years. It's never once felt off. Why now?"

She stretched her legs out in front of her. "Because the universe hates happiness?" She wiped at her eyes. "That's not even true, though. Things have been great between us, haven't they?"

"The past week has been great, Julia. But there's something wrong here. I can't think of things to talk about with you. I don't know how to act around you. And, yes, Gretchen's on my mind. Too much for it to not mean anything."

He was not ready to see her face crumple into tears. He'd seen her get sad once or twice. But this? This was uncharted territory. He thought back to the night of the "BEER" party, how hurt she'd looked when he called her a cliché. This was like that, but worse. She hid behind her hands and wept.

His chest felt emptied out. Outside, the sun was still shining, and it felt weird that moments like these could happen in the daytime. Fights, like phone calls delivering bad news, those only happened in the middle of the night, didn't they? Shrouded in darkness?

Julia stood up from the bed and went over to the box of tissues on his nightstand. She wiped her tears and blew her nose, then took a seat at his desk chair, composing herself. Dave could only watch.

"I don't want to be miserable with you, Dave," she said, scrunching a tissue in her hand. "I want to be with you. More than anything I've ever really wanted. I think things have been a little off, yes. But I also think maybe we can fix that." Another tear started to scurry down the bridge of her nose and she quickly brushed it away, not giving it a chance to interrupt. "But I don't want to start getting paranoid about whether you want to be with me or someone else. I don't want to start analyzing your every action. I don't want us to start hating each other because we don't know how to be in a relationship together." She tossed her scrunched-up tissue in the garbage beneath his desk. "I think this can work between us. I really do. But I'm going to let you decide, because otherwise I'll always have the doubt. Are we going to try this out, or do you think we shouldn't?"

After a long moment with his eyes closed, his head resting back against his wall, nausea knotting his stomach, Dave let out his breath. When had everything he'd ever wanted changed? "I love you, Julia. But maybe I'm not supposed to love you like this."

WITHOUT HIM

JULIA WAS ON her side, staring at the map on her wall. The dads came by and tried to convince her to come watch a movie with them downstairs, but she couldn't bring herself to step away from the bed. She wanted the comfort of the room slowly darkening as the day went on without her. Burying her head beneath her sheets, she imagined the folds of the cloth as caverns, imagined that she was underground, if only to give herself something to think about to ease the pain. For hours, she didn't move. She tried to empty her mind of Dave, though she had no idea how. She'd been thinking about him for years.

This hurt. In a way she couldn't shake, in a place she couldn't pinpoint, this hurt more than anything Julia had ever experienced.

MESS

DAVE SETTLED INTO his bench at the harbor. He'd skipped school for the second day in a row because he thought staring out at the cool waters of Morro Bay might be comforting. The bubble tea he'd bought an hour ago was on the ground by his feet, almost full. He'd made a mess of everything, and it served him right to sit there and feel every little bit of guilt that came his way.

MORE OR LESS

ANYTIME SHE COULD get away with it at school, Julia lived within the world of her headphones. For days now, music had been playing almost nonstop. Whenever she was forced to hit pause, the air around her was fraught with tension. No one else seemed to notice it. In fact, everyone else seemed to be drunk with happiness. That sense during school Julia had had only a couple months ago that everything had been dipped in butter, that time had slowed down to a torturous crawl, it had disappeared. The end of the year was in sight and everyone but Julia was giddy for it.

She waited in her car in the parking lot until the bell for first period liberated her from seeing Dave, and even then she'd still be late, waiting until she knew he would be seated dutifully in class. If she saw blond locks anywhere on campus, she turned the other direction. During lunch, she steered clear of the tree house, choosing to sneak bites of her sandwich by the graphic novels in the library, or leaving campus a couple of steps behind the throng of seniors who were known by their first names at the pizza shop.

Music was her solace and her refuge, and rather than trying to cheer herself up, she found herself playing the saddest music she owned. Songs about breakups and their messy aftermaths offered the most consolation. When John Darnielle would sing to her, something like, *I will get lonely and gasp for air, and send your name off from my lips like a signal flare,* she'd think to herself: Goddamn right. People were always belittling teenage heartbreak. But heartbreak was heartbreak was heartbreak.

What was almost as bad was the increasingly obvious fact that she had no other friends. She and Dave had clung to each other for so long and now she was alone. She ate by herself. She drove home by herself. Her phone's battery life seemed eternal thanks to inactivity. At night, when she felt like crying, Julia watched the Travel Channel, wrote her mom e-mails, asking when she was going to come. When she reread them, they sounded desperate. Even as she wrote them she knew they were desperate. She had fantasies of her mom whisking her away from San Luis Obispo right after graduation, taking her on a trip around Southeast Asia. They were cinematic clichés, these fantasies. Her mom pulling up in a *Thelma & Louise* convertible right on the lawn of the ceremony, honking the horn, scarves blowing in the wind, though Julia did not own a scarf. Sometimes, Julia felt like an only child wishing for siblings, like a girl making up imaginary friends.

Thursday morning, she was convinced she had exactly this to look forward to for the last month of school. Lonely moping, tearful nights, music, music, music. She was sitting in her car, waiting for the first period bell to ring when Principal Hill walked out into the parking lot and she was forced to pretend to be on her way. She gathered her bag and walked in a hurry through the front doors with her earbuds in, then walked straight past homeroom, not daring to look inside. She checked her e-mail again and her hear leapt when she saw her mom's name come up. She almost smiled for the first time that week.

Then she opened the e-mail and saw that it was long, and tears immediately formed in her eyes. Her mom was only wordy when she was apologizing. Julia skimmed the e-mail, looking only for that "no" she knew was in there. When she found it she wiped the tears from her eyes and slipped her phone into her bag, listening harder to the music. This was all she could handle right now. Just the world inside her earphones.

Skipping class and just doing laps around the school would probably get her caught. The school librarian was famously lax on almost every rule except for only allowing you in the library if you had a pass. She flirted with the idea of sitting in Dr. Hill's office, since he was outside, but she wasn't feeling particularly bold, so she decided to go hide out in the tree house. She was looking forward to the few hours of uninterrupted solitude on the floor among the pillows. But when she walked inside, she jumped at the sight of Mr. Marroney sitting at the counter, grading papers.

He was so hunched over the stack of papers that he almost looked humpbacked. A blue ballpoint pen rested in his hand, streaks of blue ink all along his forearm, like he'd been testing out the pen or had no idea how to use it. He turned around, sensing her presence.

Julia stood at the entrance, frozen. She saw his mustache move. For a second she didn't even understand that he'd spoken, she just thought that was something his mustache did that she hadn't ever noticed before.

"What?" Julia said, pulling an earphone out.

"I asked if you're supposed to be in class."

Julia shrugged. "Are you?"

Marroney chuckled and tried to cap his pen but ended up adding a blue streak to his hand and then dropping the pen through a crack between the floorboards. "This is my free period. I like coming up here to do my grading. I've heard that I have you to thank for this place."

"Not really," Julia said. She looked over her shoulder, wondering if anyone had seen her come out to the tree house. Then she set her bag down on the floor and nestled down by the pillows, out of view. "I'm just gonna hang out here for a while; please don't get me in trouble." She got ready to put her other earphone back in, maybe take a nap.

"I was just thinking," Marroney said, swiveling on his stool to face her, "that you've been very distracted in class. Even more so than usual."

"Oh, just the end of the year, you know," she said with a shrug, hoping that was enough to get him to go. A couple weeks ago she would have done anything to keep him there and have more to tell Dave about afterward. But now she couldn't see the point in laughing about it on her own. Music kept playing in one ear, a sad soundtrack that she wanted to envelop her.

Instead, Marroney crossed his arms in front of his chest and furrowed his brow at Julia, the way he did when anyone in class didn't seem to understand his ill-conceived math jokes.

"I've been teaching long enough to know when a kid is distracted and when it's something else. Are you okay?"

Julia's instinct was to laugh. And for a second she even smiled, amused at the thought that the teacher she'd basically harassed was concerned for her well-being. Then the smiled faded and she found a knot rising in her throat because he cared enough to ask, though she'd pretty much made his life hell for a few weeks. Her mom didn't give a damn but Marroney did. Julia tried to stifle the sob that she felt coming on, but was powerless against it. The last few days, she had felt completely abandoned. Dave felt like he'd just disappeared from her life, and as for her mom, Julia wasn't even sure she had ever been there. But now, looking at Marroney, who seemed not frightened or uncomfortable with her breakdown, but concerned, Julia realized that if she was alone, it was her own damn fault. She'd closed herself off from everyone but Dave, and this was what she got for it.

Sinking into the pillows around her, Julia let loose. She covered her face with her palm, tasting tears, struggling to breathe normally. "Song for Zula" by Phosphorescent was playing through the earphone she still had in. It was a fitting song; it made her heaving gasps for breath feel justified.

She could have reached out to her dads, or maybe even to Brett, or to the dozen other people who'd surprised her in quiet ways since the Nevers began. Apparently, she could even have reached out to Marroney, who was maybe a perfectly cliché math teacher, but had heart enough to ask her if she was okay. Her mom would probably make fun of him like Julia had, but her mom was kind of an asshole, and Julia was done wanting to be like her.

By the time the song played out, Julia had regained some control. She looked up at Marroney, who did not look frightened or uncomfortable.

"No," she said finally, chuckling to keep something else from taking over again. "I'm not okay. I guess I wasn't hiding it too well."

"I only started worrying when you stopped joking around." He shifted his weight, putting a foot up against the wall and struggling not to lose his balance. "And just now, I guess."

"Maybe I just ran out of material," she said.

"If that ever happened, I'd really be worried about you."

"I will take that as a compliment." Julia removed her second earphone and wrapped the cord carefully around her phone, slipping it in her bag and knowing that it would be a knotted mess when she pulled it back out. "You really want to know?"

"Please."

Julia wiped her cheeks dry. "You remember the only guy at the Broken Bean who was more embarrassed than you were by my performance?"

"Dave. Your friend."

"Yeah, my friend." She sighed and brought her knees up to her chest, hugging them close for comfort. "The gist of it is, I'm in love with him and it's not going to work out."

Marroney nodded, looking down at his lap. He ran his forefinger and thumb over his mustache. "It's always hard to tell whether you kids are bored or in love. I guess it's about fifty-fifty, but I can't ever tell. I figure that most of the time I'm over-romanticizing, since I was your age when I met my fiancée."

Julia felt a flush of embarrassment that she hadn't even paused to consider Marroney's personal life when she did all those things to "seduce" him. "I hope she didn't see the cupcakes."

"Oh, worse than that, she was at the coffee shop."

"I'm sorry."

"It's okay." He seemed to consider this for a second and then shook his head. "It's not okay. But, you know. Don't worry about it. Tell me more about Dave."

Julia rested her head back against the wall. "Typical high school drama. Love unrequited, other women, sex on the beach." She felt herself blushing immediately. "Sorry."

Marroney chuckled through his own blushing. "I've gotten good at taking what you say with a grain of salt, so we'll pretend that was just a joke. Let's stick to the emotions and leave out physical descriptions."

"I don't know what to say. The emotions are not good."

Julia looked over Marroney's shoulder at the always-blue sky, slightly tinged this morning by a few streaks of dark fog clouds coming in from the bay. She rested her cheek on the top of her knees. Julia hadn't ever felt nauseated by sadness before. "I don't know how you can be best friends with someone for so long, be in love with each other, and have things fall apart so quickly."

Marroney nodded. He leaned back against the counter, his legs stretched out in front of him, a large coffee stain on his pants. A quiet moment passed, and Julia thought that maybe he had nothing else to say. She closed her eyes and thought of Dave in homeroom, not listening to music the way they always did, thought of their literal lack of connection, the days it had been since the white cord of her earphones had stretched between them. She thought of his hands, thought of Gretchen. Then Marroney spoke. "Human beings are more or less formulas. Pun intended. We are not any one thing that is mathematically provable. We are more *more or less* than we *are* anything." He massaged his mustache for a second. "We are more or less kind, or more or less not. More or less selfish, happy, wise, lonely. Just like things are rarely always true or never true, we aren't ever exactly one thing or another. We are more or less.

"It's like that in our love lives, too. We like to think we're formulas that even out exactly, that we are perfect matches with each other. But we're not. We match up with lots of people, more or less."

Julia groaned. "That's deep, but how is that helpful?"

Marroney laughed, just as the bell rang, the sound muted by the tree house walls but still an insistent cue to leave. Julia stood up, brushed herself off as Marroney uncapped his pen.

"The equation might not balance out, even if you and Dave are more or less a match." He gave her a smile, then turned back to his papers. "Think about it."

o o o

School let out and Julia had not listened to music since the morning. All day long, she'd been turning over Marroney's words. She'd written down formulas in her notebook that made no sense, even to herself. She'd crossed out her writing and torn the pages out and then gone searching for the crumpled sheets in her classroom's trash bins, only to toss them again. By lunch, though she kept trying to organize her thoughts, she knew exactly what she was going to do.

She gave herself the last two periods of the day to think it over. She repeated the phrase "more or less" so many times to herself that the meaning attached to the sounds was starting to fall apart. She read her mom's e-mail fully, then deleted it without a response.

When school let out, she searched the crowd for a blond ponytail. She spotted Gretchen headed toward the exit, a black backpack bouncing on her shoulders. Julia squeezed past the crowd of slow movers, saying, "Excuse me," and immediately pushing through the oblivious groupings of people blocking the hallways. Before she could second-guess what she was doing, she found herself walking right behind Gretchen. She needed to say what she had to say before she lost her conviction to do what was right.

When Gretchen turned around, Julia knew right away that she was getting exactly as much (or as little) sleep as Julia was.

"He's yours," Julia said, unable to stop herself. Despite the pain at the sound of the words, there was an enormous relief. "I don't want to give him up. But I know him better than anyone else. I could have had him, once. I almost did for a little while. But you have him now. No matter how I feel, he wants you."

Gretchen's mouth opened slightly. Dozens of people passed by them, oblivious to the conversation. Julia wondered where Dave was, what he was thinking or doing or hoping. She missed the sound of his laugh, though it'd only been a few days since she'd felt him do it right against the side of her neck, the warm exhalations turning into a series of kisses that had seemed endless at the time. "You two are the better equation."

CEILINGS

IT WAS THURSDAY EVENING, and Dave was watching the typical crowd at the harbor. Road trippers on their way to San Francisco or L.A. stopping for some pictures of the bay, twentysomething couples sitting at the coffee shop, families taking strolls. Some surfers were getting changed out of their wet suits, their boards, gleaming with salt water and wax, propped up against the sides of their cars. Dave could barely people-watch without thinking of how often he'd done this with Julia, how many hours they'd spent on the bench just watching the crowds pass by. He'd pretend to look at something happening in her direction so that she'd be in his sight. Sometimes he'd count to see how long he could go without looking at her, the game always losing steam after about fifteen seconds, when he couldn't keep himself from it any longer.

He couldn't remember the exact moment he'd fallen in love with Julia, but it had probably happened on that bench. It would have been easier if he had chosen to go somewhere else, somewhere that wasn't dripping with memories. Except San Luis Obispo was small and if he and Julia hadn't been to a place a thousand times throughout the last five years, then he and Gretchen had passed by it in her car while GPS-drawing in the past couple of weeks. Every landmark in town, every restaurant or shopping plaza or tree, Dave could suddenly recall exactly what song he and Gretchen were listening to as they drove past it. His memory had never been sharper. Which was kind of a shitty thing for his memory to do at this particular time.

The sun was starting to turn orange, casting everything in the harbor in the same emblazoned light, making silhouettes out of all the people in Dave's line of sight. He watched the bundled shadows of the homeless guys gathering their belongings and moving on for the night. A couple of sophomore girls from school walked right in front of Dave, not noticing him sitting on the bench, like he was more liquid than solid.

"I'm serious," one of them was saying, "it's a real thing. We have to try it."

"There's no way that exists."

"I read it online." The girl was a brunette, wearing dozens of bracelets on her wrist that jingled audibly. "Oreos fried in Mountain Dew. Just saying it out loud gives me goose bumps."

They kept walking, their conversation fading out, contextless. Dave's butt was asleep. His feet were asleep. Everything else was painfully awake. He felt like a guttural groan would nicely summarize how he was feeling.

"Dave."

At first he just craned his neck, thinking maybe the sophomore girls had recognized him and hadn't picked up on the social cues that said he was miserable and didn't want to chat. Then he saw a silhouette coming his way, the wavy locks unmistakably Gretchen's. He stood up as quickly as he could, which was not all that quick thanks to his stiffened muscles.

She wasn't crying. That was something. She was in front of him and not crying and she'd said his name without affixing an insult or a curse. Not that Gretchen was the type to throw insults or curses around, even at people who deserved them.

"Hi," he said, not quite holding his breath, but waiting to see what came next. Since that day at school, Dave hadn't talked to Gretchen, except over and over again in his mind. He'd glanced at her once in class, then immediately flushed with shame, hiding himself away, feeling exactly like a dog with his tail tucked between his legs.

She was wearing a black zip-up hoodie with the school's name on it. Her hands were stuffed into the pockets. The smell of honey wafted over to him and he knew that it would be a long time before he'd be able to forget what it was like to be near her.

"I figured I could find you here," she said.

"The bench helps me feel less like an asshole." He rubbed the back of his neck. "Gretchen, I'm sorry. I know that's not enough but I need to say it again. I don't deserve to feel like less of an asshole."

She nodded, rubbed one foot against the other. "You hurt me, Dave."

Dave wanted to whisper another "I'm sorry," but there were still no tears and he didn't want anything to push her to that point, so he kept quiet. He'd stand there and let her yell at him, take the full force of her sorrow if it meant easing some of it. He'd absorb her pain, and Julia's too, if he could. But he didn't know how, and so he stood there, a hand on the back of his neck, looking around the harbor, stealing glances at Gretchen, who seemed almost confused about why she was standing there with him.

Gretchen took a step closer to Dave, so she was less of a silhouette, the details of her face coming into focus. He couldn't tell what she was feeling, if she was about to slap him or hug him. The moment stretched on and on without a clue as to what was on Gretchen's mind. People walked all around them as if on fast-forward, like a film-editing trick. Dave realized he had no idea what was on anyone's mind, not even a little. Before the Nevers he and Julia had assumed they knew exactly what was going on in strangers' minds, that people felt and thought in clichés. During the Nevers Dave had discovered that they hadn't been exactly right, or maybe that the assumption that he didn't fit in with those clichés was wrong. Now everyone just seemed like a mystery. He couldn't even tell what the hell he was thinking and feeling, if he was angry or sad or guilty or hopeful or curious.

"I need you to promise nothing will ever happen between you and Julia again," Gretchen said, eyes still on the ground.

"I promise," Dave said quickly, before he really understood the implications of what she was saying.

"I can't go through that again. I was a wreck. Even more than when my ex cheated on me."

"I swear, Gretchen."

Gretchen let out a sigh, shaking her head at the ground and then looking up at him with a smile of all things. "You make me happy, Dave. And as pissed as I was at you, it's been hard to forget that. I want you to keep making me happy. I want you to leave things a little better than you found them."

Relief washed through Dave, even before she took another step and wrapped her arms around him, enveloping him.

"That was the longest you've ever held a straight face," he said, taking a whiff of her hair, kissing her cheek, almost jittery with gratitude. His hands were shaky, and he felt his voice waver, as if he were on the verge of tears, not laughter.

"I thought you'd be proud of me." She broke the hug and took his hand in hers, then leaned in to kiss him. It'd only been a few weeks since they'd kissed, but the pause in between had felt eternal.

Gretchen burrowed herself into his chest, wrapping her arms around him tightly. "I missed you."

He hugged back. "I did, too."

People did not speak highly enough of hugs. Yeah, they had a good reputation, but it didn't really compare to how great they actually were. People should be walking around hugging each other all the time, amazed.

The sun kept dipping down into the ocean and the lights came on at the harbor, casting sudden shadows on the ground, illuminating the faces that were just a second ago silhouettes. The sky was golden and purple, the ocean a darker shade of violet.

FLOAT

IT WAS A Friday night and Julia had not seen a movie in far too long. Really seen one. She drove past the theater in Pismo Beach that showed all the indie flicks and saw that it was packed, as she should have known it would be. Her heart knew exactly what it wanted, though, so she found a parking spot a couple blocks away, leaving her phone in the center console, her earphones wrapped around it.

Julia splurged on some popcorn, since she'd brought a bottle of hot sauce with her, a quirk she tried out ever since her mom had mentioned in a postcard that that's how they ate it in Mexico. It pissed Julia off that her mom still had this hold on her even after that whole meltdown at the tree house. She should have been swearing off all things mom-related right now, idolizing her dads, who lived quiet lives but knew how to love. Except here Julia was, squirting hot sauce onto her popcorn. Disdainfully, sure, but still.

The theater was mostly full, and she took a seat close to the front, where the screen would take up her entire view and she could immerse herself in the movie. It was one thing she and Dave had always disagreed on, how close to sit. He hated craning his neck, she didn't like seeing the little silhouettes of other moviegoers in her periphery.

Julia munched slowly on her popcorn, trying to save most of it for when the movie started rolling. She stared absently at the trivia questions they played on the screen before the previews, questions she'd seen on easily a dozen different trips to the theater, since before the whole Nevers thing began. Struck by a realization, she riffled through the contents of her bag. Flip-flops her dads made her carry around, just in case. Earrings she hardly ever wore, her agenda, a couple of tampons, *Heart of Darkness*, still mostly unread. Her wallet, which was full of receipts she didn't need. In one of the side pockets she finally found the list, and she pulled it out, unfolding it. One of the creases had started to tear.

She'd used three different colored pens to cross off the items she and Dave had done. Now she grabbed the simple black ballpoint pen that was tucked into her agenda, used *Heart of Darkness* as a writing surface, and touched the tip to the paper. Her eyes passed over each item, quickly recalling all the things they'd done. When she got to number seven she laughed out loud. A heart-to-heart in the tree house was good enough. She crossed out *Never hook up with a teacher.*

The only one they hadn't thought to cross out yet was number ten: *Never date your best friend*. She ran a finger over the subtitle that Dave had added on when they were fourteen: *Dave and Julia's Guide to an Original High School Experience.* His boyish handwriting was so much like her own that sometimes she found notes they'd written each other and couldn't make out which side of the conversation was hers and which was his. She didn't let herself wonder about what would have happened if they'd never found the list, or let herself wish for anything else, not now, not in public—since when those trains of thought took over it always ended with her in a crumpled heap, trying not to cry into her bedding. This was enough for now, this at-ease sadness. A cliché, maybe, to let someone go because you loved them. It hurt, but it was better than any of the alternatives.

Dave deserved happiness, even if it wasn't with her. This wasn't a case of letting the thing you love go and hoping it returns to you. Dave wasn't some winged thing, Julia wasn't a perch.

She folded the sheet of paper back up, tapped it meaningfully against her thigh a couple of times, then leaned over and slipped it into a cup holder a couple seats away. She took the hot sauce bottle out of her bag and shook a few squirts out onto the first layer of popcorn. Then she propped her feet up on the seat in front of her and waited for the lights to dim, trying and failing to pace herself on how quickly she reached for more popcorn.

Since she was so close up, she couldn't see all the people who had come in and filled up the theater. A few people had ventured down to her row, but everything in front of her was clear. The audience murmured with a hundred different conversations. Out of the corner of her eye she could see someone coming down the aisle toward her and she lowered her feet in case they needed to pass. But the guy took a seat right next to her.

Julia turned to look at him and saw that it was Brett. He kept his eyes on the screen and reached over for some popcorn casually, jerking it back when he felt the wetness of the hot sauce.

"What the hell?" He examined his fingers.

"Hi, Brett."

Brett sniffed at his fingers. "Is that hot sauce?"

"Indeed it is."

"Weird." He reached over again and grabbed more cautiously.

"What are you doing here?"

"My friends brought their girlfriends, so instead of fifth-wheeling it I'm gonna sit next to you, if that's okay. I spotted you from back there." He motioned vaguely behind him. "Your hair makes it easy."

"No, I mean, what are you doing watching this movie? It's based on a book. No explosions. No boobs that I'm aware of."

"Don't be naive, all these artsy flicks have boobs in 'em." He smiled through a mouthful of popcorn and reached over for some more. "Just kidding. I've been looking forward to this movie for a while. Didn't read the book, but I'm a fan of the director. Hey, I like this popcorn–hot sauce thing."

"Yeah, me too."

The theater turned dark and the chatter quieted to a murmur. Brett leaned in to Julia, close enough that she could smell something fruity on his breath. "You don't mind if I sit with you?" he whispered.

"It depends. Do you talk during movies?"

"All the time. It's my favorite thing to do."

Julia shoved him away with her elbow. "If you finish my popcorn, I'll kill you."

"Or I can go get us a refill. I've got one of those rewards cards, so I get 'em for free."

"Look at you, moving up in the world."

Brett grabbed a piece of popcorn and tossed it at Julia. Then they quieted to watch the previews.

After the movie, they walked out together, Julia taking one last quick glance at the corner of notebook paper sticking out of a cup holder in the third row. Julia thought about her mom—how Julia had, in many ways, done the list for her mom's sake, and how little that would mean to her mom.

They didn't say anything for a bit, following the slow-moving mass of people making their way outside. A few people rushed to their cars; some stood around discussing the movie, making plans for dinner or drinks. The night was absolutely lovely, and Julia thought she might go get a cup of coffee, sit outside somewhere with a book, leave her phone in the car all night.

"I'm sorry about you and Dave," Brett said. He had his hands in his back pockets and was looking sheepishly around.

Julia laughed. "It's not really your fault."

"I know. But maybe I can make it up to you?"

"It's okay," Julia said. "You don't have to do anything. You kept me company during the movie; that's more than enough."

Brett's friends came out of the theater and called him over, and he said he'd be with them in a second.

"I'm parked this way," Julia said, pointing down the block.

"I'll walk you," Brett said, still looking embarrassed, which was the only time Julia ever saw similarities between him and Dave. He was bigger and more self-assured, but right now she could see a flicker of insecurity, too. She wasn't sure why she'd never thought of it before, but Brett had at one point lost his mom, too.

They walked slowly, not saying much until they reached Julia's car.

"I know you said I don't have to make it up to you," Brett said, breaking the silence. "But I want to anyway. I know up until the promposal, you and Dave were always planning on going to prom together. Now you need a date. How about I take you? Not like a pity thing," he added quickly. "This is a little embarrassing, but I've had a crush on you for a while."

He wasn't nervous, like Dave might be. But he wasn't as sure of himself as usual. He gave her a smile, raised his eyebrows.

"What do you say? I know you were looking to go with the future prom king, but maybe a past one will do?"

Julia smiled. "That's so cheesy."

"Dammit, I know."

She took her keys out of her bag and played with them, rubbing her fingers over her keychain amulet.

"No," she said firmly. "I appreciate the gesture, though. That's nice of you."

"Oh." Brett lowered his head, nodding like he'd seen it coming.

"It's been a pretty crazy few weeks for me. I need some time to just"—she gestured with the hand not holding her keys, searching for the word—"float." The sound of that felt great. It put an image in her head of a lake on a windless day, not a single ripple on the surface.

Brett nodded, almost eagerly. "Fair enough," he said, scratching at his chin, which, like Dave's, could barely grow any facial hair. "That makes sense." He lingered for a second before saying good night and turning away.

When he was about to turn away, Julia stopped him. "Thanks for keeping me company," she said, standing on her toes to plant a kiss on his cheek.

Brett smiled, looking momentarily dazed. "Anytime," he said finally, putting up his hand as a wave before going back the way they came.

Julia watched him retreat down the street, taking long, hurried strides to return to his friends. He pulled a beanie out of his back pocket and slipped it on before he reached the growing crowd of midnight-showing attendants, still visible among them thanks to his height. Julia opened her car door and slid in, taking a moment to mentally recover from the quick exchange, reassessing what she knew about Brett. Then she put the key in the ignition and started the car, buckling her seat belt in and lowering the windows. Her phone remained in the center console, quiet and ignored. The dads knew she'd gone to a movie, and they wouldn't worry about her for a while. She had the rest of the night to just float.

PROM

DAVE AND GRETCHEN were walking to school, the sound of their dress shoes clunking down the sidewalk. Gretchen was in a blue dress, which was more of a nice dress than a prom gown. Her hair was done up in curls and she was wearing a light smattering of makeup. She looked beautiful, and Dave caught himself glancing thankfully at their hands clasped together.

Dave himself was in a tuxedo, a cliché he felt okay taking part in. He loved dressing up and often wished people still wore suits everywhere they went. It was light out, though, and tuxedos looked significantly less impressive during the daytime. Tuxedos were meant for the glamour of nighttime, and Dave looked forward to when the sun would set and the tuxedo would finally fit perfectly.

They'd skipped the limo, and the pictures on the front lawn. Corsages matched up with boutonnieres were tacky, so they'd skipped that, too. It seemed lame to show up to prom early, but it was in their nature to avoid being late, so they were walking there slowly.

"Do you think there'll be snacks?" Dave asked.

Gretchen thought about it for a second. Her eyes flicked up, like she was looking for the answer somewhere right above the tree line. "I don't know. I feel like prom at our school will be too classy for a bowl full of chips, but not classy enough for hors d'oeuvres."

"Really? Half the reason I'm going to this thing is because I'm expecting fountains."

"Oh, those will definitely be there. As soon as we get there I'm jumping into the milk-chocolate one."

"Jumping in? Gretchen, what do you think a chocolate fountain looks like?"

"No, I know they're small. I'm jumping in anyway."

"Do I get to lick the chocolate off you?"

"Only the spots I can't reach."

"Awesome. Chocolate and elbows. My two favorite flavors."

Gretchen laughed, grabbing their linked hands and playfully hitting his side with their combined fist. She was wearing a flowery perfume that masked the smell of honey, but he could still taste it when he kissed her. Sunlight danced on the leaves of nearby trees and Dave thought, *That's what this feels like.*

o o o

Screw the gymnasium; this was California.

The prom committee had rented these huge roll-out carpets and spread them out over the football field. Concert-worthy speakers were set up at every twenty yards. A wobbly stage took over the entirety of an end zone, and when Dave and Gretchen arrived, bands were still unloading their equipment from their parents' vans. A few teachers in suits were gathered in a circle beneath the CONGRATS SLO SENIORS! banner that hung by the bleachers. They drank coffee and chatted, not yet concerned about being vigilant. The drinks table was lined with sodas and bottles of water, and no one really seemed to care about the lack of spikeable punch since the Kapoors were hosting an after-party.

"No chocolate fountains in sight," Dave said, snapping his fingers in an "aww-shucks" kind of way.

"Good. I was thinking about it and I'm terrified of ants. Being covered in chocolate would attract ants, and that does not seem like a fun idea."

"How are you afraid of ants?"

"I just can't trust anything that has eyes too small to look into. I don't know what they're thinking. They could be plotting my demise and I'd have no idea."

"You're adorable."

"Don't patronize me, ants are a legitimate thing to be afraid of. All those legs. Have you seen an up-close picture of one? That's the stuff of nightmares."

Still holding on to her hand, Dave swung her close to him. She didn't like being too touchy in public, so he kept himself from hugging her and just stood as close to her as was surreptitiously possible, happy to be close enough that he could stand with his side pressed lightly against hers. He reached for one of the blond tresses that spilled down her temple like something falling in slow motion. "How do you feel about picnics?"

"Dave, you're going to give me a panic attack."

"Did you say a 'picnic attack'?"

Gretchen burst into laughter, smacking him playfully across the chest and then leaning in for a quick peck on the lips. They each grabbed a bottle of water and took a seat along the rows of fold-out chairs that had been positioned in a rectangle around the stage, with plenty of room left in the middle for the wooden dance floor.

They watched the prom fill up. Dr. Hill came by the stage and announced a few official rules, which had been repeated over and over again on the PA system: no alcohol, no inappropriate dancing, no letting chickens run loose in the crowd (an SLO tradition). Then he wished everyone a good time, and the first band took the stage, a group of sophomores that played electro-pop covers of classic rock songs. Gretchen's friends joined the two of them off to the side of the stage. They'd started warming up to him again recently, and Dave was thankful for the second chance, happy to prove to them that he wouldn't hurt Gretchen again. Soon enough the dance floor started to fill up. Dave didn't feel at all like dancing, and he was thrilled when Gretchen didn't push him to.

Instead he watched the stars come out. It felt silly, a bit too much like someone having an end-of-high-school epiphany, some big life lesson washing over him. Except it wasn't really like that. He looked at the stars with a simple delight, the same way he looked out at everyone on the dance floor, or at the people standing along its perimeter: couples holding hands, friends getting emotional or behaving like they would any other night.

He spotted Julia walking out onto the field. She wasn't in prom attire at all, just jeans and a T-shirt, her hair a brighter shade of pink than he remembered it. No shoes. He hadn't expected her to come at all. She scanned the crowd a little, probably looking for some source of amusement. Dave imagined that if he was nearby, she'd crack some joke, funnier than anything he could come up with. He watched her cross the crowd toward the drink table, read her lips as she mouthed, *Where the hell are the real drinks?* He felt a momentary pang of longing to be at her side, but then it passed. Gretchen was chatting with Vince, but Dave could tell she'd noticed Julia coming in, too. She'd tensed up a little, the way she did when Julia said hi at school, those handful of times when they stood by making small talk. Gretchen had admitted to jealousy, but she'd insisted that she didn't want Dave and Julia to stop being friends because of her. If it hadn't been for Julia, the two of them might not be together at all.

Dave looked back up at the sky again and at the floodlights pointed down at the football field, casting everyone in an unflattering pale glow, blocking out all but the brightest stars. Music filled the night, coupled with the sound of hundreds of people talking and laughing, living their young lives in tired, unoriginal, and completely unimaginable ways.

o o o

Dave tapped Julia on the shoulder. "May I have this dance?"

Julia turned around, her brow furrowed. Then she saw who it was and relaxed into her usual deadpan. "Dude, I am about to throw up on you."

"Wouldn't be the first time. I didn't know you were going to be here."

Julia shrugged. "Figured I'd stop by and check it out. Skipping prom because it's lame is kind of a high school cliché."

Dave smiled at her. "Would a hug be weird?"

"Don't be an idiot," she said, stepping close and pulling him in. They squeezed each other tightly and briefly, letting go at the same time. "By the way, have you seen Marroney around? It's embarrassing to be here without my date."

"I think he went to go make the hotel reservations."

"I hope he's getting the honeymoon suite like I asked."

Dave laughed and picked at the label on his water bottle. "I never thanked you for talking to Gretchen."

Julia bit her lip and looked away. He could see her toes digging into the carpet. The band finished a song and awkwardly transitioned into the next one, false-starting a few times before the drummer counted up to four and got them going on a slower cut, one where the electric violinist could finally be heard over the other instruments. "You're welcome," Julia finally said, her voice uncharacteristically quiet. "You would have done the same for me." She quarter-turned to face the stage so Dave could barely see her profile. "If Marroney had seen us, that is."

He thought he saw tears welling up in Julia's eyes, but then she turned away, grabbing a bottle of water from the table. She opened it, then held it up in the air between them, as if she were toasting a glass of champagne. "To the fire in our hearts," she said with a smile.

They watched the rest of the song play out, Dave turning every now and then to look at Gretchen, to reassure her with a smile and a wave. Then Leslie Winters, the class president, came onstage. She was wearing a baby-blue tuxedo, her hair molded into a fauxhawk and dyed to match her outfit. Dave and Julia exchanged a look and shook their heads in silent recognition of the fiasco in Julia's bathroom. Julia's hair was in a simple ponytail, with those two strands looped around her ears the way they always were. "Did you dye your hair again?"

Julia actually blushed. "Shit, you noticed."

"Did Debbie survive this time?"

"I went to a salon." She took another sip from her water, clearly trying to be casual. But she must have noticed Dave gawking at her. "What, I'm not allowed to embrace a cliché or two? I like it, okay? Gimme a break before I pop your collar."

Leslie grabbed the mic. "Another round of applause for the band with the name that is officially too inappropriate to say at a school-sponsored event!" She waited for the crowd's lukewarm cheers to die down, then pulled an envelope out of her tuxedo pocket. "Now the moment you've all been waiting for." She slid her finger down the envelope's closure to tear it open. "Not really. We're all waiting for the after-party and to receive our diplomas next weekend and be done with high school forever. But about six people are quite excited about the contents of this envelope, so I'll get to it." She rummaged through the envelope for the paper inside.

Leslie announced the prom queen and a wave of whoops and cheers moved through the audience. The Miss America song started playing through the speakers, Dave couldn't tell if it was ironically or not. Dave kept his eyes focused in Gretchen's direction, like someone staring at the sky waiting for meteors. Then Leslie said, "…and your prom king is…" and Julia tapped him on the shoulder and whispered into his ear, "If you don't win it was all such a waste."

"James Everett!"

"You were robbed!" Julia yelled.

"Tonight, I'm going to weep like a jock whose glory days are over."

"You and me both," Julia said. James Everett and the prom queen, Rosie Barajas, took the stage and were crowned, still to the Miss America song.

"You know," Dave said. "I'm glad it happened." He looked at her, gauging her reaction, making sure what he was saying wasn't insensitive. She seemed at ease, though, calm.

"What part?"

"All of it," he said. "The Nevers, the beach, even those few hours where I had the worst-colored hair on the planet." Everywhere around him there were ecstatic people, kids drunk on covert alcohol and inappropriate dancing, drunk on the feeling of summer within reach, drunk on the thought that they were done. "You were the first girl I loved, as a friend or otherwise. You're my best friend, Julia."

"You're my best friend, too, David Sporkful McGee."

"Sporkful McGee?"

"Shut up. Wasn't my best." Looking around the football

field, her blue eyes were thoughtful, intense. He wondered what she was thinking, how hurt she still was. The royal couple left the stage and another band came up, fiddling with the connections, setting spare guitars up on racks, sending ripples of feedback into the night. "You know, I was thinking of a new list," Julia said. "The Always. A list of clichés to do throughout college. Frat parties, editorials in the school newspaper about the evils of the administration, paying some creepy dude fifty bucks for a fake ID. There's a whole new world to be explored."

Dave laughed and bumped her with his shoulder. "You have a pen and paper?"

★★★★★

ACKNOWLEDGMENTS

FIRST OF ALL, a huge thanks to the fantastic team at Harlequin Teen, who've made my publishing experience such a good one that my previous dreams about being published feel tame in comparison. From the editorial team to the sales team and everyone in between, the support has been humbling to say the least.

Tashya and TS, of course, for their editorial guidance. Lisa Wray, for all she does for me on my bookish travels. Amy Jones and Michelle Renaud, for hanging out with me all over the place. Dave Carley, Heather Foy, Melissa Anthony, Brent Lewis. Sigh, there are so many to name. I never quite understood how many people are involved in putting together a book. Now I've seen it firsthand, and I've met so many of them, and it's still pretty hard to wrap my head around it. Thank you for all you do.

Laura, who begged me for information about this book for a long time before I gave anything away, and yet loved me just the same. Also, for taking me on adventures, and for helping me cowrite the greatest pop song the world will ever hear.

My family, who begged me for information about this book for a long time before I gave anything away, and loved me a little less for it. Just kidding, Mom. Everyone who's met my family knows they're all great, and supportive, and deserving of their own paragraph in the acknowledgments sections of my books.

Annie Stone, for not leaving me completely orphaned. Emilia Rhodes, who, though she orphaned me, had a significant role in the creation of this book. Sara Shandler for her wisdom, particularly in improving the second half drastically. Josh Bank, too, since the pitching room would not be the same without him. Partially because it was his office.

To the incredibly supportive community of YA authors whom I've had the great pleasure of meeting since first getting published, either in person or online. Of course, the supportive community of readers, librarians, bloggers, booksellers, random one-time e-mailers, whom I've either met or e-met. I like meeting people, is what I'm saying, especially bookish people. It's been my favorite part of being published: all the people I've met since.

My teacher friends at the American School Foundation, who let me sit in on high school classes in order to draw inspiration for made-up teens from actual teens, since, as much as we like to pretend, adults forget exactly what it's like to be a teenager as soon as we're not one. Brett Sikkink, Carlos Kassam-Clay, Perri Devon-Sand, Renee Olper, Julien Howeveryouspellyourlastname, Mark Abling, Guy Cheney, Amy Gallie, others I'm sure I'm forgetting. John Powell, for giving me a coaching job and still allowing me to run off to do author things. Harry Brake and Daniel Thomas for allowing me to crash their Open Mic nights. I promise no one in this paragraph inspired Mr. Marroney. The students of ASF, of course.

One last paragraph of friends whose names deserve to be in print: Chris Russell, David Isern, Maggie Vazquez, Edgar Gutierrez, Gonzalo Scaglia, Sergio Rodriguez, Paul Donnelly, Cassie Harrell, John Kennedy (real name), Gillian Horbach,

Chris Farkas, Lundon Boyd, Ryan Troe. Joshua Zoller, who always has a hookah ready for me. Dawn Ryan, for her role in making it all happen. Cris de Oliveria, who will one day print my name in her acknowledgments section. Whytnee, Dennis, Bugs, Leah, who are always there to welcome me in NY.

Finally, a big sarcastic thanks to the jerk who made acknowledgments sections a common practice. I'm very grateful, to a lot of people. But this was stressful.